THE
STEAM MOLE

Dave Freer

an imprint of **Prometheus Books**
Amherst, NY

Published 2012 by Pyr®, an imprint of Prometheus Books

Cover illustration © Paul Young
Jacket design by Nicole Sommer Lecht

Inquiries should be addressed to
Pyr
59 John Glenn Drive
Amherst, New York 14228-2119
VOICE: 716-691-0133 • FAX: 716-691-0137
WWW.PYRSF.COM

16 15 14 13 12   5 4 3 2 1

Library of Congress Cataloging-in-Publication Data

Freer, Dave.
    The steam mole / by Dave Freer.
        p. cm.
    Sequel to: Cuttlefish.
    ISBN 978-1-61614-692-4 (cloth)
    ISBN 978-1-61614-693-1 (ebook)
    [1. Science fiction. 2. Australia—Fiction. 3. Insurgency—Fiction.]
I. Title.

PZ7.F8788St 2012
    [Fic]—dc23

                                                        2012025647

Printed in the United States of America

To Rowena Cory Daniells, Marianne de Pierres, and Garth Nix,
without whom we would not be here in Australia.
Thank you from the bottom of my heart.

ACKNOWLEDGMENTS

I've had a fine agent, an excellent editor, and a great cover artist for these books. That's more good fortune than most writers get, and I am grateful to both Mike Kabongo of Onyxhawke Agency and Lou Anders from Pyr books for their advice and patience, and to Paul Young for his covers and Lou, again, for involving me in them. This is my first entirely Australia-set novel, and I want to thank the huge number of people, particularly the islanders, who have made moving here a happy and wonderful thing, and who have helped me to try to understand the culture and people I have written about. Jamie, Pippa, Peter, Russell, Mel and Eric, Bill, Tania . . . and many others who I will be in trouble with for not naming. Thank you all. And as always, thank you to my loyal first readers, and especially to Barbara, who makes my work readable.

CHAPTER 1

"**F**ire one!" bellowed the controller, dropping his hand to signal the order.

Tim Barnabas pushed his long brass igniter into the hole. He was rewarded by a hiss, a blast of heat, and a deep, stuttering rumble as the vast digging drill head began to turn. The drill heads flashed in the acetylene light of their lanterns in the smoky tunnel.

"Fire two!" called the controller, timing it. The next drill-man inserted his igniter. The rumble grew deeper, the stutter less pronounced. By the time they got to "Fire five," the drill head was a blur and the rumble had become a grumbling roar. The digging head spun so fast, it, and the rotating drill heads on it, were a silver blur, ready to start cutting the red earth, clay, and shale ahead of the vast steam mole. Despite the heat, Tim pulled the leather earmuffs down over his ears, and his scarf over his mouth, and joined the mole-men heading back for the hatch. The air in the tunnel would be unbreathable soon. Already it was full of dust and smoke.

It was a world away from the coal-fired submarine that had brought him to Australia, but, in some ways, very alike. The crew of the steam mole also had to live in a narrow tube, with no real view out. Only they were underground, tunneling, not underwater.

The physical similarity was about where it ended, however. Tim had loved being a submariner. He was hating being a mole-man.

He was part of a crew, but it wasn't his crew, and he wasn't fitting in. His crew were scattered, and Tim missed them badly— nearly as badly as he missed Clara. He got a rough shove forward from the foreman. "Get to your station, boong. You blackfellers are all the same, dreaming all the time."

※

Clara Calland wasn't sure when the dream of reaching safety in the rebel Republic of Westralia—the part of Australia abandoned by the British when the Melt made it into a desert—had turned into something of a nightmare. It wasn't a real nightmare, more like one of those half-feverish dreams entirely too real to tell from life, where every time she woke she slipped back into the same dream. The *Cuttlefish* had limped into Ceduna under the cover of Westralian rockets. For a brief few hours, life had been pretty good—they'd been home free. From thinking they'd be trapped underwater, with the submarine cracking open like a dropped pumpkin under the water pressure, or, if they did manage to surface, being machine-gunned in the water, to the Westralian cheers as they came in to the quayside.

And then it started getting complicated, as if it hadn't been bad enough before.

Respectful and very complicated: The two hadn't been natural partners in Clara's mind. Nasty and complicated, yes, but she hadn't expected a mix of polite and terrible.

She'd known that reaching Westralia meant the end of her life on the submarine. It meant that she and Tim would probably go their separate ways . . . at least for a time. But she'd started to believe, somehow, that nothing could beat them, that it would only be a matter of time before they could be together.

Right now that seemed too much. Australia was too different— different from the warm wet of Ireland since the Melt, different from the flooded streets and musky damp tunnels of London, and different from the closed-in world of the submarine. Mostly it was the dryness. The air itself had dried up here, as had her supply of friends and people she could turn to for help.

The officers of the Republic of Westralia had taken her and her mother to a lovely bungalow guesthouse. It had broad verandahs and looked out onto Murat Bay over the sand rampart defenses for the huge water desalination plant, smoking away inland of it, and the city of Ceduna, huddled behind the wall.

Mr. Darlington, the big, bluff-faced official from the Westralian government, with his muttonchop sideburns and suntanned face, had smiled at her as they'd been introduced. "Pleased to meet you, Clara. Welcome to Westralia. You look to be about the same age as my daughter Linda. I was just about to pass on an invitation to dinner— erm, you'll find our hours here rather odd. We sleep during the heat, and get up once it starts to cool down. Most people in Ceduna would consider this the middle of the night." He waved a hand at the sash window and the blue of the sky and the sunlit sparkle of the bay. "But I was wondering, as it'll be a rather crusty affair tonight, with nothing much for a young lady, whether you would like to come and take tea with Linda and milady wife. I'm sorry, Dr. Calland, m'wife won't be home with them all of the time tonight, but they're not children that need constant overseeing, eh?" He straightened out the neatly embroidered antimacassar on the back of the Morris chair next to which he stood. "My wife chairs the local Westralian Women's Association, and they have their annual general meeting tonight. She can't miss it! But she will only be away for a couple of hours while we're out—this dinner is unlikely to finish much before one in the morning. I could have my driver come pick the two of you up, bring you to our home, introduce you to my daughter, and then take us on to our dinner at the Clarion. Professor Henderson and a number of other scientists and several industrial people will be there."

Clara had been a bit wary of being parted from her mother in this strange environment. But she didn't want to sound like a baby. Her mother smiled encouragingly at her. "Thank you very much," Clara said in her best St. Margaret's Girl accent. "That would be lovely."

And oddly enough, it had been lovely. Linda proved to be the sort of person Clara had always thought she might like to have as a friend, had all the girls at St. Margaret's not been so set on ignoring someone whose father was in jail, and worse, whose mother was divorced. After a first polite, but slightly uneasy exchange, Linda said something about her stepmother being home soon.

After an awkward moment Clara said, "I'm sorry. Did . . . did your mother die long ago?"

"She's not dead. Just divorced." The way Linda said it struck a chord in Clara. "She's living in Sydney. She didn't like Roxby. Honestly, I sometimes think I should say she is dead."

Without thinking about it Clara had reached out and squeezed Linda's hand, which startled the primly dressed young lady. "I know. I used to get the same back in Ireland. My . . . my parents divorced, too." That this was a paper divorce, designed to protect her, was not something she needed to mention just then.

Linda blinked. "It's like that . . . back in England, too? I heard in America nobody cares."

"Well, I'm Irish." It was odd to say that with pride. "But people treated me as if I had lice because of it. It used to make me so mad. It wasn't *my* fault."

And that was enough to seal the friendship. Within ten minutes Clara had heard a great deal about Linda's mother, stepmother, the other girls in the new school in Ceduna, and life in Westralia, and was soon subjected to an inquisition about her own life.

"Oh, I would love to have been on a submarine! You've had such adventures. All I ever do that's fun is ride. I have my own horse."

Clara had left out a few adventures that she'd rather not talk about yet. "It was fun. I miss it."

"And all those young men . . . My stepmother won't let me alone with one."

Clara blushed. Linda noticed, read it at least partly right, and looked warily around as if scared someone would notice. "A boyfriend?" she asked in a hushed tone. "Don't tell step-mama, but I've got a beau, too, now. But . . . well, he's a bit older. He keeps asking me to sneak out to meet him, but there's not many places you can go in Ceduna. And I'm not going to Murat beach with him . . ."

The door opened. "So do tell me more about the food on the sub-marine," said Linda as a plump lady with curls and a kindly smile came into the drawing room. Clara stood and was introduced to Mrs. Darlington. They'd talked, eaten a meal the locals called "tea," and drank tea, which was also called "tea," and then . . . the bell on the telephone-instrument on the wall jangled.

And things started getting far more complicated.

Her mother had been whisked to the hospital, having fallen ill during dinner. Fortunately one of the leading physicians of Westralia had been there. He suspected some kind of tropical mosquito-borne disease. She was in quarantine . . . Dr. Leaming would come and examine Clara shortly. Could she spend the night here rather than go back to the guest house? No, she couldn't see her mother.

The next day Clara had at least got to speak to her mother. It hadn't been comforting. Mother had barely known who she was talking to let alone making any sense. And apparently she'd come out in a rash and was running a temperature. Dr. Leaming came to check Clara once again for any signs of either. Apparently the sub-marine crew had been checked too.

The Westralians, particularly Linda's stepmother—she wasn't at all the kind of wicked stepmother from the fairy stories, but rather one who tried too hard—had been very kind.

Kind, but not understanding. "Oh, we can't let you go back to the submarine crew, my dear. Not without your mother. It . . . it wouldn't be decent. No, you must stay with us, mustn't she Linda?"

Linda agreed with her stepmother immediately.

And thus the days had dragged on . . . and then things got worse.

Far worse. In an attempt to distract her, Linda and her stepmother had taken her shopping that day . . . in the pale pre-dawn when Ceduna got most of its work done.

And she'd got the message.

A message from a spy, and a rendezvous she couldn't make.

※

Linda Darlington was annoyed at being used as a babysitter, this evening of all evenings. With the certainty that her stepmother was going to be out of the house for hours and that her father was going to be at this dinner at the Clarion, she'd been very daring. Nicky would visit her at home. And now . . . well, Father had said she must try and be nice to this foreigner. His idea of "someone your own age" was anything from newborn to about ten. She was, she had to admit, a little curious about life somewhere—anywhere—beyond Westralia. Or Ceduna. "Deadunda," as Nicky called it. He was a clerk on one of the rail companies, and she'd met him quite by accident at Strunkenwight's Lending Library. He'd turned around and bumped her pile of books out of her hands and apologized and picked them up for her. And then, well, he was there every Thursday when they went to change books. He was much older, and quite a catch because of it. Most of the girls at her school weren't allowed beaus. She might not be allowed one either, but she simply hadn't mentioned it.

It took Linda a few seconds to realize that this time at least, her father had been right. It had to happen if only by accident sometimes. Clara was only very slightly younger, and made up for it with a certain degree of assurance. And she didn't set her rules by Ceduna schoolgirls.

Linda had been quite looking forward to having made friends first with someone who, compared to everyone else, knew the world, who understood that your parents having gotten divorced wasn't a disease . . . and had the kind of confidence that the girls at school who ran everything seemed to have.

And then Clara's mother ended up in hospital.

And then something else happened—something Clara wasn't talking about. It was probably her boyfriend.

❋

Tim Barnabas had had quite high expectations of Westralia, mostly thanks to Cookie, the submarine's Westralian cook. Cookie was a good 'un, kind to a hungry young submariner, full of jokes, and decent to work for. Tim didn't mind being up to the elbows in greasy water or any other dirty job. They had to be done, and Cookie did them, too.

Cookie never made Tim feel that he didn't think of him as quite human. That had happened in Westralia, quite a lot, and it was worse working on the steam mole. It seemed the overseer really didn't like "Abos" on his machine, and did his best to make their lives so miserable they left, even though it was hard to get anyone to work on the drilling machines.

Tim staggered along toward the boiler under the weight of the two steam-biscuits he carried to the furnace.

"Get a move on boong-boy!" shouted Shift-captain Vister, swinging his fist against Tim's ear.

"Ouch!" Tim ducked a second blow. "You don't have to hit me. I'm doing my best."

"If you don't like it, you can get out. Go back to your own kind. We don't want you here, anyway."

Tim didn't have his own kind to go to. Not here, out in the middle of the Australian desert. Besides, he wasn't from Australia at all. His "kind" were the submarine crew, and most of them came from Under-London. Tim's father had once come from Jamaica, long ago, before the Melt. "I wish I could," muttered Tim as he swayed down the rattling gap to the conveyor, clanking the steam-biscuits—compressed coal shaped into ovoid perforated slabs—into place in the fire-dropper.

"Aw, next time we stop, take off into the desert. It's home for the likes of you. Hot as hell out there, which is why you beggars are all burned black," said the foreman, who was nearly as bad as the shift-captain, only stupider.

As all of them were covered in coal dust, Tim wondered just how he could say that, but arguing only made them worse. The recruiter back in Ceduna hadn't prepared Tim for this. He'd come to the submarine the day after the *Cuttlefish* had been pulled into the dry dock and Clara had vanished into the Westralian city. He'd come the day after Captain Malkis called them all together to give them the difficult news.

The coal-fired submarine had made it all the way to Westralia with a very precious cargo: a cargo the British Empire had gone to huge lengths to try to capture or destroy. They'd failed, and Captain Malkis and the *Cuttlefish* and her crew had successfully brought Dr. Mary Calland and the secret of ammonia synthesis to safety. It was something that the Liberty, the government that ran Under-London, and had built her submarines, would have backed them in doing.

But right now . . . the ship was broken. They'd had to leave her valuable cargo of nitrates in their drogues on Flinders Island. And though the people from the government of the Republic of Westralia had been glad to welcome the scientist, they weren't paying the *Cuttlefish* for bringing her to them.

"As you know, gentlemen," said the captain, "we do have small reserves of gold for paying for expenses. Normally our ventures are profitable, but this time . . . we have no cargo to sell. And the damage to our good ship is extensive, and it will cost us a great deal to repair her. It's also going to take three to four months. So it will be that long before the boat can leave, and then that'll only be for a local trip, to Flinders Island to pick up our cargo."

He looked around at the crew and went on, "The Liberty will of course be good for your wages, but in the short term we're going to have trouble paying you. Actually, we would find it impossible to afford food for the crew, and you wouldn't be able to live on the submarine while she's being repaired and refitted. Food is very pricey in Westralia, and accommodation is just not easy to find."

He took a deep breath. "You have been a great crew, and I would hate to lose you. But . . . we have another problem."

There was a long silence. Tim couldn't imagine life now without the *Cuttlefish* and her crew. They'd all been through too much together.

"Nothing that we can't solve, sir," said Lieutenant Ambrose stoutly. "My fiancée says the Westralians are yelling out for labor of any kind in their mines and factories. And they pay well. They have to. Most of the mines provide bunkhouses and food, too. We could do three months and then come back to the boat."

"Too right we could," said Cookie with a grin. "And yer's will all get to see me country a bit. I reckon after a bit of time in the Gibson Mines or the like yous'll be glad to be back to me cooking. It's easy to find jobs. There's blokes recruiting all the time. If yer give me shore leave, captain, I'll try to get someone decent and honest to talk to the lads."

Tim had been rather looking forward to the experience then. The recruiter painted a glowing picture, too: free food, bunk-space, and a short contract. And for those crew members the captain had especially commended, jobs in the toughest and best paid service in Westralia: the steam moles.

"They're like land submarines," said the recruiter. "You'd be at home in one, young man. And your captain has given you a glowing testimonial. Good experience for you."

"What's a steam mole?" asked Tim.

The recruiter grinned. "Something like a cross between a tunneling machine on rails and a termite."

The joke fell flat to a boy from the tunnels of a drowned London. "What's a termite?"

"My word! You really don't know?"

Tim shook his head.

"Well, they're like ants—white ants, people call them. They eat wood, but the sun will kill them, so they make mud tunnels up trees and poles so that they can get to the wood while staying out of the sun. We have to do the same north of the Tropic of Capricorn. It's so hot in the sun in summer, you can't sweat fast enough to cool down. So the tracks to the mines up there are covered over. Shallow tunnels, if you like. The steam moles make them. They're busy with a big push to get a whole new network going, especially to the north."

Tim liked being in a submarine, and he was used to tunnels. He'd spent his whole life in them, up to the last year. The one rub had been Clara. He wasn't even sure where she'd gone, or how to contact her. One moment she'd been there, and the next whisked away by the Westralians. She'd promised to come back and see him just as soon as she could.

"Of course you get a week off after every month, back here in Ceduna if you like, if you take a steam-mole job. Most of the mining jobs you'd get a day off a week, and you can't get away from the mine for that day. It's too far to travel to anywhere. You'd get a month after twelve months from them, but you blokes aren't planning to stay that long. Mind you, when you get among that kind of money . . ."

No kind of money was enough to keep Tim from the *Cuttlefish*. But the figure the recruiter talked about was very tempting indeed to a poor boy from the tunnels. He could do a lot with that money. Maybe even think about a snippy girl who took going to university as inevitable.

But all that was before he got to the steam mole, and before he found out he was the only one from the *Cuttlefish* on this machine.

And before he'd found out that they hated him for the color of his skin. He was the youngest and smallest person on the steam mole, and he really didn't know how he was going to survive for a month, let alone three.

The steam mole was one of two pushing south from the Sheba mine to meet the northbound rail. She'd work for two days then, as the new-cast tunnel needed to set for eight hours, go back along her tracks to the last station. There was a station like this every twenty miles, and a big one every sixty. When the line was complete they'd provide the power station for that section of track. The trains running on the tracks down here wouldn't have locomotives, but would be towed along in the dark by a long, endless steel cable. All the coal smoke and steam could be vented from the power station, leaving the air in the termite tunnel cool and breathable. But the steam moles had to have their own power. While they were building, the air out in the tunnel was full of coal smoke. A long, floppy air hose made of leather stretched back to the power stations, and one of Tim's jobs was to attach new sections to the air pump then wind them in and detach them as the steam mole backed up.

It was hot, hard work, and you risked losing your fingers with every unhook, but it meant he was away from the steam-biscuit line and Shift-captain Vister, so Tim preferred it. It was that or being a greaser on the brass piston fingers of the drill head, and that was noisier and even more dangerous. It was also where the news from outside first came to the steam mole.

"Hear they're upping the contract period from three months to six," said one of the other hose-men to one of his companions. "You're stuck for another four months, Fred."

"Bunch of Welshing b—" swore the other hose-man. "They promised they wouldn't do that. They're tryin' to push to Sheba before the Ogg-Nullabor line. I was lookin' forward to gettin' out of here."

Tim felt as if he'd been dunked in ice water. "But . . . but surely they can't just change our contracts without—?"

"Oh, yes they can, boong-boy," said Fred. "Do anything they please. Only that means they battle to get men to work . . . so they makes it worse for the men who *are* working. Makes perfect blooming sense, really, to some feller in a cool office in Augusta or

Ceduna. And it's not worth breakin' the contract, see. They'll put you in stir."

Tim had been in Westralia long enough to know what "stir" was. Jail. He swallowed, unable to speak.

"Someone gunna have to rein these blooming companies in. Bunch of Ned Kellys," said Fred's mate, angrily tossing down the brass connector. "S'oright for your kind, boong. You can always go bush and they can't find yer."

Tim just stared helplessly at him. Six months? The *Cuttlefish* would be gone by then. And as for "go bush," well, he might just have to. He didn't really know what it meant, but he'd lived out in the wild pipes under flooded London for a day or two.

If he could get back to the submarine in time, he was sure Captain Malkis would hide him and take him away when they left. The awkward part might be ever coming back to Westralia, and he wanted to, as Clara would be here. He'd have to check out the practicalities of it all when he got his time back in Ceduna. Mind you, it had taken two whole days and nights of traveling along the termite track in a jostling, clacking carriage with one dim Bakelite fitting to get here. His week off in Ceduna was going to amount to three days there, and four days traveling.

She was worth it, though, thought Tim. He'd get to see Clara somehow, and talk it over with her.

※

Jack Calland was dying. He knew this because he'd just seen his wife and daughter. And that, some small, rational part of his mind said, was impossible. He was in Australia, transported in a rusty iron hulk into this hell, and they were in Ireland.

He said so.

"They're in the rebel-held part of Australia," said the tall, slim man in tropical dress whites, who had been holding the picture.

Jack laughed.

That was a bad idea, or so said the excruciating pain that followed.

"Stop that," said another man, in a cool, dispassionate voice. "You'll kill him and that would be of no value to us, and I am not going to tell Duke Malcolm that we killed his pawn early. You . . . Martins, take him to the doctor. Tell McLennan I said to fix him up. I need the next letter."

Jack was vaguely aware of being dragged out into the heat and then back into the shade. And that was all he knew for some time, as he wandered in troubled dreams, looking for, and never quite finding, his beloved Mary and little Clara, catching glimpses of them under the gaslights and in the narrow, sooty streets of Fermoy. Calling to them . . .

When he finally awoke, weak and exhausted but in his right mind again, it was in the palm-thatched "hospital" of Denong prison camp. He was somewhat cloudy as to how he'd got there, but he remembered some things very clearly. He remembered the part about Duke Malcolm and being a pawn not to be killed early.

It had to be true. The hospital, such as it was, and the medical help, such as that was, were for the warders only, not for the prisoners. The prisoners had even fewer facilities, and mostly just died where they fell.

Jack Calland, the Irish rebel, didn't know what his ex-wife Mary had done to make Duke Malcolm, the feared head of British Imperial Intelligence take a personal interest in her. They'd divorced on anything but amicable terms when he'd been arrested. As far as the Imperial Intelligence Service knew it had been very ugly, and Jack's value as a pawn there was nonexistent. Of course, he and Mary knew differently. Or at least, Jack hoped and believed that she did. They had a daughter to care for, and if the Imperials had thought his wife might be involved, or might even be sympathetic . . . well, Clara would have been left alone.

For Clara they would both have done anything. And she was their jewel.

Jack was terribly afraid that Duke Malcolm had worked that part out—terribly afraid he might have betrayed something in his delirium. He remembered they'd brought him paper. Made him write. That was all right, Mary knew their code. She'd know that it wasn't something he'd write of his own free will. But the fact that Duke Malcolm wanted him as a lever . . . that was worrying.

It meant he had to do one of two things: He either had to escape, or he had to die.

Only . . . here in the deserts and steaming jungles of Northern Queensland, to escape was to die.

Being Jack Calland, he decided he might as well do that, then.

CHAPTER 2

"Mrs. Darlington, can't I at least talk to my mother?" asked Clara, doing her best to be polite and not sound desperate.

"But my dear, you spoke with her only two hours ago. She was delirious and confused. The hospital says she's asleep now. What do you need to talk to her about, my dear?"

The question flatfooted Clara. She couldn't tell this woman—who was the wife of someone important in the Westralian government—the truth. "Um. I'm just terribly worried about her."

The truth she couldn't tell took her straight to the gas-lit halls of Hansmeyers Emporium, the finest department store in Ceduna, and possibly all of Westralia, exclusive suppliers of all the finest drapery, haberdashery, ladies footwear, fabrics, and fine linens, as well as things of lesser importance. Clara had been relieved to be spared the ironmongery and other departments Mrs. Darlington considered barely worth noticing. One could get anything in Westralia, Imperial embargo or not. The prices could make a girl's eyes water, though. Either everyone was rich or no one bought anything. Mrs. Darlington plainly did, though, and she thought it a high treat bound to distract Clara.

It might have done so, too, on another day, when Clara didn't have such worries on her mind. Mrs. Darlington had been distracted by various shades of pale lilac cotton chiffon, and Clara had wandered off a little, lost in thought, among the roof-high towers of rolls of fabric. A rat-faced little man stood just at the end of the stack. He beckoned to her, looking about as if afraid a cat might suddenly arrive. Clara backed off.

"I have a message for you," he whispered. "Come over here."

Everything about him made her hackles rise. "From whom?" she asked.

"Jack Calland," he replied, holding up a small envelope.

She couldn't help herself. She reached forward and grabbed it. As she opened it, the furtive little man said, "If you want to see him alive, you'll meet me here tomorrow at nine. We can make arrangements. He's in Queensland."

Clara was too busy staring at the grubby piece of paper to answer him . . . or notice that he'd disappeared. She was torn from rereading the letter from her father for a third time when she was forced to shove it hastily into her reticule by Mrs. Darlington's summons.

He was alive. And in a prison in Queensland. And if she cooperated, she could see him again.

Clara knew the rat-faced man with the ginger whiskers must be a spy. An Imperial agent. She knew it was a trap. She also desperately wanted to see her father. She wanted him so badly, now, with mother sick. And she had not been able to get to the rendezvous with the spy. Rat-face probably didn't know that had been her only chance to see her mother, and that she'd been with Mrs. Darlington the entire time.

He probably thought she didn't believe the letter.

She did.

She knew Daddy's writing better than she knew anyone's. She'd read his few letters to her to pieces. This letter . . . it was his writing, just not his normal way of saying things.

The other letter made it clear that they were offering her father's freedom in return for her cooperation. In other words, in exchange for her mother's secret method of making ammonia from the air . . . something that Clara couldn't tell them how to do, even if she were willing to.

Mrs. Darlington sighed. "Clara, my dear, I don't quite know how to put this to you, except quite bluntly, but you're quite a big girl now."

Clara gritted her teeth, determined not to say anything. If she were a boy, like Tim, she'd have been out and working by now. The plump, elegant, perfumed, terribly kind Mrs. Darlington continued, not noticing the effect her choice of words had on her young guest, "There is, sadly, a real chance your mother won't get better, dear. The doctors and the hospital are doing their best, giving her the best care possible. And you will be looked after. I promise."

Clara ought to have been upset and shocked. Instead she looked stonily at the ground, refusing to let herself cry, because it was no surprise, and she'd cried herself dry last night. And as if she cared about being "looked after . . ."

She wanted *them* looked after. And while Mother had half the doctors in Westralia fussing about her, her father had nothing. She needed help. Someone she could rely on, someone she could trust. "Mrs. Darlington, can I . . . can I get hold of Captain Malkis? Or Lieutenant Willis?" She didn't say "or Tim Barnabas," because this woman would never understand.

"Who . . . ? Oh, the captain of your submarine! I'm afraid they're out in the desert right now, Clara. You could write to them, I suppose. But really dear, you'll be well looked after, I promise." Her tone said what she thought of nasty, rough submariners.

I will not scream at her. She thinks she's being kind. "How could I obtain their addresses, Mrs. Darlington?"

It had all happened so quickly after the *Cuttlefish* had been towed into the quayside. The Westralian officers might have been wearing strange, broad hats and uniforms the color of sand, but they looked like officers and they had gold braid on their shoulders. Mother still hadn't been ready to trust them, but Captain Malkis had vouched for the Westralian major, and before Clara had been able to say "Jack Robinson," let alone her proper farewells to the crew and to Tim, they'd been whisked away, promising to come and see them all soon.

After all, the submarine wouldn't be going anywhere in a hurry. Clara knew the boat would have to have major repairs before she could leave.

Clara hadn't guessed then that her mother would fall sick and be put in quarantine. She'd assumed they could come back tomorrow, and the next day . . . and, well, until the submarine left, which was somewhere in a future she hadn't thought of.

Clara found she'd been right about the submarine not going anywhere for months, but by the time she'd been able to get Mrs. Darlington to take her down to the quays, she found that the *Cuttlefish* had been moved, and that although the submarine might not be going anywhere for months, her crew were already scattered, working, while their boat was repaired and refitted. Westralia had no place for people who didn't work . . . except for her, it seemed.

"My dear, you're looking a little pale. Are you feeling all right? I know you've had a terrible shock, and I know dear Dr. Leaming examined you, but are you feeling quite all right? Health-wise, I mean."

Clara could almost see the perfumed and powdered lady lean away from her. No one yet knew quite what disease Mother had picked up, or how infectious it might be.

"I'm feeling fine," Clara said. "Just worried. And a little hot. Can't we go outside for a little?"

Like most of the houses in Ceduna, this one was made of corrugated iron, with wide verandahs. During the day it was shut up to keep the heat out, and they only opened the big sliding windows and drapes at night. Clara was used to the enclosed air of the submarine, but when they'd got out onto the deck the air off the sea had at least been cool. Not so here. The town and port, and most of all the desalination plant, had huge sand walls to stop the Royal Navy from shelling them—thus keeping the sea breeze out and only letting in the hot wind from the interior.

"It's nearly a quarter past ten in the morning, dear," said Mrs. Darlington. "We don't want to go out now. You'll get heatstroke, and the sun is so bad for your complexion, even with a parasol."

Clara gritted her teeth again. Welcome to Australia, where people sleep in the daytime and work at night. The "day" started in what her body clock said was the middle of the night, when it was cool enough. It was spring now. Clara didn't even want to think about summer. In Ceduna the people lived on the surface. In the interior of Australia, far from the cooling influence of the sea, it got even hotter, and anyone who lived there, lived underground, like moles. She was feeling like a mole herself, blind and digging. "Can you please ask someone for the addresses for the *Cuttlefish* crew, ma'am. It would only be polite if I wrote to them to thank them."

This obviously impressed Mrs. Darlington. "Of course. So good that you've been a well-brought-up little girl. I wish you'd learn from her, Linda. 'Bread-and-butter' letters are so often neglected. I'll call Maxie, and he can have them dispatch one of the black boys to run over with a list."

Maxie—Mr. Darlington—seemed to work as many hours as he possibly could. And the black boys . . . well, she'd seen them. They were aboriginals, and it seemed it was all right to ask them to run in the heat.

※

Across the world, in London, Duke Malcolm looked at the report in his hands, looked out at Pall Mall Canal outside his widow, pursed his lips, and looked back to the medical man in front of his desk. "Dr. Weltztraimer, just what is the prognosis?"

The doctor looked uncomfortable. He always did, but the duke had him fast in his web. Weltztraimer had already killed before Duke Malcolm caught him and made him provide poisons for Imperial Security instead. "She should be dead, Your Grace. That amount of aconite should have killed her. I can only assume that somehow she did not get the full dose."

The duke sighed. "I know Dr. Calland should be dead, Adolphus. The point is, she isn't. So what are her chances of recovery?"

"Good, if she can avoid any more of the poison," said the doctor.

"And if she doesn't? I have arranged for further small doses to be administered."

"She is, by all reports, not far from death, Your Grace."

The duke nodded. "There's no knowing how much she was able to tell them before it took effect, but still, hopefully the damage will be limited."

The duke's brother Albert, the Prince of Prussia, came striding into the stateroom, not even bothering to knock.

He smiled, and that was enough to irritate Duke Malcolm even more. "I hear nature succeeded where you failed, little brother."

"What do you mean?" asked Duke Malcolm, keeping a rein on his temper.

"That scientist. The chemist. What was her name? Calland? The one with some breakthrough with nitrate synthesis that you were trying to stop from escaping. She's got some disease. Delirious, apparently. That buys us a little time, and with any luck she'll die. I have ordered my scientists to redouble their efforts."

Duke Malcolm gave Dr. Weltztraimer a warning look.

The doctor kept his silence, but Albert hadn't finished talking. "I thought you had some plan for her husband."

"I did," said Duke Malcolm, who disliked revealing too much to anyone who didn't need to know, and didn't like the doctor being party to this conversation. "It will be called off. We've just had some trouble with our radio-telegraphy into Queensland."

"I might tell you that our dear brother has actually interested himself in matters down in Queensland. The other project."

Duke Malcolm blinked. Thank heavens Albert was being at least a little cryptic. Their older brother almost never concerned himself with anything more than fashion. But he was the King, the emperor, the commander-in-chief of the Imperial forces. "You may go, Weltztraimer," said Duke Malcolm.

The doctor bowed and left at a hasty scuttle. When he was safely out of earshot, Duke Malcolm turned to his brother. "I didn't even know Ernest was aware of it. What's going on here, Albert?"

The prince's responsibilities in the emergency interim government—convened when the Melt disaster had destroyed governments across the British Empire, and House of Windsor-Schaumberg-Lippe had stepped in to save the British Empire—included almost everything no one else wanted to do.

"What is it ever with Ernest?" the prince asked.

"Money," Duke Malcolm replied, rolling his eyes. Their brother managed to waste vast amounts of it on palaces, boats, pavilions, and clothes, but resented expenditure on unimportant things, like intelligence or the Royal Navy. "What's he on about? The cost, or the prize?"

"He's got wind of the silver in your prize, and he wants it."

So did Duke Malcolm, for entirely different reasons. The prize was Sheba. A mine in the rebel republic of Westralia—the part of Australia abandoned by the Imperial authorities because it was too hot or too dry, or both, after the Melt. It had once been a part of Queensland, before the catastrophe, and before the mines had been discovered. The decision to pull people and resources out of the outback and focus on maintaining the east coast had been justifiable then. There was no value in a desert where the summer daytime temperatures soared to over a hundred and twenty degrees.

"The railroad construction is relatively slow," Malcolm said, "and we've had to maintain secrecy, which adds complexity."

Albert tugged his goatee. "This 'railroad' business seems unnecessary. Don't our troops have feet? Horses? Or sufficient motortrucks? I know this is your business, Malcolm, but it would be wise if you could present Ernest with a *fait accompli*, rather than letting him stick his tasseled boots into the affair."

That would be nearly as disastrous as having Albert conduct military exercises, thought the duke. But he needed Albert, so he answered, "The motorized force is ready for railing forward. I think the rail link is about twenty miles short of striking distance. We're two or three weeks off completion. The military was concerned about their supply line given that the strike at the mine would leave them isolated and unable to hold it. The terrain and problems getting petroleum for their vehicles makes the rail link doubly vital. Besides, it's needed for shipping the ore from the mine out."

"And the cake is definitely worth the candle? Not like that diamond mine in Baluchistan?" asked Albert, naming a military folly the duke would rather forget.

"This time we're as sure as we can be. The rebels are even building a second, slightly shorter one of their underground railways to it. The cost of that is so high they wouldn't be doing it if they weren't certain. The Sheba mine is one of the most productive in the world. We need the silver from it, yes, but that's a pittance compared to the value of the huge output of copper, zinc, and lead. You know, or should know, how badly we need those. And in political terms . . . the output of that single mine makes nearly one-quarter of the wealth of that upstart republic thorn-in-the-flesh. The smuggled mineral wealth is what's keeping them, and, oddly, us afloat. It will be a lot more profitable going directly through us." The duke didn't mention his deeper strategy. If they succeeded in cutting communications before the Westralian government was alerted, striking via their own railroad at Ceduna, the Royal Navy could relieve and supply that, and then Roxby would be in striking range. With those gone, only the gold of Kalgoorlie remained to keep the rebels afloat. The many mines around there might let them survive, but the Republic would be weaker and smaller.

"Still," said the prince, "it's been on your agenda for what . . . three years? I remember us talking about it."

"The project's been ongoing for that long. It's the only one of their major mines that we can take on without a marine landing or impossible supply lines. Their other major mines at Roxby and the Kalgoorlie area are simply impractical to recapture. But the

Dominion of Queensland is still a part of the British Empire, and the covered-over railway—a simplified version of the method the Westralians are using—stops it being detected from the air, and keeps the troops cooler. That's important in those temperatures." It was, the duke had been assured by the tropical military experts, vital. The sun was a killer.

It was killing work for the prisoners sent to dig and build the railroad.

CHAPTER 3

Clara got the list of addresses for the *Cuttlefish*'s crew a few minutes after Mrs. Darlington had replaced the trumpet-like receiver back on its brass and ebony stand. It struck Clara that someone in Westralia was keeping very close tabs on the crew of the *Cuttlefish*. The names of the places were strange. "C/O Power Station 1786, Dajarra, Cloncurry Shire." That was Tim's address. She had to go and find an atlas to work out just where that was.

It was very, very far away.

She wrote letters into the heat of the day. It was a chore trying to keep from smudging the ink by turning the pages sideways and dipping just enough of her pen to get the bare minimum of ink on the steel nib from the inkwell on the little writing desk. Some of them were simple enough. But to the captain, and Lieutenants Willis and Ambrose . . . she asked if they could contact her . . . as she had questions about her family. She dared not say too much, just in case the person who had all the addresses also read all the letters. That was the way living in Ireland had made her think, she realized. It had been so relieving to be away from the secrecy and the spying . . . and that was when she was fourteen. What must it have been like for Mother, who had really been involved in secret things?

Then came the really hard part: the letter she'd put off to last, writing to Tim. She'd never written to . . . well, a boyfriend before. Some of the girls at St. Margaret's collected their love letters, and must have been good at it. Clara concluded she was good at starting and then wasting pieces of paper, smudging the ink with teardrops, and finally realizing she had no more paper and would have to use that sheet anyway. It was not a letter that she would have been proud to show her friends. She really hadn't had any friends after Daddy had been locked up. The letter wasn't the sort of goo the other girls seemed to like, though. It didn't say any of the things she needed to say, or wanted to say. It felt stilted, awkward, and pretentious. And she couldn't finish it with "love," let alone rows of x kisses, as she'd seen the other girls do. Instead she uncertainly settled on "lots of love, Clara." She hoped he'd understand the part about someone she was proud of, thanks to him, and no one else would. How would they know that Tim had finally helped her to be proud of her father, instead of ashamed of him being in jail?

It still didn't solve her problems, though. If only she knew what to do.

The next morning started worse. She heard Mrs. Darlington's husband's deeper voice, talking to his wife. The words were indistinct, but as they came down the hallway, they grew clearer.

"She may just be deeply asleep," said a doubtful sounding Mrs. Darlington.

"I'm afraid not, my dear. Try and stop the girl calling her on the telephone tomorrow."

"What'll become of her, Maxwell? You know . . . she's a sweet child. She's been a good companion for Linda. A good influence I think, taken her mind off horses, boys, and fashions a little. She was writing thank-you letters to the crew of that submarine until all hours last night. If . . . if the worst happens, I think . . . we should adopt her."

"If that's what you want, my dear," he rumbled. "Mind you, an extra child is a great deal of work."

"I've got one daughter, I might as well have two."

Clara lay there, rigid. Sleep did not come back. Eventually she got up and reread the letter the little man had slipped into her reticule the day before at Hansmeyers Emporium, as she'd walked around with Mrs. Darlington and Linda, buying suitable clothing for a young lady.

The writing was shaky, but the signature was definitely her father's. Tears blurred her eyes when she realized that she couldn't clearly remember his face anymore. And he was a prisoner somewhere in North Queensland . . .

Clara stared at the atlas she'd borrowed to see just where Dajarra in the shire of Cloncurry was.

The two places were not that far apart.

Her mother was getting the very best medical help they could provide. By her reading of it, her father would not live that long without help.

So it was up to her, really.

She knew precisely where her mother kept the little money they'd had with them. It wasn't much, but it would have to do.

She left the letter from her father in its place. Then she left a letter for Linda hidden behind the mirror, where Linda kept her love letters. She said she was going to Queensland, to her father, and that she was sorry to not tell her . . . and begged her not to tell anyone else. She felt a bit stupid writing it, but Linda trusted her and deserved trust in return.

Then she gathered up all the essentials of a respectable young lady—a small bandbox, a parasol, her reticule, and her breeches from the *Cuttlefish*, which might shock Mrs. Darlington rigid, but were essential nonetheless, and climbed out of the window onto the broad verandah. She stepped down the path, out the wrought iron gate, and out into the street.

It was dark, and it occurred to her that she had no idea how to get to the station, or even, in this country, where to buy a ticket or when the trains ran. There were no trams running at this time of night, either. Clara was about to abandon her decisiveness and try to spend the next "day" doing some research when a slurred voice spoke out of the darkness, "What's a pretty little white girl doing out at this time of night, eh?"

Clara gripped the handle of her parasol tightly as a ragged, dark-faced man lurched out of the shadows. "Um. I . . . er . . . am just on my way to Dajarra." It was a stupid thing to say to a ragged man breathing alcohol fumes at her and leering, but it was all she could think of.

"Dajarra!" he laughed. "That's up on the Diamantia. No place for your kind up there. Give us a kiss." He lunged at her.

Instinctively Clara threw herself backward and pushed at him with the rolled-up parasol, hitting him in the stomach. He doubled over and she dropped the bandbox and ran all the way back to the house she'd just climbed out of. She lay on her bed, shaking for a while—furious and worried. Partly she was angry with herself for being so frightened. But common sense said that running had been the best thing she could have done. But there was the issue of the missing bandbox and the clothes in it. She wondered if she dared go back to look for it, and decided that she didn't. She had another bandbox—one of Mother's. And Mrs. Darlington probably wouldn't notice the missing clothes for a day, if Clara didn't tell her. At least she still had the money.

But it meant that leaving soon was not only an option but a necessity. If the bandbox was found and returned, the Darlington's would surely take steps to stop her going. And then there was the note she'd slipped in behind Linda's mirror . . .

She crept into the girl's room and was just pulling it out when Linda said, "What are you doing?" It was a very cross, suspicious, low-voiced "What are you're doing?"

"Um. I can explain."

Linda turned on her light, and her eyes were hard and angry.

"What are you doing with Nicky's letter? Give it to me!" she hissed.

Clara had little option but to hand it over. "It's not one of Nicky's letters. It was from me to you. Only I thought I better get it back," she whispered.

Linda unfolded it and looked at it. "Oh." She looked at Clara again, taking in the fact that she was not in her nightclothes. "You mustn't *do* that, Clara. You'll get in such trouble."

"I'm not. I came back . . . I had such a horrible experience out there. I want a pistol, I think!"

Naturally, then she had to tell the whole story. Linda, now that she'd got over thinking Clara was stealing her letters, was desperate to talk Clara out of running away.

"Look, it can't work. And why Queensland? It's so hot there. Your mother might get better . . . please don't do this. Please. Promise me."

"Promise you won't tell."

"Of course I won't. But you mustn't do this. Anyway, you can't get there. You'd have to go with the smugglers across the Spencer Gulf. You've got no one to go with you. You can't go without a chaperone."

"I know. I'm going to bed now."

"Promise you're not going?"

Clara shook her head. "Not now. I'm going to bed."

The next predawn "day" Clara spent being cloyingly sweet— which Mrs. Darlington seemed to adore—and doing some careful investigation. And at about eight in the morning, she said she had a headache and would like to lie down.

"Shall I get dear Dr. Leaming to come and have a look at you?" asked an anxious Mrs. Darlington.

"No. I'm just tired. I didn't sleep well last night, worrying about my mother."

"You poor dear. You should have a little lie-down. And Linda's such a little bagpipe, I should think you need a rest."

Clara smiled at her new friend, and then at Linda's mother, feeling like a complete fraud to both of them. "Thank you. Linda's been so nice. But . . . I'm tired. I don't think I will get up for tea, if you don't mind."

"My dear, you have to eat!" said the plump Mrs. Darlington, who lived for her food—especially macaroons.

"I'll be fine. I just need a good sleep."

That at least was true, even if it wouldn't be happening. Ten minutes later Clara had slipped out of the window and boarded the trolley-bus to North Central Station. The man at the ticket office didn't even question her buying a ticket to Mandynonga, where the farms fed by the drip-irrigators with desalinated water grew the expensive food. It was a common enough destination. It was also where the food for the power stations on the Northern Sheba line, which Tim was working on, was loaded. Clara had to smile wryly to herself. It was quite possible that she'd beat her letter up there.

It was also sure that people would ask awkward questions about her traveling alone all that way. So she'd better have a story. She already had a kitchen knife from Mrs. Darlington's cutlery drawer, in case of any more unwelcome attentions.

The Mandynonga line was still above ground, and Clara got her first look at the Westralian countryside outside the sand walls of Ceduna.

It was not quite as bleak as she'd expected. There were plants: a few scrubby, spiky, odd-leafed trees in little coppice-like clusters; yellow patches of grass . . . and something that hopped away from the train. In spite of her anxiety and all the things on her mind, Clara couldn't help but be delighted at her first sight of a kangaroo outside the pages of books. But the trip made Clara realize two things about Australia. It was flat, and there was a lot of it. She knew it wasn't all flat, of course. But the broadness of the horizon and the searing blue sky made her feel very small.

The chaos of Mandynonga station and the termite run workers getting off their odd-shaped carriages made her feel lost, too. But she hadn't got this far to be put off. There were glum-looking groups of men getting on the curious white, flattened carriages, swinging their bedrolls and bags aboard, as well as the raucously cheery ones getting off. Clara studied the train, and the first thing she realized was that it wasn't really a train. It hung from an overhead rail.

There was no locomotive. Maybe that would come later . . .

A whistle blew.

"Departure five minutes. All passengers and freight for the Alice and Diamantia Line, last call. Embark or load now or we leave without you!" bellowed a florid faced man in blue dungarees and a little frogged waistcoat.

Clara wasn't even sure how to get a ticket, let alone if this was the right train. But that horrible drunken man had said something about Diamantia. And Clara was nothing if not decisive. Wrong sometimes, yes, but she'd decided she'd rather do things than just worry about them. Mother kept saying it would land her in trouble.

Well, it might. But still she swung herself into the nearest carriage. The men sitting on the wooden benches with their swags gaped at her as if she'd crawled out of a piece of green cheese.

"Here, Missy," said one finally. "You can't get on this clanker. She's going up north."

"So am I. I am going to find my brother. He's at Power Station 1786, Dajarra," she said airily. "I have to talk to him about our father, and seeing as he's on a contract, he can't come to Ceduna. Or that's what he said in his letter."

The audience stared at her. Finally one said, "Are you *sure* he's your brother, Missy?"

Clara surprised herself by starting to cry, having her carefully constructed story come apart before she'd really even started on it. She put it down to being dog-tired and over-worried. "My mother is unconscious in hospital. And my father's a prisoner in Queensland. I need to get to Tim."

It took a few seconds for the sandy-haired fellow—the one who'd asked if she was sure if Tim was her brother—to react. "Eh. Simmo. Davo. Gimme your swags. We'd better tuck you under the bench, Missy. Conductor will be here in a few minutes and he'll chuck you off if he sees you."

Hidden behind bedding rolls, Clara heard the conductor

demanding, "Where yer all goin'?" The men sang out various numbers, then the clanking started as the carriage rattled and rolled away
into the darkness toward the hot red center of Australia.

"Orright, Missy. Yer can probably come out now," said someone.

So Clara crawled out from under the bench into the dimly lit,
swaying, low-roofed carriage and the stares of the men there. She felt
rather like telling them it was rude to stare so, but they had helped
her, after all.

"Um. Good Morning. So, er, where are you all going?" It was,
in a way, rather like the submarine in the carriage.

She could see teeth in the answering grins. "G'day to you, too.
North, I reckon. Nowhere else the clanker goes," said one of them.
"So where are you from, Missy? Never heard of no nice girls catching
the clanking white ant." He seemed to be implying she was a "nice
girl," so that was all right.

"Um." There seemed no real point in pretending she was a local
girl. Her accent betrayed her. "Ireland."

"Me da came from Ireland," said the sandy-haired one, smiling
and nodding. "Best thing he coulda' done, he said to me."

"Me mam, too. You came in with the submarine?" asked a fellow
with a handlebar moustache. "The one they blockaded the harbor with
half the Royal Navy to stop? I heard there was some women on her."

That simplified things nicely. "Yes. My mother and I came on
the *Cuttlefish*."

"Aye. Wish they'd bring more girls. It's a good country for men
is Westralia. But even in Ceduna there's two men for every woman.
Up north, it'll be about two hundred to one, I reckon. I'm gunna
earn some money and go back to Dominion I reckon. It's crook there,
but there's girls. What's it like in Ireland, Missy?"

So she told them. From there it was a short step to telling them
of her adventures leaving Ireland . . . and basking in their adulation
because her father was in jail for fighting against the British Empire.
That was a new experience. She stopped short, though, of telling

them about the message. About the fact that, for some reason, the British Empire had sent her father to Queensland. In the meantime she talked to them about places they'd never see and heard about the hot, bleak interior, and of why the coaches were painted white. "They can be, see. No coal smuts. And it reflects heat best in the couple of bits the clanker comes out."

"But where is the engine?" She was puzzled by the lack of coal smuts. Soot and smuts were a way of life in a world that ran on coal.

"Oh, the clankers don't have 'em. Can't burn coal down here. The carriages have clamps on them that snag on the belt, see."

Clara didn't, but they were happy to explain, if a little surprised that she didn't know. There were power stations along the route, outside the tunnels, that wound huge drums of continuous cables. Ten miles was the practical limit, so every twenty miles there was a power station, providing a cable to haul the trains along ten miles to either side of them. It meant, of course, that the segments were mostly straight. They could do curves, but that started to get more complicated than Clara was following, or wanted to. Submarines and navigation interested her. Cable cars in tunnels, not so much. But the carriages were so flat because for every one running north, there was another coming south. The tunnels were round, and they had to fit.

"Why not just make them bigger?" she asked. "The tunnels I mean."

"Cause the drill heads on the steam moles are round. So the tunnels are round."

He hauled out his pocket watch. "We're crossing the gap soon. You'll get to see it."

"She's a lovely sight. Never get tired of it," said one of the other, older men, with a smile. "There's a few other aerial sections, but the gap's the biggest. Mind you, it can get hot out there."

"Yeah, but Power Seven is just the other side of her. She blows good cool air into the tunnels."

They came out into late-afternoon daylight, the shadows long across the landscape of reds, browns, and ochre below the cable-train, as she hung on a silver rail above the rocky valley below. The rail was suspended between enormous pylons, coming up from the dry valley. Looking carefully Clara could see there was some sparse vegetation. "It's so beautiful. But I thought it was all desert."

"My word, I seen her in flood once," said one of the older northbound workers. "Was nothing but water as far as the eye could see. It runs into Lake Eyre. That's not been full for a while, but when we get a wet, here, Missy, we get a real wet." He looked at the entry to the tunnel on the valley wall ahead. "Better tuck you under the seats again. The conductor comes around to check no one's drunk and starting fights, and the food-sellers on the platform might rat on you."

And so Clara's journey into the red heart of Australia continued. She ate with them—they wouldn't take her money—and talked, and eventually dosed, learning more about the miners and rail workers heading into the north, a part the British Empire considered virtually uninhabited and uninhabitable. And they were even running cattle up there.

The one thing that was even stranger was how many of these young men had come from the Dominion of Australia, and how many were planning to head back there, with good Westralian gold in their pockets. If *they* could go to-and-fro, surely she could?

※

Linda had just picked up a message from Nicky—hidden in the hedge in their secret spot—when she heard her stepmother scream.

She barely had time to tuck the note up her sleeve before her stepmother bustled in. "Do say you know where Clara is. Her bed . . . her bed had a pillow in it. I thought she must still be asleep," she said, her speech fast and voice a little shrill. "I thought with her mother being so unwell it was best to leave her . . ."

"No, Mother," said Linda, feeling sure her face must betray her as an absolute liar. But fortunately her stepmother was neither observant, at the best of times, nor looking at her. She rushed out, calling, "Clara! Clara? Where are you, Clara?"

Linda was fairly sure she was not going to get a reply.

One thing was certain. It would be a rotten time, for the next few days, to meet Nicky at night as he suggested. If Clara had run away, police would investigate every young woman they could find out on the street.

※

"Gunna have to change at Mooree," said Sandy. "I'm on the Tjarri Power Station, that's sixty miles from Dajarra, but we're pushing north. Dajarra is the last power station pushing south from Sheba. So you'll haveta change tonight at Mooree. That's where the Alice Line splits off. You go on to Alice, across to Sheba, and then down to Dajarra. That's the last part of the back-cut towards us. They've got maybe thirty miles to go, and one more power station, before the line opens all the way to Ceduna. They're pushing hard, but it's hard rock country."

He tapped the fellow with the handlebar moustache on the shoulder. "Mick's going to Sheba. He'll see you through and onto the supply clanker to Dajarra. Not many going that way on this trip, I reckon. They got some real crook bastards workin' the shifts up there. My shift-captain worked there for a while, but he don't like some of that crew. The station boss, he's all right, though, I reckon. Feller called McGurk. Talk straight to him, I reckon. No use pretending you're not there."

※

The big difference, Tim decided, between the exhausting work on the steam mole and the submarine—where work could be exhausting, too—was the power stations. The steam mole would do thirty-six hours at the bore-face and then be pulled back to the power station, and the next mole would be cantilevered in. The crew would get some proper sleep, then re-tip the drill heads, then have some more time off in the cavernous power station. You didn't have to live with the crew in the confined space of the mole, which was like the submarine in that sense, for months on end. His cubby on the steam mole was smaller, and the noise and vibration were such that it was hard to sleep well—but for thirty-six hours you could get by on exhausted catnaps. It made, however, for even more bad-tempered companions.

"What you writing, Blackfeller? I didn't know you blacks could write. I thought it was too much for your brains," said the burly steam-biscuit foreman, staring at Tim, huddled in his cubby-bunk, trying to gather his thoughts with a precious piece of paper and an indelible pencil. Writing to Clara wasn't easy. He didn't want to moan. And he didn't want to say anything about needing to break his contract and get back to the *Cuttlefish.* Heaven alone knew what that girl might do. The thought made him smile. Capable of taking on a wildfire with a thimble full of water, was Clara.

It wasn't what the steam-biscuit foreman wanted. "I said, what you writing, Blackfeller? You answer me when I talk to you."

As far as they were concerned he was one of the aboriginals, and that, it seemed, was enough to make some of the steam-mole crew nasty. And a fight with this big bruiser wouldn't help.

"A letter," Tim answered.

"Oooh . . . a letter now. Black boy's writing a letter. I didn't think you boongs could write your own name. Lemme see." And he snatched it from Tim's hand.

"Give that back!" yelled Tim, stretching for it. He didn't have any more paper and he'd gone to such effort to clean his hands before touching it. Now this oaf with coal-black thumbs was smearing it.

The foreman held it out of reach. "Dear Clara," he read. "Ooh, black boy's got hisself a woman. I didn't know you wrote to them. I thought you blackfellers just pulled their skirts off." And as he turned to the rest of the watching audience in their cubbies, he ripped the letter in two.

Something in Tim just snapped. The foreman was much bigger and older than he was. He was looking for a fight. Looking for a soft target to bully. Tim knew that. What the man wasn't expecting was a furious volcano of rage. Tim dropped his head and charged with wildly flailing fists—not exactly fighting science. His head caught the bigger man in the wobbly belly, and he went over and down with Tim on top of him, yelling, and punching everything he could hit.

The others pulled him off, and Tim, sanity returning, was horrified at himself. His heart still thumped furiously, as his tormentor got up off the floor, helped by several of the crew. His nose was bleeding and one eye was already swelling shut. Tim saw the initial shocked fear in the foreman's eyes turn into a publicly humiliated rage. Tim knew that, short of a miracle, he was going to be killed. The foreman grabbed him by the shirt-front and swung a massive fist at his head. Tim managed to duck sideways and most of the force of the blow slid off his cheek and temple. Tim's yell was outdone by a bellow from his attacker, who hit the steel stanchion so hard it vibrated. "My bloody hand! You little black . . ."

"*What* is going on here?" demanded a chilly voice.

Tim really disliked Shift-captain Vister. But right now he was glad to see him. Warm wetness trickled down Tim's cheek, and the pain started.

"This boong attacked me, sir. Attacked me without reason or provocation. I think he's mad," said the foreman.

And it just went downhill from there. It was obvious that the shift-captain was not going to let Tim speak or defend himself.

"I can't demote you, because you're already as low as an employee can go, but I'm going to dock you three weeks pay. Next step is to fire you. And unless you fancy walking back to Sheba, don't make me do that," said the shift-captain.

"Go ahead," said Tim, sullen.

That finally got Shift-captain Vister to stop his rant. He shut his mouth like a steel trap. Finally he snarled, "I can't. But I'm going to lock you up until we get back to the power station, you insolent pup. And the report I'm going to write on you will make sure you never get another job in Westralia. That sort of reputation gets around."

Tim looked around at the watchers. Almost the entire shift was there, as the steam mole made its way back to the power station after their thirty-six hour shift. Not one soul had said a word in his defense.

"Go ahead, throw me off," he said again. Anything had to be better than being in here with this lot.

The shift-captain looked like a trapped rat, eyes darting around. Obviously he'd threatened something a bit beyond his power.

And then someone sniggered.

The shift-captain slammed his hand down on the central reservoir, echoing, silencing everyone. "Stop the train," he said.

No one moved. "You heard me," he shouted. "Stop the mole. This boong gets off *now*. He can walk back to the power station."

"You can't do that, sir," said someone.

"Watch me, Samuels. And don't you give me any of your lip or I'll dock you three weeks pay, too. And any of the rest of you!"

The mole came to a shuddering halt.

"It'll kill him out there, sir. He can't breathe in the tunnels."

"See if I care. Only good one of these blackfellers is a dead one."

"At least let him out at the emergency exit."

"A weeks pay, Samuels. But yes. He can hold his breath, or breathe his own stink that long, and then walk back to the power station. All he has to do is follow the termite run for six miles."

Tim found himself hauled off by the shift-captain and the foreman and hustled along to the lock.

And pushed out into the darkness.

Tim fell off the high step, down and out into the dark. He managed to catch himself on his hands, landing against the wall of the termite run, half the breath knocked out of him by the fall. He had little choice but to breathe the smoky stuff out there. Fortunately, they were a long way from the cutting edge, and the air pumped from the power station to here was not quite unbreathable . . . not for a breath or so.

The lock clanged shut. And with a dragon hiss and a shower of sparks, the huge steam mole began to move away. Tim had to flatten himself against the wall to avoid being crushed by drill bits sticking out of the drill head.

In a sudden panic Tim ran after the steam mole, falling over the sleepers they laid for the mole rails. Gasping. Trying to yell.

He couldn't run very far in this air. Panting, he leaned against the wall, trying to think, trying not to panic. Surely they couldn't just abandon him here.

The sparks of the mole and its *clack-clack* sounds grew farther away.

The air in here would surely kill him before he could walk out. He felt nauseous and weak already, but tried to think calmly, which was just so difficult. There were breather holes and emergency exits every half a mile. The question was, was he near one, or just past one? He stood still trying to decide, swaying on his feet. Then he moved forward, feeling the wall. It was totally dark, and the steam mole's sounds grew ever more distant.

He was just getting to think he might try crawling when his hand hit wood instead of cast concrete . . . and then the heavy wheel of a door screw.

It took all he could offer of his strength to haul the screw open and pull himself into the shaft. The air there was stale, but better. Still, climbing the metal staples to the upper hatch was incredibly hard work—not because it was, but because of how Tim was feeling. At the top, he hauled at the latch, nearly falling from the ladder as it suddenly opened.

To a blast of heat . . . and air.

Hot out there or not, Tim clambered out on hands and knees. The sun beating down on him was hot . . . but joyous. He crawled away from the hole. There wasn't much logic in doing that, he just didn't want to be near it.

CHAPTER 4

Jack Calland was unceremoniously turfed out of bed. "Move. Yer back on the work squads."

"I thought I had to be looked after. I think I'm dying," said Jack, groaning for all he was worth.

"Go ahead and die," said the warder, kicking him in the ribs. Jack rolled away, weighing his chances. They didn't seem too good. There was another warder in earshot. "Orders from the commandant. He must have had word from on high that we don't need yer anymore. So I can get the dogs, or yer can get moving."

Jack cursed to himself and staggered to his feet. It had to be today. Just when things were finally so close. He'd planned to become a corpse tonight. Well, a living one. But he'd found out where the morgue was, and that he could get into it. And the corpses of the prisoners were dumped into the river for the crocodiles. Only Jack had seen the river from the camp perimeter. It was more dry mud than water this time of year. There were crocodiles, but they took the first few corpses and took their time to come back for the rest. Jack planned . . . well, hoped, to either get away before that, or be at the back of the pile.

He'd actually been getting better, not sicker. Fluids, rest, and some food . . . and he was no longer walking on the edge of death. He'd taken care not to let the "hospital" know that. But now . . . they didn't seem to care anymore. Something had changed, and it had to be something to do with Mary. He wished desperately he knew what it was.

Well, he'd just have to play dead and get dumped with the corpses. In the huge prison compound there were at least four or five every day, victims of the tropical heat and diseases. Jack knew the Empire put scanty value on their lives. He was just puzzled as to why they bothered to have a camp here, where even the warders suffered. Prisoners arrived, and prisoners were taken away. And when they went, they didn't come back.

Jack's plans were cast into turmoil again when he found himself being leg ironed and forced to shuffle out of the camp attached to six other prisoners. He was going to find out for himself just where the prisoners went.

They did not have to walk far. The railway line had a crude roof over it, with a narrow slit in it to allow smoke out. The prisoners were herded onto cattle trucks going west. The manacles were locked onto the bars of the truck and the guards retreated to a caboose that gushed out a fog of cold air as they opened the door.

"Freezer wagon. For meat. Hope the bastards get stuck in it and freeze," said his neighbor on the line of manacles, a dark-skinned man with lank, curly hair. Jack guessed him to be one of the aboriginals. Quite a lot of the prisoners were black.

"So where are we going?" Jack asked. It was no time, yet, for the infamous Jack Calland sense of humor. He needed serious answers first.

"Work on the railway," said his companion in a tone of voice he might have used if he'd said "step out in front of the firing squad."

It soon became apparent that this was pretty much exactly what it did mean. Jack's fellow prisoners knew very little about this railway going to the west. Except that no one came back, and only the irredeemable had gone . . . at first. Now, they were sending everyone. Even those who'd got drunk and been in town after curfew and got into a punch up with the police, like his new chain companion, Quint.

"So what did you do, man?" asked Quint.

That was an interesting question. "Headed up the efforts to

destroy the British Empire's hold over Ireland," was an answer he'd avoided giving so far. Protesting innocence might not be a good idea either. This was a one-way trip, and it was unlikely Quint was a spy. "I'm Irish. I was involved in the rebellion."

"Yeah. Seen a few o' your kind."

It didn't sound as though he was too happy about the experience. But then, this was not a place for joyous meetings. It was dark, hot, and the air smoky. The "tunnel," with its hand's width of gap in the roof, did keep off the direct sun, but that was all you could say for it. Jack was an engineer by training, and it all reeked of haste and incompetence. It wasn't that strong, he was sure. And the rail the leg irons were attached to was barely a quarter inch of mild steel, if he was any judge. A hastily welded rod to convert a cattle truck into a prisoner transport.

"Have you thought about escape?" he asked Quint.

"Don't be stupid. Where are you gunna go? And we're chained together." Quint paused, then asked, "I suppose you got a file?"

Something about the pause, and the spying within the prison in New Dublin, made Jack pause himself. "Just wondering."

He kept his peace after that, squatting down and surreptitiously testing the bar. It bent a little . . .

Later, when the train stopped and warders came with water buckets, he learned just how wise he'd been not to speak further.

"He's talking about escaping," said his neighbor to the warder with the bucket. It was a very valuable bucket of water. It came from the refrigeration truck—not out of kindness, Jack suspected, but just because that was where the warders were. The warders walked down the line with a trusty and a bucket. You had the time it took for them to walk it to take a dipper and scoop and drink and get it to the man next to you to use—and heaven help you if you took too long to drink and the next man missed out. He'd probably kill you, and the warders wouldn't stop him.

The warder paused, enabling Jack's treacherous neighbor to steal another dipper full of that glorious cold water. "Yeah? Ponty, you better search this one." He poked Jack with his club. And there was no water for him.

Ponty—a flat-faced warder with long, thin, hard fingers hauled Jack up by the hair, from where he sat slumped against the wall. Jack was last in the chain-gang group. "Yer looks like trouble," he said, digging fingers into anyplace a prisoner could hide anything.

It could have been awkward if Jack had had anything for him to find. As it was, he was just searched, roughed up a bit, and missed his chance at a drink of cold water.

※

"Escape," the tall man with the odd accent had said, "escape." Up to now Lampy Green had only been thinking of dying.

He shouldn't have done it. If he'd thought about what might happen he wouldn't have. If he'd known that it would lead to him being chained like a dog, he would have just walked away.

But actually, he knew he wouldn't have. Part of him hated himself to the core. The bastard had been his father. He shouldn't have done it. But when he'd come home with a stolen sheep, and his father laid into her with the stock whip, and she ran to him. And the axe had been there. If he hadn't fought with his father. If his father hadn't been drunk. If his father's woman hadn't put the blame on him. If he'd run instead of trying to stop the bleeding. If the mutton carcass hadn't been there.

If.

If he could get out of here, they'd never take him alive. Not in all his fifteen years had he been so afraid, so . . . imprisoned.

When they locked him up, he'd started to die.

He wanted to ask the new prisoner on their shackle line just how he thought it could be done. But not while they had a snitch with them. A snitch who'd just proved he would betray any one of them.

But there was another black man on the line. When Quint was asleep Lampy talked to him. He had to speak English. The man came from the far north.

"If he can break us out," said one of the white prisoners, the shifty-looking bastard who stole his bread, "you boongs c'n count me in. They'll work us until we die here. Me and the rest of us, except that Quint. He rats on us, we'll kill him."

Lampy had no trouble believing him.

※

Other men might have taken it out on the man who did this to them. Jack just stored it away. Knowing who would rat, who could be used to feed false information to the authorities, was also useful. But plainly it was terrifying the fellow next to him. The fink was obviously aiming for a place as a trusty. When the bread came around he whined about being threatened for trying to help the warders.

It didn't do him a whole lot of good, for reasons that became obvious a little later. The train stopped and they were herded and prodded off . . . to the reason that prisoners didn't come back from this trip.

It was not so much brutality, or murderous desire, but that the facts of this place must not leak out. It was brutal, of course. Some of the men hadn't even survived the trip, and the soldiers who took over herding the prisoners showed no mercy. One of the men in their cattle truck had lapsed into unconsciousness. The guards simply chopped his legs off and shot the bleeding, dying man. It provided a horrific lesson to the rest of the prisoners.

They had been taken to a military camp. A large military camp, heavily camouflaged. What was happening there was plain to Jack's eye, thanks to his experience in Ireland. This was a build-up of men and materiel for some kind of attack. It could only be on something in Westralia.

Jack had a good grasp of geography. But no one really knew just what lay in the vast deserts and semi-deserts of central Australia, besides heat that could kill a man. There were mines of great wealth there. Jack knew there was gold and iron to be had, just for a start.

It must be a prize worth a lot to the British Empire. There were, by his rough calculation, billets for maybe four thousand men in the camp. And there was a build-up in the marshaling yard they'd been disembarked at, trains and carriages, and, as he saw a little later, a fleet of trucks. The Hussars and Dragoons in their tropical undress kit intended to strike hard and fast, somewhere. They weren't colonial troops. These were elite men, out from England itself, sharpening up for an attack.

And somewhere soon.

The British Empire didn't care if prisoners died for no real reason or gain, but the British Army was a little less wasteful of its men, especially if it had shipped or flown them halfway around the world for this.

The reason they had begun taking any prisoners, and not just the few with death sentences, for the chain gangs, carrying sleepers and laying down track under the eyes of soldier-guards, was also quite obvious to Jack, within hours: They were pushing hard. Pushing to get to the last staging post before the vehicles could make their final stab across the desert.

Jack was no one's fool, except, at times, his own. In a way this meant the railway hard-labor gangs were no longer a work-until-you-die sentence. When they'd finished here, the British Army wouldn't care who knew about it anymore.

His fellow prisoners on the gang of seven, leg ironed together, didn't know that, though. All they saw was grueling work with little food, barely enough water, and other prisoners dying and being shot like dogs.

About a third of the prisoners were aboriginals or, like Quint, part aboriginal. They got it from both sides. The soldiers treated everyone badly, and them, if anything, worse. The white Australian prisoners tended to take it out on them, too. The kid in their line was a youngster, barely more than a boy, who was even blacker than Quint, and he was having the worst time of it. Deloraine, who'd obviously been a thief, stole the kid's bread ration the first day. Jack gave the kid half of his, meager though it was. He couldn't watch the boy watch him eat, even if he knew he needed his own strength. The others noticed. And the next time there was none of that, although Jack was watching. Quint was again doing his best to kiss up to the guards, but there was little chance to do so. He might have been hoping for a soft job as a trusty. The rest had seen what was happening out there, and weren't wanting anything but away. Plainly, they talked among themselves. Jack was awakened by a quiet shaking from the next man along from Deloraine, a full-blood aboriginal man that no one messed with. "Irishman. You talk 'bout escape?"

"That was on the train. The bar could have been broken. But yes. I'm for it. Just trying to work out how."

"Donner and me and Parsee, Deloraine and Lampy, we all ready to take a chance wi' you. The country out there is a killer, man. And they got dogs for hunting us. But it feels like we're in for a wet. If we're going to make a break, we need to do it soon, in the rain. You break us loose, we'll go 'long."

※

Deep in the desert Tim Barnabas dreamed of rain. His mind must have been a bit messed up by breathing bad air, being nearly frightened to death, and maybe even the bump he'd taken on his head. Somehow, he'd lost the low hump of ground that indicated the termite run. It was quite rugged terrain out here, not the miles of flat sand he'd thought he'd find. The sky was a dirty red. The wind wuthered among the rocks and scattered dry, yellow shreds of grass. There were the scattered, twisted, wind-desiccated bones of trees here for him to fall over, too.

He really wasn't sure where he was going. His head throbbed and his mouth was dry, but at least he wasn't sweating so much anymore. Surely that must be good.

It was just so hot.

Eventually he stopped staggering along and took some shelter from the sun under the overhang of a large boulder. He lay there, looking at the cracks and shades of red, and watched them twine and make strange patterns before his eyes. It was slightly cooler under the rock—anything was better than the beating sun. Mind you, that was half hidden in blowing dust, a fierce red disk up in the sky.

Tim must have slipped away into a sort of sleep, or at least unconsciousness, because when he woke up he was shivering with cold and it was dark, and his head wasn't quite such a mess. He was still desperately thirsty.

He was pretty sure that he'd come from that direction . . . he'd certainly crawled under the rock from it. And therefore, logically, if he walked back that way, he'd come out at the mound that marked the termite run. If he walked along it, only at night, he had to come out at the power station, and water. The mole had been on its way back. That was why he'd been so busy trying to finish his letter to Clara, to put it with the mail on the supply train returning to Sheba. It couldn't be more than six . . . seven miles, surely. Walking at night was the right thing to do. He could manage seven miles.

Somehow.

If he was walking the right direction.

The sky was hazy, so he couldn't even use the stars to navigate by.

And walking straight . . . well, that was out of the question. It was broken, stony ground. And dark.

He just had to do his best.

Slow but steady.

He wasn't sure how long he'd been making that slow but steady progress, with occasional falls, when the moon came up.

Tim's head was in that exhausted, cloudy zone where nothing

made much sense except to put one foot in front of the other. At first he was just grateful for the extra light. There were scrubby bushes here to fall over, too, but then something struck him as wrong.

He'd learned navigation on the submarine. It had been one of the subjects he'd needed for his submariner's ticket. The moon rises in the east.

He was walking the wrong way. Except . . . except, had he walked east or west when he first wandered away from the termite run?

He honestly didn't know. His head was whirling.

So thirsty.

And there were more of these bushes, and even a tussock to fall over between the stones. He chose the path of least resistance, no longer caring if he walked straight or east or west. Just . . . one foot in front of the other.

And then things got worse. He fell into a hole. A sandy, scrabbly edged hole, far deeper than he was tall.

He tried to clamber out of it, too weak to grab the crumbly edge and haul himself up. He slipped and fell again, and for a while he just lay there.

And then it dawned on him that his face was laying on something damp.

Damp . . . in the desert.

That gave him, from somewhere deep inside, a spurt of energy and clarity he'd thought lost to him forever.

Damp sand in a hole . . . It was definitely damp, sticking together the way the sand on the edge of the pit had not.

On his knees, Tim dug—he could feel the damp through the knees of his dungarees now. He scraped away sand. And more wet sand. And more.

Eventually he stopped. He wondered if he could try sucking the water out of the sand. After a few minutes he sighed to himself and tried to swallow around his swollen tongue, then reached into the hole to start again. He was down nearly a full arm-stretch by now.

He stuck his hand into water.

It was barely enough to cover his palm.

It was still water.

It might have been muddy, but he didn't begin to care.

It trickled between his cracked lips.

Nothing had ever been quite as welcome.

He could have drunk gallons and gallons of it . . . except it was a slow process. A little bit of the precious stuff cupped in his fingers to each mouthful, and it seeped in very slowly, too.

After far too few mouthfuls to slake his thirst, but enough to help his thinking, Tim started on a second, bigger hole, a little farther across. He found a stick to help dig, and it went easier. With two holes he could let one seep while he drank from the other.

The sky was beginning to pale for another blistering day in the desert by the time Tim had had enough to drink. His head was much clearer, and he started to work things out. This must be a watercourse. Not so much a river as where the floodwater ran when the desert saw rain or run-off from elsewhere. That was why there'd been more vegetation to fall over.

And the hole . . . well, someone must have dug it. His feet choosing their own path—the course of least resistance—in his state last night had somehow put him on a trail of some kind, to this hole that someone must have dug to reach the water.

Tim had his wits about him enough by now to know that he needed to drink and get himself into as much shade as possible before the sun baked down on this hole. It would be cooler in here for a while yet, but the sky was already a relentless blue, very different from yesterday's wind-blown red.

He knew he had to stay out of the sun. He knew a few hours in it could easily kill him. He just didn't know quite what to do next. He couldn't stay here forever. And yet . . . to leave the water was simply terrifying. He steeled himself for at least a clamber out of the pit. Now, in daylight, not in the state he'd been in last night, it wasn't that difficult. It still left him panting and tired, just that little bit of exertion. But in the morning light he could see that this was indeed a river bed—or had been once in wetter times. Walking, except along the trail he'd stumbled onto, would have been difficult. There were more plants here, even some scrubby coppice-like trees up to seven or eight feet tall, with waxy green leaves. In the distance he heard a bird calling. But there was no sign of which way the termite run was. Tim could tell east and west and north and south, but besides the path he'd followed, he had no idea where any humans might be. It was quite a well-trodden path, though. He wondered if he ought to follow it. Surely it couldn't be far to wherever the digger of the hole lived. Unless . . . unless of course it was an animal. Tim literally had no idea what kind of wild animal might live in Australia. It was too far from the tunnels under Drowned London. He needed some kind of weapon. Or fire . . .

That would do. People would see the smoke. He should be able to see the smoke of the power station . . .

Only he had no means of making fire, and the sky showed no trails of smoke.

How had he come so far?

CHAPTER 5

The opportunity to escape came for Jack and his fellow prisoners two days later, thanks to the rain the young aboriginal prisoner, Lampy, had predicted. They were carrying sleepers, and very grateful for that rain and the little bit of cool that came with it. They'd just got back to the pile that had been dumped off the rail car when one of the soldiers pointed to them and said, "Right. You lot. Onto that cattle truck with the gravel. Been a washout at Three-mile Creek."

So they found themselves shunted down there, to off-load three tons of crushed rock in the rain while the two guards sat and smoked in the cab with the engine driver and fireman. There were five other gangs, each in a cattle truck half-full of gravel. It wasn't, to Jack's eye, going to work. That was fine. He helped to make sure it wouldn't. He dumped his sack-load carefully into the culvert, and tipped a wink at the others—barring Quint—to do the same. They'd got good at working around the would-be trusty. The man was nervous, but still working toward ingratiating himself with the new military guards. And Jack bided his time. They carried load after load, while the rain sheeted down.

"Big rain," said Jack.

One of the others laughed grimly. "Nothing to what'll be comin'. North end gets plenty . . . but all at once."

"Guess we won't tell them the culvert is blocked and the bridge is going to wash away," said Jack with grim satisfaction.

Naturally, Quint did, as soon as they got near the engine, singing out and pulling them closer, the others angry and reluctant.

Jack had to smile to himself. You couldn't fake this kind of stuff. And Quint had already made himself known to the troopers on guard duty. They weren't the elites training at the camp. They were just sappers, and sour with the job, too.

"Ah, hell's teeth," a soldier swore as he got down from the cab. He turned to his fellow. "Come on. I'm not getting wet while you sit here like Lord Muck."

"I'll get my rifle wet," complained the other.

"Leave it in the bloody cab. Mine's wet already." He pointed at the prisoners. "Go on, you lot, get back to it."

They turned and began their chained shuffle while the guards jogged toward the water. When they were a good distance off, Jack fell over, pulling Quint down, and at the same time hitting him with the fist-sized rock he'd picked up in the stream. "Pick him up with me and walk closer to the engine," he said quietly. "Sorr? Mr. Driver, sorr," he called out, "this feller's fallen and hit his head."

The driver put his head out and Jack pitched the rock as hard as he'd ever thrown a cricket ball—but from a lot closer. And he'd been a first class player, once. It hit the driver on the side of the head, and then they were running forward. The fireman, who had come to see why his driver had pitched out of the cab with a groan, took a swing at them with a shovel and found himself grabbed by six desperate men hauling a groaning seventh. They sat on the fireman and held a sharp shovel to his throat.

Jack knew how to get a steam engine going. "More coal, boys," he said, opening the fire door and the dampers. "And any of you who can shoot, deal with the armed guard if he comes back. He'll be out to kill us, so I suppose we may as well play by their rules."

"They don't seem to have noticed. They're down at the water," said Deloraine. "Man, have you gone crazy? Taking the locomotive? They'll shoot us all for this."

"They'll kill us or work us to death anyway, Rainey," said Donner.

"It's too late now, anyway," said Jack. "Here we go." He turned the lever and the engine began to roll slowly but steadily away up the hill, with the squealing of metal on metal. "More coal. Come on! More coal."

Behind them in the rain, someone shouted. Jack opened the throttle as far as it would go. Looking back on the slow curve away from the creek he could see two uniformed men running toward them. And one knelt down.

"How's your shooting?" asked Jack, as something ricocheted off metal farther back on the train.

The adult aboriginal, Marni, had taken the rifle with the calm assurance of someone who'd used one often. "Better n' his," he said, and shot. "Blast. Winged him."

Jack could shoot, too, but from the cab of the rattling train, he doubted he could do anything like as well as Marni. The other man still ran after the train, the driver now up and running behind him, with blood on his face.

"Give them the fireman."

They flung the man off into the bushes. Jack managed, in all the fear and tension, to feel a little sorry for the fellow, but he might be better off of the train.

It was not a very fast little steam locomotive, and there was a slight upgrade from the creek before a flattening, and then they were on a long upgrade away. The runner might almost catch the train, if he was fit enough, on the second grade. Jack had noticed it was the old three-link coupling joining the carriages. He knew enough to know what that meant. He grabbed the fire-door lever and a short section of bar, knelt down next to Lampy, and inserted the points into the leg iron chain. He twisted the two bars in opposite directions, and the chain snapped.

"You need to jump from carriage to carriage to the guard's van," Jack told Lampy. "The caboose . . . there'll be a big brake wheel. Release it and get back here as fast as possible."

※

Lampy relished being free of that dog chain on his leg, even if it meant he had to make the terrifying jump from the coal tender to the cattle trucks and then onward to the next and the next to the caboose, a little four-wheeled van with a running board and a small verandah. He clambered across to that, and down. And the door was locked. He got onto the running board. Clinging to the rail, he edged his way around to the back verandah, the wheels clickety-clacking on the rails inches from his feet. The back door was open.

The room wasn't empty, though. It had a guard in it. A guard who hadn't . . . yet . . . put the brake on properly, because he hadn't . . . yet . . . stirred from his drunken stupor. A bottle of cheap rum lay on the floor next to him. Lampy had seen that often enough with his father. But the clack and rattle was bound to wake him eventually, even if the shouts and the gunshots didn't. And it looked like the other prisoners had caught on. There was fighting going on.

He could jump—at this speed that was not that much of a risk, and then he would be free, and given the weather, they would never catch him.

If he went in there . . . that big drunk might either catch or kill him. It was no time for thinking or hesitating. But he couldn't help but see in his memory his father bleeding, dying, but still swearing at him and trying to get up.

He swallowed, then opened the door quietly. Not that it would make more noise than the steel wheels on the rails, but it was all he could do to soothe his fear. The hot little cabin stank of the cheap rum, only helping bring the bad memories back to his head as he wrestled the brake wheel, with half an eye on the guard. It finally came easily. He could feel the train start to accelerate. The clatter and rattle far louder now than the dragging squeak of the brake had been. But . . . if the guard woke, he'd just put it on again. The wheel was attached to the shaft with a split-pin.

Lampy hauled at the pin. It didn't move. He looked around for something, anything, to stick through the eye to give him leverage.

Next to the guard's hand lay a clasp knife. The man was definitely stirring. Gritting his teeth, Lampy grabbed the knife, stuck it in the pin eye, and hauled the pin out. The heavy cast iron wheel fell off with a *clang*. Lampy snatched it up . . .

The drunken guard was awake, staring blearily at him. Lampy flung himself out of the door and hurled the wheel and knife away as the guard staggered toward the doorway. Lampy realized, too late, that he should have hung onto the knife. He had to vault onto the running board of the swaying train and swing himself onto the front verandah, as the guard turned and came staggering back to the locked door. The few seconds it took for the guard to open the door were all it took for Lampy to jump the gap, haul himself up, run frantically along the cattle truck, and jump to the next. And on. At the tender he found the others already busy, still chained, but making a human chain down to the coupling.

The Irishman hung down there.

"Jump, boyo!" he yelled. "Well done."

Lampy clung to the edge of the swaying tender, and there was another jerk, and the carriages banged the buffers . . . and then began to slip back as the locomotive accelerated again.

※

Freed of its load, the little engine surged upward toward the grade.

"Haul me up," shouted Jack, and they did. They crawled, dragging the semiconscious Quint along, back to the bucketing and rattling little loco's cab.

"I forgot the brake in the caboose," said Jack. "Devil away, I nearly lost my hand down there."

"You forgot about the guard, too," said Lampy.

"To be sure, I never thought of it!" exclaimed Jack. "Sorry lad. You did well, then."

It was another five miles to the end-of-the-line camp, and Jack

had no intention of being with the train then. He also had very little
intention of being chained up for longer than he had to be. The engine
had tools, and it had levers. He pulled the various fire irons from the
rack. He held them out as he adjusted the throttle with his other hand.

"Break the chain, and we take these with us for the rest later."

The other prisoners were used to taking his orders by now.
"What's the 'rest' you're talking about?" asked Lampy. Maybe he had
doubts after Jack had forgotten the guard. Or maybe he just thought
faster than the rest of them.

"We get off in a creek and shake off the dogs by staying in it.
We let the engine trickle on. I'd like to send it to blow up and crash
at the end of the line, but there's no sense telling them something's
wrong before someone gets there from Three-mile Creek."

"And him?" One of the men pointed at the treacherous Quint.

"It'll be for the best, for now, to take him with us," said Jack,
looking at Quint's frightened eyes.

Jack knew the value of a known traitor, even if those who followed him might easily kill Quint first and listen later.

Besides, he didn't like killing people, least of all in cold blood.

※

Lampy had spent the last two years around his father's "friends," if
you could call them that. He hadn't had much contact with other
white men, besides that kind. This one with the strange accent and
mad ideas was something different.

He was a bit soft. He didn't want to kill Quint.

But then . . . he hadn't held back, either, taking the train,
dealing with the guards and the fireman. And he wasn't stupid.

There was something else, too. Thanks to the Irishman, Lampy
knew he could get away from all the things that crowded in on his
head. Away to the desert and the open land where things were . . .
cleaner. Clearer.

He'd come back to his father when his uncle had been shot.
Now . . . he wasn't sure how or where he was going to go, but he was
never going back to the city fringes again. He was staying out here.
Free.

CHAPTER 6

"End o' the line. Get out all you layabouts. End o' the line," bellowed the conductor, as the clamps on the rolling line released and left the carriage stationary at the Dajarra platform. He hadn't bothered to check the baggage wagon that Mick had smuggled her into. It was odd to not be moving after two days. The clank and rattle were almost part of her now.

Clara took a deep breath, adjusted her hat, took a tighter grip on her parasol, and picked up her reticule and bandbox. She wondered what Mrs. Darlington would have said of her appearance after all this time sleeping on the train, with quite inadequate facilities for washing and no mirror to do her hair properly. Huh. She liked clothes, but this was more important.

She stepped out onto the platform and walked away. The key, she'd decided, was to make sure that the train had left before they could put her onto it. After that . . . well, she really didn't have a plan, beyond vague ideas about how close this was to Queensland. And now that she'd seen the scale of the country, she wondered if she'd been absolutely silly. In hindsight the whole idea was just crazy. She'd had too little sleep and too much worry . . .

And now she was here, walking along the platform to the wrought-iron stairs, trying to look as if she walked this way every day. Above her, steel girders soared to the high, pitched roof of the power station, to her left were the huge winding drums rolling endless silver cable. The smell of coal and the wafts of hot oil pervaded the place. And so far, although they stared, no one had challenged her. A lot of the men looked as if they might, though.

And then someone did. "'Scuse me, Missy," said a tall, young man with a puce Spencer-coat with green epaulettes.

Her stomach knotted.

The big, young man beamed at her. "Can I carry yer bag, Missy?"

"Er. Yes, please." She handed it to him gratefully.

"Where are you going, Missy?" he asked.

"I would like to go and see Mr. McGurk."

He nodded. That obviously made her being there perfectly all right. And having someone escort her was obviously all the passport she needed. "We could walk a little slower, please," she said.

So they positively dawdled. It would have driven Clara mad . . . if she hadn't been playing for time. Mick from Sheba had said the clankers normally only stayed as long as it took to off-load mail, men, and supplies, and to take aboard anyone who had to go back. Her bag carrier was doing his best to engage in small talk, but, Clara realized, he must have used up nearly all his courage coming to talk to her. He couldn't be more than three years older than her. Every time he said anything he turned puce enough to match his jacket. She did her best at small talk for him. He was, she discovered, a sub-foreman on the steam mole *Passara*. He told her of the *Passara*'s virtues, and the number of tons of coal she used, and the number of chains they dug, and of re-tipping the drill bits, as they walked along corridors lit with brass fittings . . . rather like those in the sub-marine. And then they came to a large wooden door with a brass nameplate that read: H.M. McGurk, Forward Operations Manager.

Her escort set her bag down.

"Thank you kindly, sir," Clara said, curtseying as if this was Dublin not Dajarra Power Station.

He bowed. "It's an honor, Missy." He blushed to the roots of his hair. "If I could ask your name, Missy?"

"Clara. Clara Calland," she said, offering her hand politely.

He shook it as if it were a flimsy piece of porcelain. "Tom Whelan, Missy. Anything, absolutely *anything* that I can do for you, just ask for me."

It made her smile. She wasn't really used to boys falling over themselves for her yet. But as Sandy had said on the way to Alice, they didn't see many girls up here. Her escort blushed all over again, and having run out of things to say, fled. Clara braced herself, a little lifted by this, and knocked.

"Enter," said a slightly testy voice from inside. Clara's courage shrank down again as she did. The little, round, bald-headed man behind the desk full of papers, tapping away at a small pneumatic abacus, didn't look up for a moment . . . and then did.

He dropped his pipe, and hastily had to rescue it and his papers. He stood up. He was shorter than she was. "Good gracious. To what do I owe this pleasure?" He sounded, now, more amused than irritated. But just a little wary, too. "What brings you to Dajarra, young lady?"

There was no point in delaying too much now. The train had almost certainly headed back to Sheba. "Please, sir, I have to speak to Tim Barnabas."

He blinked. "And I assume he's here at my station. You're a very determined young woman, to get all the way here. Has he got you into the family way? I can put a garnishee on his pay for that."

Clara was shocked. "No!"

McGurk took this in. "I think I may have started on the wrong foot," he said, more gently. "Perhaps if we start again. Your accent says to me you're not from Westralia."

"I'm from Ireland. I only arrived in Westralia about two weeks ago, with my mother, on the submarine. Maybe fifteen days . . . It's hard to keep track with the funny hours."

"Ah," said Mr. McGurk. "Yes, I do remember noticing that one of the new contract workers came off a submarine. We do get foreign people trickling over the border with the metal smugglers, but not many submariners. Pardon me. We don't often get young ladies here. Actually, I don't think we've ever had one here before. A bit of a surprise to me. I . . . um . . . do get letters about . . . other matters from women. I was mistaken. So, you've come from Ceduna to see Mr. Barnabas. Alone?"

Clara nodded. "I didn't know how else to speak to him."

"There is telephony as far as Sheba. And we get telegrams relayed to us on the trains."

"It's not something I could explain on a telegram. It's . . . well, my mother is dying." Clara felt a tear run down her cheek.

McGurk was silent for a while. And then he said, quietly, "I'm sorry. I completely misunderstood." He stood up and looked at a huge list pinned to the felt on the wall of his office. "Here you are. Tim Barnabas. He's on the steam mole that's currently at the cutting head, under Shift-captain Vister." He rubbed his chin, awkwardly. "I'm not sure how much good it will do you, young lady, to speak with your father. The company is very inflexible about leave from contacts."

Clara gaped. Her father? Then she realized what the man thought. Fortunately, he was looking at another list.

"They've finished their shift and will be on their way back soon. They should arrive in three hours." He smiled at her. "In the meanwhile . . . maybe you'd like something to eat? A cup of tea? I could show you around the station. It's not often I get to give the guided tour. I think the last person was our Minister of Science and Agriculture, and he used to be an engineer himself."

It had been a while since Clara had last eaten . . . but even longer since she'd last washed. "I'd love that. But . . . is there any chance of . . . of some ablutions. Or is water too short here?"

He laughed. "You'd be surprised, Miss Barnabas. We're on the great artesian basin and we have a good strong bore. Besides, it's as dry as a . . . well, very dry out there now, but when we get a wet, we've got flooding problems. It's why the termite way follows the higher ground, although it would be very much easier to keep to the lower areas. We try not to burrow too much. It's keeping the rails at as slight a gradient and with as few a curves as is possible that's important. We have to do a lot of scouting and surveying to get it right, my word we do. Anyway. Let me organize a bath for you."

A little later, clean, refreshed, and fed on a meal that reminded her of submarine cooking, complete with tea with condensed milk, Clara got a guided tour. It was plain that Mr. McGurk loved his power station and knew it backward. He also loved showing it off. She would have pretended to be impressed anyway, but there was no need to pretend.

"The station makes use of evaporative cooling—we copied the design from the magnetic termite mounds. The roof is designed to avoid the sun, and the building is three-quarters underground. We built it in a slight hollow, and have valved vents at the rooftop to let hot air out at night and draw in from the cooler air at ground level. During the day air is vented at ground level and drawn in from the top of the roof and across the damp-wall to cool it before coming out into the halls. We're also using the heat in the smokestack to power the ammonia-expansion chillers. Out in the desert it can go from a hundred and twenty degrees in the daytime in summer to near cold enough to freeze at night. Here we keep the air much cooler in the day and warmer at night. It's a full-time job for the station air men, keeping it so, opening and closing the right vents, cranking up the screens . . ."

"I thought it was just a building," said Clara, slightly humbled and awed.

"My word, no. Westralia is far ahead in ways to make the desert livable," he said proudly.

It had to be, Clara realized when he took her out to the sheds. At the end of a long adobe tunnel, the sheds were there to keep the dust off material stored there. They were made of adobe with a lime plaster but were roofed in corrugated iron. The heat in the shed was terrible, sending little runnels of sweat down her back, but the machine in it was fascinating. It had huge, tracked wheels and a vast boring head—and a little tower above it that was obviously intended to telescope in.

McGurk hauled open one of the double doors and said, "The team will be going out in an hour or so. Stand out here in the shade, Miss. It's slightly cooler.

It was. Slightly. Compared to the inside of the power station it was hot to the edge of unbearable, and Clara could feel her linen blouse sticking to her, sweat beading along the band of her chip-straw hat. "That's a scouting steam mole. I wanted you to see it because it's as near as you'll get to seeing the big steam mole as a unit. The machines working on the tunnels are just so big it's hard to visualize the whole thing. They, of course, have to run on rails, whereas the scout here runs on these endless tracks. It can drill, just like the big ones—it needs to get the samples so we know what the terrain is going to be ahead, and so it can shelter during the day. They sometimes spend a week or two scouting the best route for-ward. It's difficult planning a termite way. We need to consider the soils, the gradients, the run-off of the water . . ."

Clara was relieved to go back into the coolness of the station. She understood now why they built these termite runs. She was glad to bathe her face and hands, drink a cool glass of lemonade, and go down to meet the steam mole with Mr. McGurk. She wasn't entirely comfort-able about how it was all going to work out when he saw that Tim was obviously not her father. But she was going to see Tim again, and in just a few minutes. Her heart beat faster for that. They watched the tunnel.

McGurk consulted his watch and chain and said, "They're a little late."

Clara began nervously imagining disasters. The time from then until they heard the mournful hoot of the steam mole from the tunnel seemed to have been hours, but it was probably only five min-utes. The long, digging train, like a sort of land submarine, slid up to the platform. The hatch was un-dogged and men started coming out. Clara looked eagerly for her Tim. Yes, he was hers.

They were rather silent and subdued looking men.

McGurk stepped forward to a tall man with a grim expression and a rather flushed face. "Ah. Shift-captain Vister. You look like you've had a problem. This is Miss Clara Barnabas. She's come all the way from Ceduna to see one of your crew, a Mr. Tim Barnabas, I believe. Where is he?"

Clara watched the ruddy face of the man turn ghostly white and him start to stutter something incomprehensible.

"Mr. McGurk, he put him off the mole!" said one of the other men there.

"Shut up, Samuels," hissed Vister. "You're for the high jump. I will not have you on my shift—"

"I will not shut up!" said the other man, as red-faced as Vister was white. "McGurk, he as good as murdered the kid. Pushed him off at the eight mile."

"The black bastard made me do it. He went mad!"

Clara stood there, clutching her parasol and reticule, mind full of horror.

McGurk stepped closer to the shift-captain. "What? What did you do?"

"Nothing," said Vister, waving his hands as if pacifying a big dog. "He insisted on getting off. We tried to stop him. He was dangerous." Vister pointed at a big man with a swollen black eye and blood still on his clothes. "Look what he did to poor Foreman Gore. I had no choice."

"You're going to be doing some explaining to the WMP!" grated McGurk.

"He was only a damned abo! Why did you put a blackfeller on my mole? And the company won't like you calling in the WMP!" blustered Vister.

McGurk paid him no attention. "Move this mole!" he commanded. "You. Barrett. Get the Puffing Billy crew. I want this mole on the carousel and the Puffing Billy ready to roll down the tunnel in five minutes. You hear me? Five minutes! Run to it. Samuels. Not you. You stay right here. I want the story. And you. Get a seat for the young lady."

The shift-captain opened his mouth to speak. "Shut it," snapped McGurk. "When I get back, Vister, you and every man jack involved are going to be in more trouble than you can imagine. Now get out of my sight."

The man fled, and someone brought Clara a hard chair out of an office. No one stayed on the platform. Not with McGurk in that sort of mood.

Clara sat there, wringing her hands, as McGurk grilled Samuels.

"Gore picked a fight with the boong, sir. He don't like them. Only, well, the kid tore into him so bad he knocked the big bast—uh, pardon me, Lady . . . knocked the big bloke down. And Vister heard the noise and got nasty stopping it, and the kid . . . well, he give Vister some cheek and Vister lost it. Put him out in the tunnel. I tried to stop it, sir. But, well, Vister got most of the crew on the mole so spooked, no one was backing me up. I begged them to let the kid out at an emergency exit. Vister said he would, but I wouldn't believe the bast—um . . . bloke. He's a piece of work, sir. Gave us a lecture about how we'd never work again if we says a word about what he done. He and that Gore. I was coming straight to see you when we got in. Honest, I was."

A little green locomotive came hissing and belching up to the platform.

"Excuse me, Miss. I'd better go with it," said McGurk. "Come on Samuels."

"I'm going, too," said Clara, hastily getting to her feet and grabbing his arm. "Please. I can't wait here."

"He's probably dead, Miss," said McGurk, quietly. "What a mess. You'd best stay here. It . . . it could be ugly."

"I've seen ugly. I need to know," said Clara, desperate.

He sighed. "I suppose as you're the next of kin, you'd see him sooner or later. Up into the cab, Miss."

There were four of them there, and very crowded it was, as the little train sealed its airlock double door and the driver sent it down into the black tunnel mouth. The locomotive had a powerful forward lantern and little porthole windows. Clara had to stand on tiptoes to see out of them, but there was nothing to see but the concrete ribs of the adobe tunnel and the furnace of the engine. No one shoveled coal, though, and despite her worry and distress she did wonder how it happened.

"Is the re-breather kit ready?" asked McGurk.

"Just changing the charcoal filters, sir," said the other engineer, warily, while undoing brass tubes on the front of a clumsy looking black leather-and-rubber mask with twin eyepieces. "It's not been used in a while."

McGurk only said, "I see," but she could read "there will be trouble about that" in his tone. Right now it seemed there was going to be quite a lot of trouble. Some of it might involve her killing that bully of a shift-captain.

"Exit one," said the driver.

It was a door rather like those in the submarine, tightly closed. The little train raced on, past exit two, three, four, five, six, and seven . . . exit eight, however, was open. With a squall of steel on rails, the Puffing Billy stopped. McGurk breathed a sigh of relief. "He must have got this far. Disciplinary hearing instead of murder charges. We'll be able to keep the WMP out of this, with luck. Get the re-breather on, Johnstone. Not that it'll be too bad with the exit open."

The engineer donned the mask and went to the airlock. Clara waited, feeling as if the weight of the entire universe had lifted off her shoulders. Tim was alive. Whatever trouble he was in . . . *they* were in, he was alive. She'd been seeing his sprawled, lifeless body in her mind's eye for the last five exits.

And they waited.

And waited.

"We'll have to get someone else out there," said McGurk, tersely. "Is there another re-breather?"

"He's coming back, sir."

"Alone?"

It was an unnecessary question, as they could all now see the engineer. Alone.

He came back in through the airlock, stripped off the re-breather, and said, "He'd been there, sir. The upper hatch was open, too. And there was blood on the lower handle." He held up his hand, stained with drying blood. "But he ain't at the top. I looked all over. And there's a willy-willy blowing up from the west. I reckon he must have started walking back. It only goes deep for a few sections. You can follow the ridge of the termite run most of the way. He's probably the better part of the way back to the power station by now."

Clara remembered the sun out there and the distant, heat-shivered skyline, when she'd been to look at the scout mole. "Ca-can," she struggled to speak through a dry mouth full of gluey spit. Swallowed. "Can we go and look for him? He's from the tunnels under London. He won't know how to survive in the desert."

"He's a blackfeller!" said Samuels. "They're at home out there in the desert, Missy."

"I was on the submarine with him all the way from London. He's lived his whole life underground . . . in a city."

"Wait a minute, young lady. I thought you said he was your father?"

"No, I said I came to see him about my mother, who is in a coma in Ceduna."

Things went downhill from there. McGurk was in no mood for believing her, and he was an angry and worried man. Clara was scared and tired, but she was also angry. It degenerated into a shouting match, and Clara could give as good as she got. It rapidly ended in stony silence from the manager and her as the little Puffing Billy headed back.

It only occurred to her when the little engine pulled into the platform that she needed McGurk's cooperation. "So what are you going to do to find him?" she asked.

"It will have very little to do with you," said McGurk, savagely. "You're going to be on the clanker out of here by five o'clock, in the charge of the guard, if I have to put you on it kicking and screaming. I've had enough of your tall tales and your using your sex to manipulate us. I should imagine he's walked the better part of the way back to the power station along the ridge. There are only a few deep areas where you can't see the tunnel from the surface."

"But . . . but you can't just leave him out there! It's hot. It's—"

"I have other problems to deal with besides your romantic daydreams," said McGurk. "If he hasn't come in by tomorrow we'll mount a search party."

They got out, Clara still seething and trying to work out just what to do next. Mr. McGurk had his ideas. "Samuels, convey this young woman to number three dry storage. That's empty and has a lockable door. She can wait there until I hand her over to the clanker guard to take into Sheba.

Clara weighed her chances and decided the best she had right now was at least to get away from McGurk and then, somehow, to take steps to avoid being put on that train. She walked ahead of Samuels.

"Erm. We didn't know he wasn't a blackfeller from hereabouts, Miss," said Samuels awkwardly, scampering after her. "I tried . . ."

"You should have tried harder," she said. Clara's sense of justice was not at its best right then, but fair enough, this man had at least made some effort.

"Not easy when the boss is spitting mad and is a bloke like that Vister. Look, he'll be all right. He got out of the bad air. They can send the scout mole to fetch him."

Clara had forgotten about the scout mole. "Oh. Yes. Look, Mr. Samuels, thank you . . . and I'm sorry. I was just upset. Can we go and ask them to do that right away?"

"Reckon McGurk'll have to order it. But I'll ask him."

"Can you go and ask him now? I . . . I promise I'll go to this storehouse on my own."

He shook his head. "McGurk would have my guts for garters, Miss. It won't be long. We've got two clankers a day coming in from Sheba."

That wasn't much comfort. And there wasn't much in number three dry storage either. It wasn't totally empty. There was a small desk and a chair and various bits of equipment. Trolleys, winches, levers, and coils of rope were neatly stacked in the corner.

"Sorry about this, Miss," said Samuels as Clara walked docilely into the storeroom. "It's clean at least."

"And will you ask Mr. McGurk to get the scout mole to look for Tim? He's never been out in the desert."

"I'll do my best," said Samuels, locking the door.

Clara took a deep breath and waited. Counted to ten. Then did it again. Locked in . . . That might work on the sort of women McGurk was used to from Westralia, but it wasn't going to work on Clara Calland, who'd passed her submariner's basic ticket. As a result, she knew how a block and tackle worked, and how to multiply the force she could apply to the door. It had a lovely solid bar handle on this side, and looked like it was bolted right through the door to a similar bar on the outside. The hasp lock might stop petty pilfering, thought Clara, setting up her pulley and threading the ropes. There were big, inch-thick staples in the walls, obviously intended for hauling loads in through the big double doors. They obviously hadn't anticipated brute force being used on the access doors from the inside. The hasp was no match for a gyn tackle. Rubbing her hands, Clara set off walking purposefully, as if she had every right to be there, and knew exactly where she was going. When the scout mole was sent to look for Tim she planned to be hidden on board. And McGurk could whistle.

But when she got up there, Clara realized that that plan wasn't going to work. When she'd been there earlier, the machine had simply been parked, inactive. There hadn't been another person around. Now it had at least eight men working on it like busy ants. Smoke came out of the stack, and coal was being poured into the tender. The water pipe was in the process of being disconnected. The men were so busy they didn't notice her.

"I reckon you're 'bout ready to go, Harry," said a greaser dropping to the floor from the big piston. "Hullo . . . it's the girl."

Obviously the news had spread. "Please, are you going out to find Tim?" she asked, giving them her very best I-am-not-the-sort-of-person-who-just-broke-open-your-storeroom smile. "Because I need to go with you."

The man up in the cab shook his head. "No. Going out to scout the next section for the northbound line. They don't have a scout mole there. It's forty miles or so, and rough country, some of it."

"Please, sir, Tim Barnabas is out there."

The driver took his pipe out of his mouth and shook his head at her. "Look, Miss. Only blackfellers out there. They can survive out there. We can't."

"I know. That's . . . that's why it's so important to find him quickly. They put him off the steam mole and he got out at emergency exit eight and started walking back. Please. He's . . . he's from London. He's not used to the desert and doesn't know what to do. Please. You've got to help him."

"Wish I could. But I got my orders," said the driver. "Mickey, you want to check the drill-head coupling is greased . . ."

"You can't just leave him out there to die!"

"I got my orders, Miss," said the driver, shifting the pipe stem in his jaws.

"You can't! Please . . ."

He shook his head. "No use bothering me, Miss. Better get back downstairs. It's smoky when she gets going. Noisy too. No place for a young lady."

"Are you just going to leave someone out there?" demanded Clara. She turned to the others. "Are you going to let him?"

There was an awkward silence, broken by the thunder of feet coming running up the passage. They must have found I've escaped, thought Clara, looking for ideas and failing to find a single one. The door burst open.

"McGurk," the runner panted, "says you're to bring all your lot down to level four, Mr. Driver, sir. We've got a problem with a bunch of men who've locked themselves into the winder room."

"What?" said the mole driver.

"McGurk tried to arrest Shift-captain Vister from in among a bunch of his crew. Told them they were all likely to end in stir. Didn't go down too well. They had a punch up, and he knocked McGurk down and things got out of hand. There's trouble down there."

The mole driver got down. "All right, lads. Let's get down there." He looked at Clara. "You better stay up here out of the way, Miss. Don't touch anything."

He looked at the panting messenger. "How long is all this going to take? The scout's just about ready to go."

"How the Hades would I know?" replied the messenger with a shrug

"Yeah, well, more than an hour and her burners will be out, we'll have to reprime her. And that'll set us back half an hour."

"I don't think McGurk cares about half an hour right now. They're threatening to break the winder unless he agrees not to charge them."

The group of men, some with crowbars and some with shovels, set off down the passage, closing the door behind them.

Clara waited until their footsteps grew faint before scrambling up the wrought-iron ladder and into the cab of the small steam mole. She closed the door and dropped the heavy latch bar in place. Now they couldn't get her out of here, she thought with some satisfaction. If they wouldn't look for Tim, she would. They could come and find their toy, and her and Tim. Or not.

Well . . . if she could make it go. Clara got up into the driver's saddle. She had no idea what to do next. There were levers and knobs and dials. She was too angry and desperate to think straight. She hit the first button. The whistle sounded, loud enough to startle her into some semblance of thought. She read labels instead of just hitting buttons.

"Coal feed."

She pulled that lever and was rewarded by the conveyor starting up, dumping more coal down a chute. The pressure gauge needle started to come up slowly. But how did you make it go forward?

There were two levers at her hand level, sticking up from the floor. She pushed one of them forward cautiously. The little steam mole began to move . . . left . . . and into the wall, which cracked alarmingly. She pulled the lever back in haste . . . a bit too far. Now the mole swung backward, the coal tender smashing the door Clara had come through and collapsing the passage behind it. Clara pulled it upright, and they stopped. Very, very cautiously, she tried the lever at her left hand . . . and the mole moved forward, turning right.

Both hands down, and it moved straight forward. Well, sort of straight. She hadn't started straight, because of experimenting with the levers. The mole was very heavy and solid . . . but quick to respond. She pulled back on the right lever to stop it scraping the wall and pushed on the left to have the little mole turn a half-circle on the spot before she stopped, completely destroying the corrugated iron shed that had sheltered it.

Clara gulped and ducked her head involuntarily as the pieces of roofing clanged on the top of the mole—but the machine was built for burrowing and was not in the least worried by that. She took a deep breath and pressed both levers forward. The little tracked mole thrust its way through the debris and out into the desert. The sky was red and so heavy with dust, looking ahead it was hard to tell where the land ended and sky began. Resolutely Clara set about following the humped ridge that was the termite run. The little mole was doing, according to the dial, eight miles to the hour. Of course, it wasn't merely a matter of driving dead straight, which she struggled with anyway, but avoiding obstacles as well. Her steering wasn't very good yet, and she tended to overdo it then correct and recorrect. Her trail, of course, would be dead easy to follow. Looking back, it also looked as if it had been made by two drunken worms crawling in parallel.

Clara knew she was in more trouble than she could imagine, that the destruction she'd caused was considerable, and that the machine she'd borrowed . . . well, *stolen*, was rather valuable. Probably worth more than she could ever earn.

Right now, she also couldn't bring herself to care.

CHAPTER 7

"**D**on't waste time on the shackles, get the point of them pry bars into the chain links and twist them opposite ways," said that bastard Rainy, who'd nicked his bread. Still, Lampy had to admit that the thief knew how to break chains. He probably knew about anything that you needed to know, when it came to breaking into locked property, Lampy thought.

Soon they were all merely wearing metal bracelets around their ankles—except Quint, who still had his legs attached together. They looted what they could from the loco's cab: two buckets, three big water bottles, a little food, a length of rope-like cord, some wire, a couple of shovels, and a penknife Jack had found in the fireman's pocket. Lampy fancied that, but Jack kept it. The mad Irishman slowed the little locomotive down to barely a walking crawl and they jumped into the flooded little creek, hauling Quint along.

"He'll only rat on us if he stays," said the Irish feller. That was true enough. Lampy suspected they ought to chop his head off or something to stop him talking. But he didn't want to do it, or even be there when they did. He just wanted to get away.

The small mob of ex-prisoners struggled through the shallow water into the scrub. Lampy knew he could run faster, but his conscience troubled him a little. He didn't owe the rest much, but this Jack . . . He'd stick with them a little while.

The land, even without the haze of rain, was flat and featureless away from the creek. There were some plants, mostly twisted little red gums barely taller than a man at the highest. At first Quint tried to drag behind, but Donner threatened to cut his throat. They must have been at least a mile from the railway when Lampy decided he'd had enough of the man, but he was beaten to it by one of the others who said, "If the Irishman won't let us kill 'im, I'm not gunna drag 'im all the way to Queensland. Tie him to a tree and leave 'im."

"Use his breeches," said Jack. "We might need the rope." So they shredded Quint's clothes, tied him to a "tree," and left him.

The feller would work his way loose in time, thought Lampy, and he'd bet that was what Jack planned. Lampy was getting some idea how the bloke worked now. He was too soft for this . . . but then . . . it was all too confusing. He needed time and space to think it over.

A little later, the group stopped again. "Need to loop back to the rail or we'll never find our way," said Deloraine. "Gunna be a long walk back to Rocky."

"I am going on," said the Irishman.

Deloraine, free now, was taking on his cocky, gang-boy attitudes again, and fast. He snorted. "You're bloody mad, Irishman. It's desert out there."

The Irishman nodded and smiled like he was missing a few screws in his head. "I'm crazy. I'll go on a bit. Can't be too far from the border to Westralia," he said. "Got to be cooler there. Anyone with me?"

Lampy nearly said something, but Donner beat him to it. He was only half bad, that big bloke. "Too right you're crazy, Irishman," said Donner. "There's no border posts, nothing. It's just wild country. No one really knows where Queensland stops and Westralia starts. No one really cares. Come with us. We owe you, man."

"Me, I'm goin' north," said Marni. "Ain't gunna find me in my people up there. But they won' take you whitefellers. I got a rifle now. They'll like that."

"Aw, we're gunna need that," said Deloraine, dangerously. "You boongs don't."

"Leave him be," said Jack flatly. "He's earned it."

For a moment it looked like a fight. Marni backed off and held the rifle ready. "Yeah. If you wasn't crazy, Irishman, I'd take you along. And call me that again, Rainy-boy, and I'll kill yer. Come on, boy," he beckoned at Lampy.

Lampy shook his head. He'd made up his mind now, he just wanted to watch a bit more. "My mother was one of the Tialatchari people. This is our country here."

They split up, Jack going west and the rest, bar Lampy and Marni, going east in a bunch.

Lampy walked far enough out into the rain to hide himself, and followed with his ears and nose, like his uncle had made him practice back there in the good country of being young.

※

Jack knew his chances out here in the desert were slim, but, except for the aboriginals, the others were as likely to be a liability as an advantage. He needed to get as far as possible from the railway line and the obvious places the guards would search for them, keep as much of the water as possible, and head west at night. He also knew he had to follow the water—flowing southwest—as far as possible. The rest of the escapees were going upstream, hoping to get over the divide to where water flowed east. He followed the creek out into the middle of Australia.

Contrary to what he'd let on, he did have a plan, and an idea of what he had to do. First, he planned to cross the railway line. To follow the flow of the water to the southwest. The little creek would probably dry up, unless more rain fell, but it might take him part of the way to this "Sheba" place. It was fairly common knowledge— gleaned from the soldiers guarding and driving them—that this rail line was being built to attack Sheba, in Westralia. They planned, eventually, to join it to the termite run from Sheba to ship ore out.

Jack wasn't too sure what Sheba was, besides a mine and a rich prize. He hadn't known what a termite run was either at first, but he knew now. There was a covered rail line running north-south. And they had to be nearly within the range of those trucks. Jack understood the logistics of capturing and holding such a place. They'd need a lifeline to bring in more troops and ship out whatever it was they were after.

The question was just how far they were from that Westralian covered rail line, and whether he was strong enough to walk it.

He'd never know by standing still. He had a penknife and some cord that was close enough to rope, and a fire-bucket . . . and half a sandwich. Not much for a walk of seventy or eighty miles across what would become an even worse desert. Across temperatures that, when this rain abated, could kill him. They even stopped the prisoners working during the midday heat, let them lie in the shade. They couldn't sweat fast enough to cool down.

The rain at least gave coolness and water, and a haze that hid everything. He carefully skirted the area where they'd left Quint, then cut back down to next to the water.

Then he walked on, trying to stay out of the water. He wanted a scent trail going northeast, pointing them to Quint, rather than the way he was going . . . the rain might still wash it out.

Back at the rail tracks, he took two broken branches, crossed the line, and jumped into the water again, taking the branches, too, and letting the water carry them away. Now he was careful to stay in the water. The only smell-trace left behind led the other way.

He was worried about the wet and sand chafing on his thin prison sandals, but he hoped the water would hide his scent.

It was, besides the sound of the rain and the running water, strange to be so alone. It was the first time since he'd been shipped from Ireland that he'd actually been completely alone. It was a good feeling after all this time. He might die out here, but at least he would try, and die free. Alone and free.

A mile or two later he realized just how ignorant he had been.

※

Lampy had been a bit shaken, for the how many-th time today, by the way things had panned out and how fast. He'd never had any intention of sticking with the group, himself. Just didn't want to make leaving an issue, or have any arguments about the loot turning ugly. He'd not worried too much about taking things. He could live off the land, and the only thing he wanted was either the gun or the knife. He knew he couldn't get either without a fight.

He hadn't expected it all to fly apart quite so quickly, either. Or for the Irishman to stand up for Marni. Lampy had backed off, with Marni, because you don't mess with a man with a gun, and, well, he wanted nothing to do with the rest of them.

Except that his uncle had taught him to be a man, and at the same time, that a man had . . . obligations.

You paid back what was due. And you stood by family. Yes, well that was why he'd gone back to his father after his uncle had been shot. That, and not knowing quite what else to do.

He owed that Irishman. And he knew, better than anybody else around, that the desert would kill the man. Following him in the old way, keeping just out of sight, using his ears and his nose to keep Jack placed was easy . . . Well, he nearly lost him once. There was a perente flushed out of its hole by the rising creek, and he couldn't turn down food. The big goanna tried to scratch and bite, but Lampy was a match for it. He killed it, tied it onto himself, and set out to follow the Irishman again. He caught up in time to watch Jack cross the line with his bits of stick.

He was a clever one, even if he knew nothing about the bush.

Lampy followed for a while longer, trying to decide what he should do and what he should say. If the man didn't want to go southeast, well that was his lookout. So he cut ahead a little and waited for him. The Irishman was looking tired already, but he had a little smile on his face.

※

Jack looked up to see Lampy standing there, watching him.

"You go die out there, man. It's not good country for white men," said the youngster.

Jack wondered how long he'd been followed and been unaware of it. "My daughter and wife need me. And that lot'll be caught. The only way I have any chance is to do what they don't expect. I'll follow the water as far as possible."

"You doin' clever, Irishman," acknowledged the boy. "But they got dogs and horses. Got trackers, too, back in the camp. They'll find you."

Jack nodded. "I know. I'm hoping they'll follow the group and give me a little extra time. I'm hoping to get to the Westralian termite run."

Lampy scowled. "Them railways fellers are no good. They're as bad or worse than the soldiers to us blackfellers."

"The more the fool them," said Jack, tiredly.

"Yeh. Look, Irishman. You was good to me back there. And you got us loose. You trail alonga me a day or two. I'll keep you alive. Teach you a few things. You ain't stupid."

"Can we go west?"

Young Lampy scowled again. "Hard country, that. Can take you west a bit, if you want to go that way. They not going to look west till they finish looking east. Then they find the tracks. Give us a few days maybe. But I ain't going near them Westralians. They're a bad lot. Shot me uncle."

"I wouldn't go either if it wasn't for my wife and my child," said Jack. If it wasn't for them, he'd be trying to get back to Ireland.

"Fambly come first," agreed Lampy, who was barely more than a boy himself in Jack's eyes. "I c'n understand that. Let's move along. We don' want to be this close when they turn the dogs loose. They'll smell us anyway, even if they can't smell our trail."

Jack hadn't thought of that. How far did the smell of human carry on the desert wind?

He walked faster. Jack had always thought himself a strong walker. But soon he realized that he was a toddler compared to this aboriginal boy, who walked easily barefoot where Jack struggled in his wet sandals. The cloaking rain was slacking off, and already the heat began to bake through it. The land streamed with water, but soon it would be steaming and humid, then hot and dry again. Jack wondered if the search was underway yet. The guards made sure the prisoners saw the big hunting dogs they kept. They didn't want to encourage escape, but Jack wondered just how effective they could be.

Well, Lampy obviously thought they were a real danger, and he ought to know.

CHAPTER 8

For Dr. Mary Calland the turning point had come when she swam into a sort of dizzy consciousness just as the doctor was there on his rounds. In her giddy eye he'd looked . . . less than pleased to see her looking back at him. "I thought I was to be called if she regained consciousness," he said to the sister.

That crisp woman in whites and a mask looked down her nose at him. "I've had one of the nurses sitting watching her for the entire time, doctor. This is the first time she's opened her eyes, or done more than moan. How are you feeling, Mrs. Calland?"

Mary Calland's mouth was very dry "'ater, 'ease," she said.

The sister lifted her and held a tumbler to her lips with gloved hands, smiling encouragingly. "Just a little, now."

Mary sipped. "What's wrong with me?" she asked, feeling as if the answer should be "everything."

"We're not sure, Mrs. Calland," said the sister. "Some tropical illness. We're keeping you in quarantine, although no other cases have been reported."

Mary could remember now. Pills, and feeling worse.

"Well, obviously the medication is beginning to work," said the doctor. "See that she continues with them, Sister. Immediately. She's missed several doses."

"Yes, Doctor." The sister nodded.

A few minutes later the sister arrived with the tablets. Four instead of the usual two. "The doctor said to double the dose. It's all we've got, but he said he'd bring more in the morning."

"What is it?"

The sister shrugged. "I don't know. Dr. Foster had them made up for you."

Mary took them with a very welcome drink of water, the sister supporting her trembling hand. She knew she shouldn't drink so much water, but she was so thirsty. And a minute later she paid for it by being sick.

The sister looked at the result. By the wrinkled eyes above the mask, she pulled a face. "I'll have to try to reach Dr. Foster."

A little later a young doctor showed up, still rubbing sleep from his eyes. "I'm afraid we can't find Dr. Foster. If you don't mind, I'd like to examine you."

Mary, despite having thrown up, was actually feeling a little better. She put up with the prodding quite well.

"The rash you had seems to have gone, and while your liver is enlarged and tender, and your pulse is a little fast, you seem to be doing better than the charts indicated. I'm afraid there is no proper entry of what the medication was that Dr. Foster prescribed. I believe the hospital has sent runners to look for him. In the meanwhile, we'll keep you under observation."

Mary was glad enough to rest. But she didn't sleep. And now that her mind was less cloudy, she was recapturing how she'd got here. Dinner with several officials and scientists . . . and then, just after the tea tray had been brought in, feeling unwell. Fortunately, one of the Republic's leading physicians, Dr. Foster, had been there . . . and then it got murky. She did remember something about quarantine.

"How long have I been here?" she asked the nurse watching her.

"Two weeks. You've been unconscious for nearly four days."

"My daughter . . . can you let her know I'm conscious?" asked Mary. Clara must be beside herself with worry.

The young woman hesitated. "I'll speak to Sister Beatrice."

"She'll be worried stiff. Please, I'm sure she won't mind being awakened. And I know I was sick but I am dreadfully thirsty. Can I have some more to drink? I think I just drank too fast."

"I'll ask Sister Beatrice, Mrs. Calland," said the nurse, getting up.

"It's *Doctor* Calland."

"You're a doctor?" she asked, as if a woman couldn't possibly be. Mary had found Westralia was odd like that in some ways. Free of the Empire, technologically ahead . . . socially very conservative.

"Of chemistry, not medicine."

Mary got her drink of water. She took it very slowly, it stayed down, and she felt considerably better. The sister took it on herself to offer her patient a little custard. And that, too, eaten very cautiously, stayed down and seemed to give her a little strength.

A little later Mary had a visitor. Without a mask or a cap, but with a very worried expression, she recognized him: a major figure in their government, the minister for science and agriculture. Maxwell Darlington was a mine engineer who had originally built the desalination plants. The man who had escorted her to that dinner.

"Dr. Calland, I am relieved to hear that you're doing somewhat better," he said.

"So am I, Mr. Darlington. I wanted to at least send a message to my daughter Clara."

Darlington bit his lip. "That's . . . rather what I've come to talk to you about, ma'am."

"Don't say she got this disease, too. My God, is she . . . ?" Mary thought she was going to faint, but still tried to get up.

Darlington put a strong hand on her and pushed her gently down onto the pillows. "She has not been sick. And, Ma'am, evidence is emerging that you may not have been either. You may have been poisoned."

"What?"

"When you vomited up the pills you'd been given, the hospital attempted to call Dr. Foster. When they failed to find him, they put out a call to the Westralian Mounted Police. His gig was spotted at a premises and two of our men went to ask him to attend to you. The one officer involved happens to be involved in counterespionage work. When they entered the premises, armed and in uniform, they caused, shall we say, some consternation. Foster and the individual he was closeted with did not know the officers were merely wanting him for an emergency call to the hospital. And the police officer recognized the man Foster was with as an Imperial agent. Shooting followed, ma'am. Foster won't be attending anymore patients."

He drew a deep breath, then continued, "In the midst of all of this, I had received a call that you were awake and looking for your daughter. You see, while you were ill, my wife and I fostered her in our home with our own daughter."

"That was very kind of you, Mr. Darlington."

"It seemed the least I could do. But I have . . . more to tell you, ma'am. When I got the call, I attempted to contact Dr. Foster, too, to check on your condition before speaking to you. Which is why I got to hear about the death of Foster from the commissioner of the Westralian Mounted Police. Evidence of blackmail had emerged, and although Foster and the Imperial agent are dead, and one of ours wounded, we, um, began to suspect you had been poisoned. British Imperial spies have been very busy. And I'm afraid . . . please try and take this calmly, Dr. Calland, they may have kidnapped your daughter."

Mary tried to stand up again. She nearly fell over, only to be caught by Darlington, who sat her down and handed her some water. She drank a little and calmed slightly, though her heart still hammered in her chest. "Tell me all of it."

"There is no evidence to show that she's been hurt, and it is not easy to leave Westralia. We control the metal smuggling routes, which are how most people enter and leave Westralia. We don't mind them doing so, but the British do. So our side is well controlled. Other than that, we've been hunting night and day. I'm afraid I took the liberty of looking in your belongings, and hers— those she left behind. It appears she left of her own will. There was a letter from Jack Calland—I believe he is her father? We think the girl was tricked into meeting an Imperial agent."

Mary blinked. "Why? I mean . . . I was dying. Being poisoned by them."

"Er. We don't know. Perhaps something of a delay, and the left hand not knowing what the right was doing? The letter from Jack Calland claimed to have been from a prison in Queensland."

"Jack *is* in prison, but in Ireland. And we have a code . . . so that I can know that what he wrote was not forced out of him."

"I will get it for you to look at, ma'am."

"When did this happen?"

"Nearly three days ago. The day after you lapsed into unconsciousness." Darlington pulled a face. "It's . . . actually more complicated, ma'am. You see, we're not absolutely sure she has been kidnapped. A bandbox of her possessions was recovered from a very bad area."

Mary felt faint again. "Just tell me. Are you saying my daughter . . ."

Darlington shook his head awkwardly. "No. I'm saying we just don't know. Look, ma'am, generally speaking a girl or a woman out here is safer than anywhere else in the world. There are three men to every woman in Westralia, and the result has been, shall we say, a degree of chivalry you don't see much of in the Dominion. Touch a respectable woman against her will here, and you're likely to get lynched. Touch a young girl and you will be. Of course there are always exceptions, ma'am, but, well, it's not something we worry about a lot." He grimaced. "Which is why when her bandbox was found it caused such consternation."

Mary Calland clutched the brass headboard. "Go on."

"The bandbox was found on Solitude Beach. It's a place the tramps and metho drinkers hang out. The police have been searching and questioning. They eventually got some answers out of a half-blackfeller called Hans. He's trouble, but he swears she dropped it when she ran away from him. Not even calling on some of the elders from his tribe got him to change his story," explained Maxwell Darlington.

Mary had warmed to him, slightly, after he'd broken the news to her. He didn't look like he'd slept much in the interim period either.

"I've been pushing for more effort from the Westralian Mounted Police, ma'am. And for the army to do some searches. But, well, they claim they're doing all they can. Getting labor in the Republic is a difficult job. Everyone is employing, mining companies and those who deal with them are awash with mineral money, they recruit everyone, and we're short of policemen as a result."

"So does the money not flow into the coffers of the Republic? Surely they can hire more men and keep them?" demanded Mary.

Darlington shrugged. "A fair bit of the wealth does, yes. But no, ma'am, they're not going to pay troopers more. My own sector, science and agriculture, gets a far better share than the police do. Westralians don't have a lot of time for constituted authority. After all, when we were in trouble, it was taken over by the British Empire, and the police got their orders and mostly ran off on us. But we do need it sometimes."

"If money is what it takes," said Mary grimly, "then I will have to make them part with it. Mr. Darlington, I am sitting on a secret that is worth billions, that the British Empire wants to own, and suppress. I wanted to use it to help the people of the world to feed themselves. The Empire wants to keep their dominance over nitrates, as weapons of war. I want my daughter. If the Republic of Westralia wants the secret of ammonia synthesis—beyond the information I have already provided . . ."

"Professor Henderson and his team haven't got very far. The professor claims the work was invalidated by another great German chemist, Nernst."

"The professor's brain is back in 1905, and his mathematics, and Nernst's, are wrong. I can make it work."

"It would appear that the British Empire, or at least Duke Malcolm believes that, Dr. Calland. But we'll need to convince a few more people."

"Are they people with a lot of money, Mr. Darlington? Westralia has some mining and rail magnates who would pay me very well. They'll see the value in this and be willing to back it. And I need that money in a hurry."

He smiled a little, for the first time in that shattering interview. "I can see the value, too, ma'am. I have the agriculture portfolio, too. If there is one thing we need nearly as much as water, it's fertilizer. And the miners need explosives. I'm not without influence, ma'am. I'll burn all my bridges and ask the prime minister and the finance minister to an urgent meeting. They're both in Ceduna right now, busy with other business, but I think I can swing this. And I owe it to you and your daughter. She was in our care when it happened."

"Clara, as I have learned, is never in anyone's care but her own," sighed Mary Calland. "She's her own person. And in the meanwhile, if I could have her things—and mine? There may be some clue that I may read into them as to where she's gone. I would have thought she'd go to the *Cuttlefish* if there was trouble, or to young Tim Barnabas. But he's a sensible boy and would have brought her back, or talked to Captain Malkis, if not to me. I assume you have checked with Malkis?"

"I've spoken to him myself on the telephone to Roxby. He's attempting to get a leave of absence from the work he's taken on to help the search. A very honorable man, your Captain Malkis. Unfortunately, the mining work contracts are just not flexible. It's something the government is trying to legislate."

"Work? Why is he at this Roxby place? I would have thought he was with the submarine?"

Darlington pulled a face. "It appears that the crew of the *Cuttlefish* have taken various jobs to pay for the repairs to the submarine. Someone from the Westralian government ought to have stepped in."

Mary was shocked and felt enormously guilty at the same time. The *Cuttlefish* and her crew had risked so much and had only been that badly damaged because of her. "You should have. I must do something about this."

"Westralia's a very commercial place, ma'am. Government ran away and tried to force us to leave when we were in trouble. There is a balance to be reached, of course, but at the moment the men making money out of minerals are more influential than the politicians. We're trying to restore that balance."

Mary Calland peered over the top of her glasses. "If the magnates who are making money here hand over fist can't let a man go and look for a young girl, then it's time to stop trying, and succeed."

He smiled properly. "We need you in government, ma'am."

"I need to find my daughter."

He nodded. "I'll get onto arranging the meeting, and I'll have the remaining bag and trunk sent to you, along with the letter. In the meanwhile I suggest trying to get your strength up, ma'am. I'd suggest a little food—"

She scowled. "When I can think of a way of making sure it hasn't been poisoned."

※

Linda found this a very difficult tryst. She wanted some advice. Nicky wanted some petting. She pushed him away. "Not now, Nick. Please."

"Don't you love me anymore?"

He was very elegant, but he smelled a bit of brandy just then. "Yes, but I am so worried about Clara. I think I ought to tell my father."

"He'll lock you in. And then you wouldn't be able to see me."

"I know. But . . . but she's my friend. And I *ought* to tell them. No, Nicky. Stop. I'm . . . going now."

"Don't go blabbing, Linda," he said as she got up.

He sounded very unlike his normal self. Not caressing, but cross. Grown-up. Well, not grown-up. She was that. But *old*.

※

Clara hadn't been prepared for the wind and the dust. She'd assumed that when she got going it would be relatively easy to work out where to go. That assumption had vanished into a red haze. There was a compass, but while that could tell her which direction she was going, it did nothing to tell her what way she *should* be going. And in this . . . well, she could pass Tim ten yards off and not see him.

She moved the big machine slowly and steadily. That would give her, and him, the best chance of spotting each other. For a little while she indulged in a daydream of finding Tim. But in the dust and dying light, she knew that it was only a daydream. And it was going to be night soon. How could she find anyone in the dark? She didn't even really know where she was. She started to fiddle. The shriek of the steam horn nearly made her jump through the roof. Surely he must have heard that.

Clara opened the window in one of her accidental proddings and testings. It told her two things: First, it was blowing half a gale out there. And second, no one would hear anything.

If Tim was out in this, he'd be sitting down, waiting it out. No one with any common sense would walk in it. No one would be out looking for her or their missing steam mole either. Her next button got her a forward light. That was good. She kept going, slowly. She had no way of measuring how far she'd gone or precisely what ground she'd covered. But by now she'd surely done a lot more than eight miles. She turned and tried a track back the other way, going as slowly as the scout mole would go, avoiding occasional rocks, and sounding the horn in the darkness.

And then she did it all again. And again. She worked out how to feed steam-biscuits into the machine, and pressed on. The wind dropped and the night sky cleared sometime before morning.

Dawn found her in the middle of nowhere, not knowing where to go. She decided on looking for the highest point, a range of hills she could see . . . but as she got closer, they seemed to be floating . . . and then broke up and vanished with the sun.

And the steam mole stuttered and . . . stopped.

CHAPTER 9

Mary studied the letter from Jack Calland with tears in her eyes. The writing, if it was his, showed a distinct tremor. And the code pattern telling her it was true and trustable . . . was not there. But the way of expressing things was very like Jack's. He was an insane, dangerous hooligan. But he used to make her laugh.

She could believe that Clara would have been taken in, though. And Duke Malcolm just might have done that—transported Jack to Australia, where he could be a useful lever.

She was still looking at the letter, lost in reverie, when someone knocked on the door of the guest house. She was under guard there, and it was, after the attempt on her life, for her own safety. She didn't like it, but it did mean there should be no unwelcome surprises. She still took steps to be ready in case, somehow, they'd got past the guards.

"Captain Malkis!" she exclaimed upon seeing the bearded, reliable, shrewd submariner who'd safely transported them all the way from London to Westralia. "Oh, I cannot say how glad I am to see you. Come in!"

A ghost of a smile touched his lips. "I'm glad to see you up, Dr. Calland. The letter I had from your daughter was less than hopeful. I went to the hospital first, even before going to see Darlington. Perhaps you would like to put down the carving knife?"

Mary Calland was enormously embarrassed. "I am so sorry. It's proved to be a lot less safe here than on the *Cuttlefish*, Captain. I was poisoned. Forgive me for the knife."

The captain dismissed it with smile and a wave. "I would prefer it to be a pistol, and I would prefer the guard to be some men I know I could trust to the end of the Earth, ma'am."

"I've always been rather nervous about guns, sir. But you are right, as usual," she admitted as the captain came into the with-drawing room.

"Believing that remark is likely to get me killed by a Royal Navy drop-mine," he said, smiling ruefully. "I've come about your daughter, ma'am. I had a letter from her."

"Dear heavens, I hope it's got some more clues for us. I know you've been told about her being missing."

The captain nodded. "Maxwell Darlington, to give the man credit, seems to have been trying hard to find her. I'm sorry it has taken me so long to get here, though, and I hope I've not taken too much of a liberty coming to search for her, but the crew would not have forgiven me if I hadn't, and I wouldn't have forgiven myself."

"Oh, Captain, of course not. I'm so glad to have you. But Mr. Darlington said you were having some trouble with . . . with your employers in this Roxby place. That's just wrong, Captain."

He gave a short laugh. "I've left them with more trouble than they were giving me, and they are glad to see me gone. These Wes-tralian mine owners think they're a law unto themselves, but the men working for them have just about had enough. They're going to find it's a changing world, and oddly enough, it is largely thanks to your daughter. We organized and had a strike. The men on the mine weren't impressed with management, and thanks to Dar-lington, their government isn't backing the mine owners. The owners demanded the army move in to support them, and didn't get a very good reception. So the owners were very glad to give me a leave of absence to get rid of me, which got rid of their strike. But I don't think that the genie is going back into the bottle. Now, what can I do to help find Clara?"

"Well, if you don't mind, let me see her letter? And then, well, try to find out what has been done so far. If I succeed with the Westralian government, I am going to need you to buy up the contracts of the *Cuttlefish* crew, pay for her repairs, and direct your crew in a search for my daughter."

"Bravo, ma'am. I can think of nothing I'd rather do. But it is only fair to point out that the repairs are expensive. They could run as high as fifty thousand gold Australian pounds. Even the contracts are worth hundreds."

Mary Calland gave the captain a tight smile. "They could have had my grandmother and Fritz's work for nothing, but it's worth millions. So now they will be paying."

He nodded. "But first, ma'am, I think you need to sit down. Have some tea. And, by the looks of you, something to eat. We looked after you better on *Cuttlefish*, ma'am. You look ready to fall over."

She grimaced. "I've been cautious about eating. For a start, I was poisoned by eating what I was given, and for a second thing my stomach is quite delicate as a result."

He nodded. "I think I'd better give you Clara's letter. It's . . . worded quite oddly. And then I will go and get some suitable food for you. I think one of our most pressing needs is Cookie."

Dr. Calland thought of Cookie's solid submariner food, cooked in his tiny kitchen, with something of a nostalgic laugh. "I don't think he does hospital food."

The captain acknowledged this with a wry smile. "Perhaps not. But he's never allowed any of my crew to be poisoned, either. Unfortunately, he's out in the Gibson Desert, but some of the crew have managed to come to assist us. Lieutenant Ambrose was working with his future father-in-law's company in Port Lincoln, and they've given him leave immediately. They're mineral smugglers transporting ores across the Spencer Gulf. All legal this side, but disliked by the Empire."

※

Linda had taken herself quietly out of her home and found a jarvey to take her to the diplomatic bungalow overlooking Murat Bay. There were some advantages to having a well-known father. The soldiers on guard there let her in to wait. And having got that far . . . she had plenty of second, and third, and fourth thoughts while she waited.

※

Mary Calland faced the assembled group of government dignitaries and scientists with steely determination. Some of them, by the comments she'd overheard, did not believe anything of value could come from a woman scientist. She kept her voice as level as possible. The British Empire was less retrogressive about women and their place than this frontier republic. That would have to change.

"Gentlemen . . . the method of ammonia synthesis was yours for the asking. But since you've put a financial cost on finding my daughter, and keeping the crew of the submarine that carried us here at incredible risk, as too high for you to bother with, I'm putting my own price up," said Dr. Calland grimly. "I have no interest in being wealthy, but I can see myself spending the money more wisely than you have."

It was plain no one spoke to the prime minister like this normally. But he was a gentleman and tried to paper over the cracks. "We're embarrassed by this, ma'am. We have the Westralian Mounted Police searching. We can assure you that every kind of help—"

"The process will cost you three hundred thousand pounds. And point one percent thereafter of the sale price of the ammonia. Westralia is flush with wealth from the mines. You have the money. And the synthesis process will be worth many hundred of millions, far more than your mining wealth, besides feeding the starving and making mining and chemical work much cheaper. Choose, gentlemen. Westralia is a commercial place. I can find backers who will pay me much more and give you much less."

They gaped at her, unused to being dictated to. She felt it necessary to explain . . . a little. "I need to pay for the repairs to the *Cuttlefish* and hire people to search for my daughter. I want people I know I can rely on, and to me that means the crew of the *Cuttlefish*. Their contracts will need to be bought out."

"But . . ."

"We need to accept it, Thaddeus," said Maxwell Darlington to the prime minister. "We know the Imperials are desperate. Next time they may succeed in killing Dr. Calland. And we've got the gold, but they've got the military might. We need to be able to stand on our own feet."

"We're buying a pig in a poke," said Professor Henderson loftily. "It's a waste of money. How do we know you can produce the goods, Dr. Calland? I've looked at the formulae, and I am convinced the great Walther Nernst was right. You can't produce ammonia, ma'am, no matter what the Imperials think."

Dr. Calland looked at the self-satisfied face of the Westralian scientist. "I believe I do have the essential ingredients for a tabletop demonstration. It's not ready for commercial production, but that too can be solved. Give me twenty-four hours to set up and test. If it works, the Westralian government will pay me three hundred and fifty thousand pounds and point five percent of the sale price of the product."

"I thought you said three hundred . . ." said the finance minister, warily.

"*He* just put the price up," said Mary Calland, pointing at Professor Henderson.

The Westralian prime minister tugged his moustache and nodded. "Accepted—if you can prove you can do it, and on the condition that you stay on to head the team of scientists who make it work on a commercial scale."

"Once I have found my daughter." Mary did not say "dead or alive." She would not allow herself to go there. "And now I have things to prepare. I need to collect my equipment and test some of it. And a few assistants would be of value." That would put a stop to any suspicion of fakery, and besides, she could use their labor.

The little pressure chamber she needed was carved out of a single huge quartz crystal in an iron jacket, and it was heavy. It had to be to sustain the pressure of two hundred atmospheres, many times higher than that thought possible when her mother had worked on the device with Fritz and Robert Le Rossignol. The sequence of pumps and heating and cooling units she'd need were just as heavy, and Mary was still desperately weak and tired from the aftereffects of the poison. Weak, tired, and afraid. But she dared not fail now. Her daughter needed her. Maybe Jack did, too.

※

Mary Calland walked unsteadily and tiredly into the guarded bungalow on the outer edge of Ceduna's sand berm. "You got a visitor," said the guard, cheerfully.

That was the last thing she felt she needed right now. "Who is it?"

"Young lady," said the guard. "Said she had to talk to you. She's got no weapons and I reckon she's not a poisoner," he said with a grin.

"I reckon" wasn't what Mary wanted from a guard. "Why didn't you keep her outside at least?" she snapped.

"Oh, she's all right. Big Max's daughter," said the guard. "Too hot out here."

The attitude of the military here was so different from the soldiers of the Empire, Mary reflected. But by "Big Max," she assumed he must mean Mr. Darlington. He was big, had once been a mining engineer, and seemed popular with the ordinary people. And yes, Mary had taken Clara to meet the girl the night she was poisoned.

Mary wasn't prepared for the sniffly misery that the wait had turned the girl into. And she was, if anything, not much older than her daughter. Dressed in high Westralian fashion—which was about five years behind the women of London—and looking as if she hadn't had any sleep since Clara left, she twisted her hands and looked wretched.

"Mrs. Calland," she burst out. "I promised her I wouldn't tell anyone. But you're her mother. I've been . . . tearing myself apart. I told Nicky and he said . . . He said I mustn't tell anyone. But Father says you've been so worried. Clara . . . Clara's run away to Queensland. To her father."

"Are you saying she has not been kidnapped?" asked Mary, gently. This was no time to point out that she liked to be called Dr. Calland.

"I don't think so. See, she tried to go last Wednesday night. Only she had a nasty experience with some drunk hobo. She lost one bandbox. Then . . . she came back. She'd left me a note saying she was going to Queensland. To her dad."

"I . . . I understand. My parents are divorced, too. I've thought about running away. Going to my mother in Adelaide. And she thought . . . she thought you were never going to be conscious again," explained Linda.

"It was close. Being unconscious probably saved my life, though. Now, why don't you sit down and tell me the whole story."

She did, and it plainly gave her a great deal of relief.

"Well, my dear, you've taken some care off my mind. We were terribly worried about the bandbox, and now it turns out that the hobo concerned was telling something close to the truth. I have to assume that Clara had some kind of assignation with the spy who brought her the letter from my husband Jack, which was how she thought she'd get to see him in Queensland. They didn't think I'd do anything for Jack, but they knew I would cooperate for the sake of my daughter. Thank you so much for coming to talk to me."

"I did promise her I wouldn't tell. But she didn't think she could tell you," said the girl.

"Under the circumstances, Clara would want you to tell me. You've done what was best for her."

It was a relief to know that the matter of the bandbox had been a false lead. But it got Mary no closer to finding her daughter. And now she had to produce synthetic ammonia from the air. She said so. She was surprised by Linda Darlington's reply. "Please. Please can I help you? I'll . . . I'll ask my father. I want so to do something to help Clara. And I know quite a lot about where things are in Westralia . . . if you need supplies, or someone you can trust to run messages. I can even cook," she said humbly. "I won't be as useful as Clara, but I really want to help."

Mary Calland reflected that Clara would probably never admit to being able to cook. And, unless she'd learned on the submarine, she couldn't.

※

Linda wondered if Clara had any idea how much like her mother she was. Clara's mother was plainly the kind who gave orders . . . and who was rather too used to dealing with her own daughter to let Linda do the acquiring of permission to be there. Linda could imagine Clara sliding out of that, just like she'd never quite promised not to go. "I will call your parents. I'd be happy to have the company. I miss my daughter."

Linda had to hope the call didn't include a mention of Nicky. It didn't, and it wasn't on the telephone to her father anyway. He turned up while Dr. Calland was speaking to the operator.

"I thought I said you weren't to pester Dr. Calland," he said in the sort of voice that suggested real trouble, soon.

"Mr. Darlington," said Clara's mother. "She hasn't pestered me. She's been a blessing. Actually, I was just trying to call you on the telephone to ask if she could assist me. I'm used to girls of this age, and she knows Ceduna: where the local businesses are, where local suppliers are, and more importantly where to go and not to go. It would . . . help me cope with Clara's . . . absence."

"Please, Father. Clara was my friend. I . . . I haven't been able to do anything much and I've really wanted to. And you were saying how Dr. Calland proved that women could do anything they set their mind to. She'd . . . she'd be a good role model," said Linda, digging deep.

And in the next few hours she found out that she was expected to know things that no lady educated at Ceduna's finest ladies seminary did, things that would have shocked her teachers rigid. Women were not expected to deal with that sort of thing, after all . . . She could almost hear the headmistress, Miss Caldwaller, saying that. Clara's mother, however, could see no reason why she didn't know the periodic table, let alone by heart; the symbols for the elements; how to calculate pressure; or what the Boyle-Mariotte Law was. And, when she didn't know, she was either told or handed an elderly encyclopedia, which she was supposed to read really fast when she wasn't running to carry this, fetch that, accompany a soldier to a manufactory to collect tubing, or get the operator to call yet another supplier in the search for gas and burners.

It was, once she got over the shock, absolutely what she wanted to do. And it would give her stepmother hives, and probably please her father.

Mr. Darlington dropped in a little later, as they were getting ready for the first test run. When he arrived, Linda was connecting pipes, something her smaller fingers and hands were more useful at than Captain Malkis's in the maze of them that linked the various pumps.

"I'd come to relieve you of my daughter," said Darlington, "but she does appear to be making herself busy."

"Oh, Father, please can I stay?" asked Linda. She wanted to see if it worked.

Dr. Calland intervened, looking up from her careful soldering. "She's been very useful, and I hope she'll stay a little longer. She's deft and practical. We're working flat out to get the equipment up and running. Luckily things have moved on since my grandmother's time and there are powerful mining pumps available."

Her father looked surprised. "I had no idea Linda had any interest in science, let alone being, well, any good at mechanical things."

"Do you object, sir?" There was a certain brittleness in Clara's mother's voice.

"Goodness, no," said her father, looking thoughtfully at his daughter, almost as if he'd just seen something he hadn't noticed before. "Pleased as punch, actually, now that I think about it. Well, then, I'll leave her to it. I've arranged for some food to be sent up. I'll just tell them to add one more. And no, ma'am, it won't be poisoned. We've taken steps."

"Good, but I don't think we'll have much of a chance to eat. We'll be doing our first test run in ten minutes.

"I think I'll just stay then."

"No, you won't," said the man Linda had learned was the submarine captain. He was wrestling an enormous keg of coal gas into place with cheerful firmness. "You'll see to them getting that food to Dr. Calland quickly, Darlington. She's pale and not well. You can see the demonstration with all the other officials." The captain was plainly used to giving orders and having them obeyed, and the attitude seemed to work on her father, too.

The next phase of the work involved starting the pumps and the heating. Linda's job was to watch the pressure gauge and sing out at each ten-bar mark. It crept upward as the pumps thumped away. And then there was a high-pitched whistle and the pressure dropped. So it was back to fixing piping again. That was definitely the weakest part of the entire hodge-podge, cobbled-together machine.

On the next try they got the pressure right up to two hundred atmospheres. And then a pipe joint burst, so they had to start again. This time a pump caught fire. So they ate, and started again.

And finally, as the nitrogen and hydrogen flowed in, a drop of some fluid fell out into a flask. Then half of a second drop formed. It took a long time.

Dr. Calland held her hand up, and they all went to their jobs of powering the ammonia-making contraption down. Dr. Calland sniffed the flask. "It's ammonia. But at that rate of output, I don't think it's going to change the world. Or convince anyone of its viability."

"You have proved it could be done," said Captain Malkis.

"Not sufficiently. We'll need a different catalyst."

"What?" Linda meant, "What is a catalyst?"

"Uranium, I think."

"Er. I think I'll ask my father," said Linda, who didn't want to have to refer to the encyclopedia again, and did remember uranium being mentioned when he'd spoken about mining.

"We won't need a lot of it. It doesn't get used up."

So Linda got on the telephone.

The request was met with some surprise. "Uranium? You mean there's something useful that can be done with it? Besides as a source of radium? We used to use it in glass, but it's dangerous stuff, you know. We get some out of the copper ores from Roxby."

"Dr. Calland wants some as a . . . a catalyst."

"There is some at the geological institute. How much does she want?"

"I'll ask."

The problem was not so much in getting the uranium, but in getting such a small quantity.

And this time it worked.

They shut down at three drops.

"We need witnesses, and heaven knows if this Heath Robinson contraption will survive long this time."

Linda realized that the earlier success wouldn't be the part that history remembered. The next part would. It was rather neat to think that she'd be able to say "I was there." It of course wasn't anything like the image she'd had, before getting involved, of a scientific laboratory. She'd have thought that it would be quiet, rather like a church, with everyone reverently waiting for the first drop of ammonia into the receiving flask. Of course, it wasn't like that. There was the steady *thump-thump-thump* of the multiple compressors, the roar of the gas burners playing on the reaction chamber, and the hubbub from the watchers.

But that noise at least was silenced when the droplet formed on the condenser spout and began to grow. Then the watchers were still, even if the machinery continued to make its noises. That was good, Linda knew. If they were making noises, they were still working.

The drop was followed by more, forming and falling steadily. Linda realized she'd been holding her breath, and exhaled before she fell over. She smiled for the first time since Clara had vanished. She knew, then, that this was what she wanted to do. Make things, make them work, make people amazed.

※

Dr. Calland swallowed, wishing her mouth wasn't so impossibly dry. Time to stop it now, before something failed. She knew how fragile it all was, even if they didn't. She signaled to the tense technicians to start the process of switching off the machines and the gas for the burners. It took a few minutes, but in the meanwhile she took the flask now containing a few fluid ounces of liquid across to where Professor Henderson stood with Darlington and Nathan Geldray, the finance minister.

"It will obviously have to be tested properly, but if you care to unstopper this flask and smell it, I think you will find we have the key to solving Westralia's nitrate problems in our hands."

They sniffed the liquid. "I think," said Henderson, grudgingly, "that we'll have to accept that you can produce synthetic ammonia, ma'am. But I still don't think it can be done on a commercial scale."

"As you claimed it couldn't be done at all," said Darlington, "I think I'd bet on Dr. Calland. What do you say, Geldray?"

"If we don't believe her, I can bet she'll be getting a hundred offers for the process by this afternoon," said the finance minister. "I looked through those calculations you sent me, Darlington. You've erred . . . on the side of caution, I think. Dr. Calland, I am, on behalf of the Westralian government, authorized to accept your terms for the invention. I will arrange for you to have drawing capacity to the full sum from the Barraclough Bank."

CHAPTER 10

Tim lay down in the hole, dozing, as the heat built into the cerulean sky. He'd got as far as breaking some branches to make himself a shelter. He'd even cautiously tasted one of the leaves. The bitterness took a while—and quite a lot of spitting—to get rid of. Tim had no idea what he'd eat out here, but it wasn't going to be that. The heat brought out flies that made sleep hard. So did the hunger, but at least his body was mending itself. Toward evening Tim decided he couldn't just stay in the hole and hope something happened. That thought was reinforced by something looking over the top edge of the hole at him. Tim froze—and two more long, reddish-yellow, hairy faces appeared. Were they . . . wolves? His grasp of what wild animals there were in Australia was slightly smaller than his knowledge of Japanese. They had quite big teeth, whatever they were . . . and Tim didn't even have a penknife. Then it occurred to him that yes, actually he *did* have a penknife. He'd just not thought of it up to now. He reached cautiously for his pocket. The animals didn't wait to see what came out of his pocket. The second he moved, they were off.

That was a relief. He wondered if this was their water hole. They might come back when he was asleep. However, it had made him think of his little penknife and what good that could do him. Well, he could cut things with it. Maybe make some kind of spear to fend those creatures off with. Maybe . . . although this seemed unlikely . . . kill one for dinner. He'd done that with a tunnel rat, with the other boys in the tunnels under London, but they'd had a fire to cook it. Even as hungry as he was, he didn't fancy it much raw.

What he really needed was some way of carrying water. He thought vaguely about hollowing out a piece of wood . . . but he'd probably starve to death before he finished. Resolutely, he got down on his knees and drank as much as he could, then scrambled out of the hole into the dying daylight. He'd just have to make sure he could find his way back here.

A few minutes later he realized just how difficult that might be. Away from the channel and its scrubby trees he was on a plain, and the gully he'd come out of was hidden from sight. He could see all around him to the far horizons. It didn't look any different to the west, south, or north. He could see some rougher country to the east.

Tim knew he had to find the railway, or people, or he would die out here. There was no space for pride or thoughts of self-sufficiency. He'd be nothing more than bones lying on this dusty plain with its scattered tufts of dry grass, if he didn't find help.

Only . . . where to look? He scanned the distances. A hot wind blew, making the horizon dance, then disappear into a blur when he stared at it. That could be smoke to the northwest . . .

Then his eye was caught by a wink of brightness, off to the east. There were some low hills or something there. And there was another flash. It reminded him of Clara and her Morse signaling when she was trapped on American Samoa, stuck in the old bunker. Just thinking about her gave him strength. He started walking in the direction of the flash. It meant crossing the dry channel again, and walking on. He was sure he'd come from the western side . . . but in the state he'd been in, he could have come from anywhere. He could have crossed it twice without knowing, if there was an area where the brush was less thick.

He walked on toward the flashes, into the dusk, and then, hoping he was still going the right way, in the dark. Heat still radiated off the sand as he walked, but it was definitely cooling. Fortunately, it wasn't hard walking here. Stony and sandy between the tufts of grass, but at least the ground was open . . . until he came to another dry channel. And later another. They were smaller than his first one, but there was still dead wood to fall over, live trees to push through, and noises in the dark. In the distance, howling. Something that ran away from him through the bushes in great thumping bounds. It left Tim with a racing heart, clutching his little penknife.

He was never so glad as when he saw a light on the far side of a channel. He ran toward it, relief flooding into him.

Only it seemed to move ahead of him. It was also running away! Bobbing and fluctuating, it moved ahead of him. Desperate, he yelled at the light between panting breaths, "Help! Help! Come back! Come back!" He tried to catch his breath, watching the light, listening for an answer. But all he got was silence. It didn't seem to be moving, but it was changing color, eerily pulsing brighter . . . and then, as he prepared to yell again, it vanished, and the hairs on Tim's neck stood up. It wasn't natural, whatever it was.

It was very dark and he was very alone and very, very afraid. After a while he got a grip on himself and kept walking on. But every noise, and there were a surprising number of them, on the edge of his hearing, or in his imagination, made him tense. He crossed more channels, and more of the flat, grassy plain. The night grew colder, to the point where he knew he had to keep walking just to keep warm. Dawn, or at least the first signs of it, a paling of the horizon with just a hint of bloody redness, came to the sky as Tim reached the edge of yet another channel. This was a much wider one. He decided he'd stop there and see if he could catch the flashing again, or any sign of people in the daylight. The horizon wasn't quite a flat line here. Maybe . . . maybe he was somewhere near the edge of the desert? Logic said that simply couldn't be true. But how he hoped for it.

For a while he just sat there and rested his tired, sore feet, and watched the sun tint the sky with rosy shades and edge the black of the low hills with fire then pour hot gold onto them. It was beautiful. He was tired, hungry, thirsty, lost, and totally unappreciative of the beauty. Tim would have swapped it all for a dirty cubby underground in the tunnels of London, happily, right then. For his bunk on the *Cuttlefish* you could have had the sunrise and all the gold in Westralia.

And that over there . . . that tall spike, outlined by the sun. That had to be a power station! Even if he couldn't see the smoke . . . it had to be. It was a long way off, though. Maybe . . . maybe this was the northward line! It was supposed to be only thirty or forty miles from the southward line. The jokers on the mole had reckoned the two would miss each other and keep going . . .

But that, up in the hills, that was smoke! Just a thin thread of it, working its way up into the sky. Only . . . it was nowhere near the spike.

Tim sat there, torn. Tired, thirsty, and not really knowing which way to walk. Already the sun was heating the landscape.

Eventually he decided on the smoke. It was much closer, not more than a mile or two away, or so he hoped. He really wasn't any use at judging distances on land, he decided. It was so different from looking out at the sea.

He pulled himself to his feet and began trudging across the channel toward the smoke, head bowed, but still unbeaten.

It was a fairly long trudge, weaving between the scrubby trees and out onto the plain. He walked on, as the sun stole the coolness. It was hard for Tim to imagine being cold last night, now.

When he looked up again, the smoke trail was gone. All there was in front of him was just blue sky and red, rocky hills.

Now he felt beaten, indeed. He could no longer see the spike of the power station, either, miles and miles away. All he could see were hills quivering with heat. He was desperately thirsty. He knew he'd never get back to his water hole.

He sat down on a rock. There were rocks here, and it was getting harder walking, slightly uphill. What did he do now? He looked at the hills, trying to pinpoint where he'd seen the thread of smoke. If only he had some way of making fire . . . his questing gaze spotted several birds slowly circling up into the sky above the hills. One dived down . . . and led his eyes to a narrow, darker indent. Tim had no idea if that meant anything. But he also had no idea what else to do. So he walked toward it, planning to stop in the first patch of shade he found, his tired feet dragging.

※

Clara had had to start from having only the vaguest idea how the steam mole actually worked, to working out just why it had stopped. The heat of the day was still coming and she saw no signs of the tunnel's low mound or any other man-made structure. There was just a plain with scattered grass tussocks divided by occasional scrubby channels for as far as she could see, fading into a yellow-red distance.

She set out systematically examining the whole thing. Gauges, levers for raising and lowering the drill head, and, on getting out, the conveyor to the fire box, the supply of fuel in the tender, the pistons, and the endless tracks. It wasn't exactly something any of the girls of her acquaintance up to now would have even tried. It wasn't what girls did.

Well, she'd never been any good at accepting that. And neither had her mother or her grandmother . . . Which, she thought darkly, made mother's insistence that she should also want to do chemistry so annoying. Then she wanted to cry again, thinking about her mother in hospital, her father shaking with fever in some prison in Queensland, Tim hurt and lost out here . . .

Clara wasn't much better off, or any help to any of them, stuck and lost. She seriously had no idea what to do next. Leaving the machine would be stupid, looking at the country. She had food and water here at least. And food and water, if Tim was out here, were what he was without. If she couldn't get to him, perhaps he could get to her? She had a mirror in her reticule. Mrs. Darlington had insisted on that, as an essential adjunct to any smart young lady.

So she set about eating and drinking. The scout mole had been stocked for two—by the looks of it, for weeks. Then she stood and flashed her mirror as systematically across the plain as possible. She occasionally paused to try to work out just what made the machine go. If she could do that, she could work out why it wasn't going now. That involved getting up and climbing around on the machine in the heat. The day was so hot it literally made it hard to think coherently, let alone reason things through. She was terribly grateful for the shade of the machine and its water supply.

That day produced little progress. She found tools, opened accesses, looked . . . and then, when it got too dark, she slept. There were two of the bedding rolls in the cab section, and the night did become cold. That was hard to believe after the day's searing heat, but it was so. She awoke long before first light and set to work again.

※

When Tim finally got to the darker indent in the hill it proved to be a narrow, water-etched ravine, from some long ago time when this place was wetter. There was some shade, and relative coolness in that. What Tim hadn't found there was water. What he did find were birds. They were feeding on the fruit clustered among the leaves of the tree that grew on the rock wall and sent its grey roots down like stalactites.

By now Tim felt not at all like eating. But the fruit might have juice in them. They were not above thumbnail size, and ranged from green to yellowish. Somewhere Tim had read, or been told, that not everything that birds could eat was edible to people, but he thought by this stage he might as well die of poisoning as of thirst and hunger. The small fruit didn't have a lot of taste, or that much moisture. It was some kind of fig, Tim decided, by the seedy inside. It was slightly sweet. It didn't do much for his thirst, but the sweetness must have helped him a little. Tim started to think again and look around. The tree was green and fruiting . . . it had to be finding some water. He made his way farther up the narrow ravine. There was an overhang with a crack under it, and some green moss. Tim felt it, it was wet, so he pulled it free and sucked it. Judging by the crack and the moss's wetness, if he kept that up all day he might get half a cup of muddy, mossy-tasting water. He might as well, he decided, trying the next bit. It was in the shade, and he didn't have anything else to do.

The demossing of the entire crack took him about an hour, he reckoned—and had given him less water than he'd hoped—but looking down where he'd started, there was a droplet clinging to the rock. A few precious drops had fallen already onto the dusty floor of the overhang.

It was slow, but it was wet. It took hours before he felt he'd had half enough. He left his shirt under the drip and went back down to the fig that had twisted and climbed its way into the cracks—probably getting more of the water that seeped there than Tim had managed to get to. He ate some more of the yellow little figs. Not too many, because not dying had become more important again.

The birds were not much worried by him, so his next effort was throwing a stone at them. He missed. "You throw like a girl," he muttered to himself, knowing it wasn't true. Clara hit what she threw at. He'd played darts with her on the *Cuttlefish.*

He had to wait a while for a second chance, and then a third. On the fourth attempt he knocked a bird down and managed to grab it as it flapped on the ground. It wasn't dead, but pecking, scratching, and flapping at him. Tim didn't know what to do with it, but he had it now, and had injured it, so he hit its head with a rock.

The brightly colored little thing was still and dead.

Now he had to decide what to do with it. And he really had no idea. They plucked birds, didn't they? So Tim tried. It was a lot easier to think of than to do. There were a lot of feathers, and they were well and truly attached to the bird. When they eventually did come off . . . so did the skin. After some more attempts that seemed to be more about getting the fine downy under-feathers to stick to his hands than actually getting them off the bird, Tim decided to just pull the skin off. That worked a bit better. Tim found a lot of the bird was feathers, and the end result from his effort was very small. The drumsticks were the size of the first joint of his pinky finger. He knew from cleaning tunnel rats that the guts had to come out. But doing it with a not very sharp penknife, no water, and no experience was difficult. Even under his overhang there were flies coming in to "help" him. In the end he had a gutted and mostly featherless bird, though bits of the fluffy down stuck to everything. At this point he knew he ought to cook it, but he had no way of doing so.

He wondered what raw bird tasted like. He supposed he'd have to find out, sooner or later. And it had better be sooner, before any more flies tried to settle on it. He cut a little sliver. Tried to tell himself it was good for him. A part of his mind, as he chewed with determination, told him that they always said nasty medicine was good for you, and when he really tried to pretend it wasn't raw bird, it went down. On both the positive and the negative sides, there wasn't a lot of it.

CHAPTER 11

Lampy sniffed. There was of course the wonderful smell of wet after rain, but he could smell the dust and heat on the back of the breeze coming out of the interior. It smelled of dry. It smelled like freedom, and a long way from cities and filth and being chained up. He'd never thought about it before, but now that he'd been there, he knew they'd have to kill him rather than chain him up or lock him in again.

He had to wonder if he was right in his head. He was behaving like some fool who'd been on the grog, and he wouldn't touch the stuff, not after what he'd seen it do to his pa. His father had been all right when he wasn't drinking. Except he got the shakes if he didn't. Lampy shook his head. Here he was heading straight toward where he said he'd never go near.

The Irishman played games with his mind, talking about his family. There was something about the way Jack had said it that sounded just like his uncle talking. The uncle who came to fetch him away when his mother died, who took him back to his land and his people.

The uncle who said everything in life was a circle and would come back around one day.

That was the uncle a horrified boy had watched shot down. When Lampy had run forward to help, another shot had ricocheted off the stones. And there'd been a bunch of whitefellers standing there, laughing, at the mouth of one of those tunnels, guns in hand.

And his uncle said, with his last breath, that he should go. Run.

※

Jack and Lampy eventually bunkered down in a gully with some small trees for shelter, as the rain had vanished as if it had never been. It was dusk, and Jack was literally so tired he could hardly walk another step.

"I reckon we better take a smoko and get some tucker into ourselves," said Lampy, squatting down. "You look all in, Irishman."

Jack knew by now what a smoko was and what tucker meant. He didn't smoke, even if he'd had anything to smoke, or to light it with, but the break was good. "I didn't get any more of the food, I'm afraid, but for the half sandwich I gave you back there. I think Rainy got the driver's sandwiches."

"Got tucker here," said Lampy, showing straight white teeth against the black of his face. "Only you whitefellers don't eat it."

"Watch me."

Which was how Jack ended up digging for grubs and making a show of appreciating them. Actually they tasted a bit like almond paste, if you could forget the texture and the fact that they were insect larvae. It was, he realized, some kind of test. He was right, too. "Mostly women and kids eat them," said Lampy, who plainly considered himself a man. "I like 'em more cooked, but we not gunna make a fire until we get a little more far away. I got a perente back there. We'll eat 'im when we stop in the morning."

"We've got to go on tonight?" Jack knew the answer before he even asked the question, but his feet were sore, and he was tired.

"Too right. Them dogs are good, and they got horses, man. They prob'ly pay a couple of blackfellers with a few bottles of grog to track us, too. They follow us easy, now the rain is gone. We got to move at night and hide and sleep in the daytime."

"I'm just worried about my feet. They're not as tough as yours. I'm starting on blisters by the feel of it. I want to be able to walk or even run when I have to."

He saw the gleam of those white teeth in the darkness again. "You whitefellers have got soft feet. Wait up. I go find some paperbark."

By the time Lampy had finished with Jack's feet, Jack felt as if he should be in a horror biograph about Egyptian mummies. The flat, flexible sheets of bark, like cheap newsprint, had been made into something like socks and tied in place with cord or held by the sandals. It did make a huge difference.

Lampy plainly had a goal in mind, and he kept them walking. He wasn't too impressed with Jack's fire bucket of water. By the time he'd fallen over several things and spilled most of it, Jack wasn't too impressed with it either.

By predawn they'd crossed miles of plain and returned to a channel with a cloak of small trees and shrubs. The rain farther east, where they had literally waded in the flood, had not made it here, but the water had. It was being devoured by the thirsty soil just about as fast as it flowed, which was not very fast. Still, there was a shallow stream of brown water for Jack to fill the bucket and bathe his feet.

"When a big wet comes, she'll get miles wide. We're a bit early in the season, but if that happen, they ain't gunna track nothing. They be lucky if half their railway don't wash away. Them Westralian bastards do a better job with water. They got the whole thing underground on the highest ground," said Lampy, working on making a fire.

He'd used the knife Jack had taken from the fireman to cut a wedge into some old, soft, dead wood, and line it with something rather like the paperbark he'd wrapped Jack's feet in. He whittled a blade out of a second, much harder piece of wood, and sawed furiously in the wedge until eventually the bark began to smoke. The smoldering bark he put under a pile of dry grass he'd prepared, and Lampy gently blew that into catching fire. It didn't look particularly hard, but Jack Calland wasn't fooled. He knew he'd probably try for a week and fail, and he said as much.

Lampy grinned. "It don't work as fast as a match, though. My uncle made me learn. Now we go cook this perente."

A perente proved to be the big, ugly, mottled, three-foot-long lizard that Lampy had tied over his shoulder. It tasted a bit like chicken.

"Better than prison bread," said Jack, exhausted. "What now?"

"I go cut me a couple of spears, use the fire to harden them up a bit, and we put it out, move away from it in case som'thing smell it, and then we sleep." He yawned.

Jack yawned, too. It was infectious. "Will you show me how to make a spear, too?" asked Jack. It was no answer to a rifle, but in absence of that, he'd take whatever he could.

Lampy laughed. "They chuck you out of Westralia if you show up with a spear, and maybe some throwing sticks, eh. They don't like whitefellers gettin' too friendly with the blackfellers."

"Their loss. I'd be hungry by their rules."

He was so tired that he barely managed to help Lampy. The boy was tougher than he was. Jack went to sleep, knowing this was the first time he'd done so as a free man for more than three years. And maybe . . . maybe he'd really get to see his wife and daughter again, if in truth they were in Westralia. He'd learned not to believe the stories Duke Malcolm's men told him. But there had to have been a reason for shipping him off to Australia.

※

Duke Malcolm had been watching the reports out of Australia quite intently. He wanted to know just how effective they'd been in bottling up the nitrate problem that had so upset his brother Albert. Last he'd heard the woman was in a coma, and the Westralian scientific establishment had made no headway at all with her notes. Their experimental pressure vessel had reached a hundred and twenty atmospheres and they'd had no results. Well, so much for that. What a waste of effort it had been. She was probably dead by now, and all that effort and money had been wasted chasing her. But the duke carried his grudges well. It would serve as a grim warning to other traitorous scum if she were dead. Then there was the military venture in Queensland. The Empire was of course involved in half a dozen such exercises on different scales across the globe, though few had the financial pay-off potential of this one, or would have quite such a painful impact on an upstart nation. They'd really angered him with the Calland affair. Safe havens on what had once been a part of the British Empire sent a bad message.

The head of the Australia desk brought the report up himself. That was never a good sign. The weekly digest wasn't due for another two days. Duke Malcolm looked at the report on his desk. Tapped his teeth with a new ivory cigarette holder. It wasn't as good as the old one, but it also held a hidden, poisoned blade. "Tell me the worst. Save me reading it and sending for you."

"We've had something of a problem in Ceduna, Your Grace. Griffiths got himself caught, along with Dr. Foster."

"I see. To what extent has our network been compromised? It shouldn't be too bad. Griffiths was sent in especially to handle Foster. A good agent."

"We're not too sure how much he gave away, if anything. If our informant is correct he shot Foster to prevent him from talking, but was badly wounded himself. We have a second string of agents . . . but they're finding things quite hot. The Marconi transmissions were tracked. The Westralians are quite technologically adept in some areas, and our men are being hunted rather hard right now . . . because of a bit of miscommunication."

"Tell me about this 'miscommunication,'" said Duke Malcolm evenly. He prided himself on his self-control.

"Well, it concerned the honey trap for the child. The Calland girl. You wanted her used as lever, so the father was sent to Queensland. The message included a written letter from him, and it all took a little time."

"Hardly applicable now that the woman is dead," said the duke, losing interest. Revenge was sweet, but best when accompanied by reward.

"Er . . . She appears to have recovered somewhat, Your Grace."

"What? That idiot Foster was supposed to make sure she did not recover."

"He was caught and killed, Your Grace," said the major.

"Not that it matters. The process didn't work after all. And those Rebel Australians are supposed to have a scientific edge, or so my brother informs me."

"In other fields, Your Grace. Their Chemistry is quite weak. Professor Henderson is a chemist . . . well, he's the sort you promote to politics to get rid of." The major flushed. "Outside of the Empire of course."

"Of course," said Duke Malcolm, marking this man down for an unpleasant and short future. Disrespect for power was not an attitude he needed. "So what you're telling me is that she's recovered and succeeded? That's not going to be good news for Prince Albert?"

"We don't actually know. The Westralians appear to have thrown a real blanket of secrecy over it all."

"I see. So we need to go ahead with the plan to take the girl as a hostage. Start acting on this."

The officer was silent.

Eventually, the duke lost patience. "What is it, man?"

"That side is a mess, Your Grace. You see, you gave orders . . . You told me Jack Calland was no longer a prisoner of value. He's been sent to the railway. And . . . and as I said there was a miscommunication. The message and our offer have already been given to the girl."

"Get this Jack Calland back. If the mother is involved, she's shrewd enough to want proof that he's alive, and he's too valuable for the railway. Is the girl willing? Or has that gone awry, too?"

"The girl is missing, Your Grace. And they're blaming us."

Something about the way he said that raised alarm bells in Duke Malcolm's mind. "And *have* we got her?"

The major shook his head. "We don't think so. The . . . situation in Ceduna is fairly volatile right now. Our agent sending the Marconi message may have been caught. He stopped at that point. But he did say counterintelligence agents were searching all the metal cargoes going out."

"Interesting times. Anything else untoward happening in the Australian Dominions?"

The major looked relieved to be able to shake his head. "There's the usual ferment, Your Grace. But I think we're on top of that."

"Good. Let me know if you have more news out of Ceduna. And get this Calland sent to Sydney. I gather it has a healthier climate."

The officer saluted, clicked his heels smartly, and left. Eventually Duke Malcolm got up from his desk, still not having looked at the dossier, and stared out of his grimy window at the waters of the Pall Mall Canal. The windows had only been cleaned yesterday, but thanks to the humidity of the canals of London, and the city's heavy use of coal, they just didn't stay that way.

There was a timid knock at the door. Malcolm turned. It was his secretary. She never came into the office itself. He had an excellent voice-communicator system and steam canister delivery to her office. "Your Grace . . . His Majesty's comptroller called . . . er. You are late. It's . . . The meeting is not in my diary."

"He's got his days wrong, again," said the duke with a sigh. "I am due to see him tomorrow, as you have diarized. But one does not tell the King he is wrong, Miss Farthing. Call the comptroller and say I am en route. I will take my personal watercraft."

It was worrying. The King's drinking habits seemed to be making him more prone to these lapses, thought the duke as he waved a salute at the guard on the water door to St. James. At the private quay under the roof, a young lieutenant was already at the wheel of the armored skid boat, checking gauges, and two engineers hastily poured primer into the twin Rolls-Royce Whittles. His efficient secretary had obviously called ahead.

As the turbojet-powered boat scythed through the waters of Pall
Mall Canal, sending more ordinary vessels scurrying out of its way
with its siren, its wake surging over the raised walkways, Malcolm
wondered if, for the sake of the Empire, the time had not come for
Ernest to die.

Margot had had to.

The trouble was, the succession did not offer any real improve-
ment. Albert was, Duke Malcolm admitted, not easy to control, and
unlike Ernest, he would actually keep trying to run the Empire. His
other half-brother would channel everything into the Navy and
probably into war. Duke Malcolm had nothing against war. But only
wars the Empire could win without crippling her. He was fourth in
line for the throne himself, since Margot's unfortunate death, but the
idea of being the sovereign had no appeal. He only did what he did
so that the Empire could endure.

The King had plainly been drinking already, and it was barely
eleven o'clock. "Ah, Malcolm. You're late."

The duke bowed. "My apologies, Your Majesty. A mechanical
problem with one of my engines. I had to proceed at quarter speed."

It was a successful gambit. The King loved fast craft nearly as
much as he loved being a leader of fashion. He bored the duke with
a largely wrong and incomprehensible diatribe about the Hahn-
Bentley triple jet and forgot his peevishness. He almost forgot his
reason for the confidential meeting he'd called for, too.

That would have suited Duke Malcolm well. The palace leaked
information, despite the counterintelligence effort focused there. But
a chance remark brought it all back. "Bang! Lost one of the engines
off the transom. But the triple jet didn't veer more than fifteen
degrees! Sank old Monmoth's tub, but that's what you get for nearly
beating your king. Had you lost one of your Whittles it'd have spun
you around and sent you back like one those Australian whatcha-
macallits . . . boomerangs. And speaking of Australia, that's what I
wanted to ask you about. I was talking to Field Marshal Viscount Von

Belstad at the Pavilion the other day. The subject of gold mines we'd
lost control over came up. That one in Queensland. Sheba."

Duke Malcolm knew now where the leak was and that he had
been powerless to stop it. No need to mention that the target was
not actually a gold mine. "It's an ongoing process, Your Imperial
Majesty." No one referred to the King as "Ernest." At least not in his
presence. Not even his brothers or his surviving sister.

"Yes, but it would be useful to be able to say to the Royal
Council that we've got a major new revenue stream coming on
board." The King looked a little uncomfortable, not a natural
expression for the supreme commander of British Imperial Power, of
the Empire on which the sun never set. "Thing is, they've been a bit
sticky lately. Money." He shook his head. "A monarch has expenses.
So when do we expect this to go ahead? Von Belstad said it was one
of your pet projects. Excellent idea!"

The duke hedged as best as he could. He tried to reinforce the
need for secrecy, and left feeling, if possible, even more that the
Empire needed a new head. One less capable of wasting a vast fortune.
How Ernest got through it was a mystery. Well, not a mystery, when
you considered the seven new palaces, three royal yachts, racing boats,
importing a herd of oryx for his newest hunting estate and . . . Duke
Malcolm sighed. It was a long list. Not crippling for an empire of the
size and wealth of the British Empire . . . but there were three places
to put every one of the pennies that would come from that mine. The
empire produced riches, which, in part, flowed to Great Britain. But
the cost of keeping that empire was growing like some insatiable mon-
ster. The more money there was, the more it needed.

If Ernest knew the name of the target, then sooner or later, spies
would too. And several foreign nations—the Russians, or the blasted
French—would delight in passing it on to the Australian rebels and
their upstart Republic. He'd love to crush it, but they really couldn't
spare troops from India right now. And Australia was large, and
inhospitable. Not a place the Empire wanted an extended campaign.

When the skid boat roared him back to St. James, and he returned to his office, he found the major in charge of the Australia desk waiting. "Bad news I'm afraid, Your Grace," he said, cutting to the chase immediately. "I sent off an urgent Marconi message about Jack Calland as soon as I got back to my office. I've just got a reply from the commander of the forward camp of Operation Solomon in Queensland. Calland has escaped along with about forty other prisoners. There's a massive manhunt underway. I immediately sent orders that he was to be taken alive."

Duke Malcolm slammed his fist onto the desk, sending the brass message capsule flying. "Forty prisoners? Can't they do anything right?"

The major looked uncomfortable. "Well, it is possible they didn't escape together, Your Grace. Best if I read you the transcript of the reply, Your Grace. It . . . gets worse."

"Continue."

The major read, "'There was a mass breakout by forty-two leg-ironed prisoners who had been sent to repair a culvert, including this prisoner. In the process, guards were killed and a locomotive wrecked. All the prisoners at the scene scattered, most having broken their shackles. Trackers and troops and teams of dogs have been dispatched, and there is a massive manhunt in progress across very hot terrain, hampered by rainstorms. According to standing orders the instruction was given to shoot on sight. The search is dispersed over a wide area, and the troops searching for the escapees are widely scattered and heading for the coastal forests. Messengers have been dispatched, but it is unlikely they will reach all of the troops before they find the escapees.'"

"I trust he has taken disciplinary measures against the guard commander," said the duke. "Well. Instruct him that I have taken a personal interest and wish to be informed about the success or failure to capture either the other prisoners or Calland. What is our current timeline on that project, Major Simmer?"

The major looked relieved. "They're working on the final section of rail and the off-loading ramps. Three more days. The colonel of the Dragoons said this breakout couldn't have come at a worse time for the work. They've got guards out hunting instead of supervising."

"Not likely to alert the Westralians, are they?"

"I thought of that, Your Grace. The colonel says the prisoners appear to have fled east, rather than toward Westralia. It's harsher desert to the west. A lot of open plains and very little water."

CHAPTER 12

The next morning Linda got to Dr. Calland's bungalow in time to have an early breakfast with her. It was plain that Clara's mother missed her daughter badly. And Linda had found that her new interest had given her a whole new position in her father's life, and it thoroughly confused her stepmother. Her father had talked for several hours . . . to her, mostly about the chemistry of fertilizers. A month ago she would have looked blankly at him and found something else that she needed to do. But now . . . well, she'd had a window into that world. And it was a world where she saw Dr. Calland getting a type of respect that Linda had now decided she wanted. It . . . it was different. She was used to seeing men open doors and stand up for women and girls. It was the respect caused by discovering that they were meeting with a better mind that was different and interesting. Some of them, like that smelly old professor plainly hated it.

And it had so obviously suddenly dawned on her father that his daughter might also be able to do the kind of thing Dr. Calland did. She'd never realized he wanted that in his child. He'd obviously never realized that, just because she wasn't a boy . . . he was talking about extra mathematics and deploring the state of education . . . and was very willing to see her spend more time with Dr. Calland.

They were drinking tea when Captain Malkis arrived. Linda wondered if Clara had ever realized that the captain was in love with her mother, and that Dr. Calland seemed totally unaware of it. Linda rather liked him. He always looked, without the obvious effort that

Nicky put into it, dapper and smart. It wasn't so much the clothes he wore as his manner.

"I have interesting news, Dr. Calland," said Captain Malkis. "Two important developments. The first is that I have, I believe, a confirmed sighting of your daughter. From Mandynonga station, on the day she was reported missing. That station is the railhead for the northern line of their underground 'termite ways.' I've telegraphed messages to the station master at Alice Springs, which is where the line branches. We've had no reply so far."

Mary Calland worked it out just after Linda did. "You mean . . . instead of falling in with this plot to kidnap her, my daughter has gone on a one-woman expedition to save her father?" She shook her head ruefully. "My daughter. I think once we've found her, I will have to kill her for the worry she's put us through. So, you were right, Linda. Clara was planning to go to Queensland, not with whoever baited this trap, but alone. Now we just have to catch up with her. I wonder how far she's got."

Captain Malkis stroked his beard thoughtfully. "Well, the second part of my discoveries may provide a clue. I have had my lieutenants buying up the contracts of the *Cuttlefish* crew, as per your instructions, and contacting them where possible. Mostly, at least, they've been reachable by telegraph. We have nineteen of the crew back here, most of the others on their way. We've now been successful in buying all the contracts . . . bar one."

Clara's mother closed her eyes. "Tim Barnabas."

It didn't take Linda a second to join the dots. More the dots between what Clara *hadn't* said about her Tim, than what she had.

"Correct, ma'am," said Malkis. "He's at Dajarra Power Station, working on the steam mole there. And, yes, that is accessed via the northern line, via Alice Springs. It's part of the new line they're building. The final station in the current push south . . . and yes, it would have been in Queensland before the melt. It is within two hundred and fifty miles of the location your husband was supposed to have been at when he wrote that letter."

"Clara . . . I don't think she has a particularly good grasp of just how far two hundred and fifty miles might be, especially across the desert. Her . . . her own travels beyond a mile or two have all been by train, or airship, or submarine.

"The desert is considered to be our barrier between the British Empire and Westralia, Dr. Calland," said Linda. "I've never been there, of course. But I have been told it's very bleak. They can't cross it. There is no transport of any sort going that way."

Dr. Calland sighed. "I don't think 'can't' is a word my daughter understands."

"It's a family failing, ma'am," said Captain Malkis, with just a hint of a smile.

"True," admitted Dr. Calland. "And she got a double dose of it. Jack was worse than I am, by far. Well, I suppose we now need to get to this Dajarra place."

"It's a two-day trip on their underground cable-train, ma'am, and there isn't another departure scheduled until tomorrow. Look, Lieutenant Ambrose said there was something very, very odd about the behavior of the Discovery North Rail Company. They were 'business as usual' until he said just whose contract he wished to buy. The clerk looked it up . . . and went to consult his superior. That individual came back and said that contract was not for sale, goodbye. Ambrose reported this to me immediately, and I went around to their offices with him, in the hope of reasoning with them." Captain Malkis grimaced. "We were actually forcefully ejected from the premises and threatened with police action if we came back. I have sent a message to Maxwell Darlington to enlist his help with this matter."

Linda's father arrived a few minutes later, accompanied by another man in the uniform of the local police, with added gold braid and the green slouch hat with its dingo badge. "Colonel Matthew Clifford. Westralian Mounted Police," said Max, introducing him.

"Are we in trouble with the WMP already?" asked Captain Malkis mildly. "I did specifically tell Lieutenant Ambrose he wasn't to take the crew to the offices of that railroad company."

Her father smiled. "I brought Clifford around to try to avoid you doing that."

"You might have no choice," said the policeman wryly. "See, they don't have to sell you the contract. It's not normally an issue, but if a company wants to be difficult, they can." He scratched his head. "But we can work around it, sir. I can draft the boy into the force. We're still technically at war with the British Empire, and the state may demand the surrender of a contract, for the contract valuation. I'd be willing to do so. I might tell you that we could have problems with this crowd. Their general manager, Rainor, thinks he's a law unto himself. He's got a lot of money and rides roughshod through the law, and lets his lawyers clean up the mess. He's got a lot of influence here, even within the WMP. People have relatives working for the company, and he's a vindictive piece of work."

"I see," said the captain. "Kidnapping is crime here, isn't it?"

"Of young women?" said Colonel Clifford. "My word, yes. We'll hang someone for that. And that'll be because we couldn't keep them alive in jail or out of it."

"And dealing with spies?" asked Dr. Calland.

"That comes under the heading of treason," said Colonel Clifford. "You could get twenty years breaking rocks in Alice for that."

"So, Colonel, how do you feel about drafting *several* of my crew?" asked the captain. "On a temporary basis, of course, and seconding them to this investigation?"

The colonel smiled. "A three-month drafting? Easily done, but the pay is terrible."

"I don't think we need to worry about that," said Dr. Calland. "I will match their earnings, of course. But it will save them calling on the police for help. Captain, if you would find, say, ten of your men that you consider suitable, and meet with Colonel Clifford to do the necessary paperwork, I think we could meet at the offices of this company at . . . should we say ten o'clock? Linda, you could show me where they have their offices? Do you know where they are?"

Linda nodded, hoping her father thought those were just lady-like blushes. Nicky worked there. She was still getting used to the fact that Clara's mother simply made decisions. Neither her mother—from what she remembered—nor her stepmother ever directly told anyone what to do. Dr. Calland did exactly that in her laboratory, and she wasn't that much different out of it.

They took a jarvey down to the offices of the Discovery North Railroad Company, so really, Linda's direction-finding skills were not needed. Linda noticed two familiar-looking men in telephone corporation uniforms up a ladder against the side of the building. One of them was definitely a submariner. She recognized him as having been with the captain that morning.

"I thought they were joining the police?"

Dr. Calland shook her head. "Submariners! One thing I've learned about them, Linda, is that they seem to be selected to be both audaciously daring and preventatively cautious at the same time. They're cutting the telephone line, I would guess. I think we should carefully not notice what the top-mast men are up to. Hold your parasol in the way, so that we can truthfully say we didn't see what they were doing."

The captain arrived with several men, and bowed to them. "If you'd like to follow Lieutenant Ambrose, special constable of the Westralian Mounted Police, we have deployed men at the other exit too. Let's see what answers we can get." There was steel in his voice.

They followed. Knowing that something was about to happen, Linda could see men quietly converging on the door. She wondered if anyone who didn't know would notice.

The railroad office was, for Ceduna, an impressive place, with fake marble colonnades and a doorman. Well, it had always impressed Linda, especially the doorman.

The doorman took one look at Lieutenant Ambrose and grabbed him by the arm—to find himself seized from the sides and behind by three more of the *Cuttlefish*'s crew and propelled away from the door. Ambrose took a letter out of his pocket and held it under the doorman's nose. "This is my appointment to the Westralian Mounted Police. I haven't had time to collect my uniform. Do you want time inside what they call 'stir' around here, for assaulting a police officer?"

The doorman looked at the lieutenant, then left and right at the solid submariners. "Er. No, sir. I was given orders that I wasn't to let you back in, sir. Just obeying orders, sir."

"Your orders, I'm sure, do not permit you to assault a police officer. Who gave you these orders?"

"Uh, Mr. Adam Manuel, sir. He's, he's . . . the assistant to the boss."

"Thank you for your cooperation," said the lieutenant pleasantly. He gestured to the men who had somehow just drifted closer. "Right, boys, move in, and fan out. Keep them peeled."

Linda had never found an excuse to actually go into the front office of the railroad company. She was surprised to see her Nicky behind the large slab of Tasmanian oak, gaping at her, blood draining from his face. The other clerk didn't seem shocked, just irritated. "What's going on here?" he asked frostily as Linda, the captain, and Dr. Calland followed the *Cuttlefish* crew up the front desk. Two of the crewmen calmly lifted the barrier and walked through to the other side of the desk, flanking him. Her Nicky edged toward the door, only to find a third crewman was there already, shaking his head.

"We're from the Westralian Mounted Police," said Lieutenant Ambrose, plainly enjoying himself very much. He slapped a piece of paper on the desk. "We have here a drafting order for one Barnabas, Timothy. We need his contract surrender dealt with . . . now."

The clerk stuck his finger in his collar. "I will go and call my supervisor, sir."

"We'll accompany you," said the lieutenant. "And before you even think of arguing, we're investigating both kidnapping and possible treason. I am sure you're eager to help."

They all walked through, and Nicky was swept along with them. He seemed to be avoiding looking at her.

"I don't know anything about it," said the clerk, nervously. "Orders from Mr. Manuel . . . when I couldn't find the contract in our files, I asked him what to do. He said I was to get rid of you immediately, sir. He gave orders to the doormen about keeping you out. He's going to be very angry about it."

That idea plainly terrified both the clerk, and, by the way he was sweating, Nicky. Linda wondered if she ought to help him. She was about to say something when Dr. Calland spoke in the sort of tone that could cut glass. "It sounds like this Mr. Manuel has some explaining to do," she said. "If those explanations are good enough, he may end up not being hanged." She could sound quite terrifying, thought Linda.

She obviously did so to the clerk, who nodded as if his head were on springs, but said nothing. Nicky coughed. "I'm sure you don't need me," he said, his voice a little high-pitched. "I . . . I am just a junior clerk. I know nothing about it." But before he could escape he was pushed with the rest into a plushly carpeted office containing a large brass and mahogany desk . . . and a startled, flush-faced, bald little man with a big nose, who looked more like a crow who'd fallen into a pot of red paint than someone to be terrified of.

Still, he did his best to try. "What is the meaning of this intrusion?" he demanded, staring at the mob pushing into his office. Or being pushed, in the case of the clerk and Nicky. Then he plainly recognized the captain and Lieutenant Ambrose. "I thought I warned you . . . I will have the police . . ."

"Sir. They're *from* the police," interrupted the clerk. "I tried . . ."

"Hush," said the captain. "Don't get yourself a longer sentence."

Blood drained from the man's florid face. "What can I do for you gentlemen?" asked Mr. Manuel in an entirely different tone.

"We're needing a contract surrender for a man in your employ who has been drafted into the WMP, in accordance with Proclamation 322. We have reason to believe he can assist us with an ongoing investigation," said Lieutenant Ambrose.

Manuel bit his thin lip. "Sir. I must inform you that Mr. Barnabas," he made no pretense that he didn't know who they were talking about, "is dead."

Linda looked at Nicky. Had he known about all of this when she'd asked his advice about Clara? Surely not. She hadn't known more than Tim's first name.

"So why the secrecy?" asked the captain.

Mr. Manuel continued, obviously trying to look both respectful and sad. "We didn't want to sell his contract until the next of kin had been notified."

Dr. Calland looked as if she'd been hit with a wet sack. Some of the other submariners looked just as shocked.

"How did he die?" asked Linda. She didn't quite believe him, and it might have come out in her voice, because Mr. Manuel looked as if he was about to speak harshly to her for her impertinence. And then he obviously realized that putting down a chit of a schoolgirl, right now, would be a bad idea.

"Um. An industrial accident with the cutting head of the drill," he said. "Much regretted. We're having an investigation, but it appears that he willfully breached safety rules," said the man, tugging his earlobe.

"His body will have to be taken back to the *Cuttlefish*, for a submariner's burial," said the captain heavily.

"Er. The body was buried. In the heat, you know . . ."

"Just one question," said Lieutenant Ambrose who had plainly got his wind back after the shock. "Just why hasn't this been reported to the WMP?"

Now it was Manuel's turn to look as if he'd been hit with the wet sack. He certainly started sweating. "Er. Accidental death. We're in the process of filling in the forms."

"We're going to have to exhume the body, and then get witness statements," said the lieutenant.

The official could have broken a drought with his face. "We don't know where the body is," he admitted. "Look. We had problems. Rioting at that station. We couldn't afford to lose more construction time. We've had to fly up a new station manager. I'm . . . I'm sure it's all something that can be dealt with. I . . . I really need to consult my superior."

"Good," said Lieutenant Ambrose. "I think we'll talk to him, too. Perhaps before you explain. Let's go."

"Uh. We can't just burst in on the general manager!"

"Watch us," said the captain grimly.

Someone had, however, obviously run to warn the man. His secretary flapped at them ineffectually, but the office was empty. The telephone's ear horn lay on the desk, and the speaking horn dangled from its cable. "Where has he gone?" asked the captain. It was politely said . . . but in such a way that it would have cut through a force ten gale.

"Uh. He just stepped out . . ." The secretary swallowed, looking at the hard faces around his desk. "The back exit."

"Who was he trying to call?" asked the lieutenant.

Obviously the secretary decided lying wasn't worth it. "Uh, Senator Wattly. But the telephones are out."

"Who did you have on the back door, Ambrose?" asked the captain.

"Gibb and Nichol, sir."

The captain smiled savagely. "I think we'll conduct our interview down there. In the meanwhile, Willis, I think this young man will help you to find any documents relating to this matter, and will tell you and Thorne all he knows. I'm sure he doesn't want to be hanged next to his boss."

Linda didn't know much about the law, but she was sure this wasn't the way the Westralian Mounted Police normally operated.

On the other hand, Clara was her friend, and this smelled of something very nasty that they were trying to bury, and the *Cuttlefish* crew were getting results. It might be yet another false lead. Whatever happened, Linda knew there'd be real trouble from the crew of the *Cuttlefish*, and from Dr. Calland, if Tim really was dead. She could tell by the expression on their faces, and the tone of their voices, that they liked him too.

The bluster and demands for a lawyer and complaints about police brutality from the general manager of Discovery North Railroads were met by the captain's most unpleasant, tigerish smile. "Who said we were the police? You say you have friends in high places. We're submariners. Barnabas was one of our own. He had friends in *low* places. We might even have to take you to join them . . . unless I get answers *now*."

They got them. But they didn't help much. Mr. Rainor knew nothing about Clara. He didn't care if his station manager reported that a contract worker had been possibly murdered and that he had problems with a riot. He'd told his staff to make the problem go away and get the drilling going again. The Westralian Mounted Police would take days to get there, days to investigate. Drilling would be interrupted, and might even be stopped. Rainor didn't, plainly, care, so long as that didn't happen. "We can't afford any delays. I sent one of my best men up there, my troubleshooter, Adrian Ness, to replace McGurk and get it all working as fast possible."

"And what about this death?"

"Um. I'm sure Ness will get to the bottom of it. Look, we can't afford delays. I will see that compensation is paid—generous compensation—if we can just let it go."

"Brush it under the carpet, you mean?" said the lieutenant, dangerously.

"Not, not really. Just deal with it expeditiously. Who is it going to help to hold the work up? Ness is a good man. He'll fix it up. Barnabas's family will be well compensated."

"What have you heard from this 'troubleshooter'?" asked the captain.

"Er. Just that work had resumed. He wouldn't trouble me with details."

"I think we need to speak to him," said the captain, in a voice that said "now" if not sooner.

"Impossible, I'm afraid. You could send him a telegram. There is a train from Sheba every day."

"How much compensation are you prepared to pay if we don't pursue enquiries about what happened to Barnabas," said the captain.

"Oh. Should we say, a hundred pounds?" said the managing director, looking like a weasel who has just spotted a way out.

"I think that very cheap for one of our own," said the captain evenly.

"Um. Five hundred? But I'll need a signed agreement you won't pursue it."

"Ten thousand," said the captain. "And we'll have that agreement signed right here. Get me paper, pen, and ink, boys."

It was brought. "In your own hand," said the captain. "Write 'I, Robert Rainor, do hereby agree to pay the *Cuttlefish* and her crew the sum of ten thousand Australian pounds not to pursue the matter of the suspicious death of Timothy Barnabas.' Sign it."

"What's to stop you pursuing it anyway?" asked Rainor.

"We'll sign a similar document, you can choose the wording, on our receipt of the money," said the captain.

"But I don't see that I have to sign this at all. I'll get you your money right now."

"Of course you do need to sign it. We're not making you do so, but we won't believe you unless you do. We can't take the money, because we don't know if Barnabas is dead or not, until we hear from your man Ness. Unless," snarled the captain, "you are lying to us about being able to talk to him."

Rainor scrawled his signature.

"Right. We'll need a couple of witnesses," said the captain. "You, miss." He pointed at Linda. "You are not one of the crew. Write 'witnessed by,' and sign it, please."

Linda did, despite her horror at the idea of them taking money and leaving. But she had to complain. "You can't do this, Captain Malkis. The police . . . Clara . . ."

He winked at her. "We can deal with that. Lieutenant, please sign it too."

Lieutenant Ambrose did, while Linda was still wondering about it all.

"Right," said the captain. "I think you can escort Mr. Robert Rainor to Ceduna Central, Lieutenant. They should at the very least be able to hold him on the intent to pervert the course of justice on the basis of this offer. Might manage bribery charges, too, as you *Cuttlefish* crewmen are now police officers."

"I can't begin to tell you how much trouble you are going to be in," snarled Mr. Rainor, as he realized he was being escorted to the police station and not to the harbor.

Linda could imagine. The big six companies had huge influence and controlled nearly everything.

That didn't seem to worry the captain, or Dr. Calland. The captain laughed grimly into the man's face. "You've lived too long in a world where everything has a price, Rainor. The lives and honor of my men are not for sale. I might have let you loose, if you hadn't tried that. You'll try to bribe and lawyer your way free, no doubt. I think we'll go and call on your friend Senator Wattly, too, before you start squalling about wrongful arrest. You can claim we forced it from you, but then you're going to have to explain your earlier cover-up. You find yourself on the receiving end of what you were doing, Rainor. You've got away with this sort of thing for too long, and I'm guessing this will be the dam-burst. You'll find your staff telling the story of the boss running away and sneaking out of the back door to everyone they know. And a fair amount else, I suspect, or I've no experience of being in command of men."

"Wait until my lawyers get into you," snarled the man.

"They'll have to come north to find me," said the captain. "I have one of my crew to search for, and a young lady to find."

CHAPTER 13

"Your Grace, the news in from Queensland isn't positive. They've so far recaptured or killed all the escapees but four. Unfortunately, some of those killed early on, before orders were given that Jack Calland was to be taken alive, were just shot and left where they fell. And in the tropics . . . well, the bodies are in no state to be identified. One of those may be Calland. Or not. The captured prisoners . . . They are aware that they're in danger of being shot. And somehow that we're after one prisoner, alive. So they're not being cooperative about identifying themselves."

Duke Malcolm pursed his lips, shook his head, and sighed in irritation. "And of course there are still four missing. They've been gone nearly four days now. Calland could be one of those, I suppose, knowing the luck we've had so far. Well, what chances do they have of capturing them? Does Colonel Debrett in Queensland give any assessment?"

"They've got some aboriginal trackers on the job now, Your Grace. They're exceptional trackers, the natives, and are going to find them, if possible. But a lot of the prisoners are aboriginals too, and it could be that those are the escapees, and Calland could be dead or in custody already. It's harsh country. The only positive thing seems to be that they're sure they've stopped them before they got farther east to the more populated areas. They're fairly certain the prisoners are inside their cordon. They've had to use some men from the Hussars to make it effective. Those were men who were being saved for the push to Sheba." The officer sighed. "It's a mess, Your Grace."

Duke Malcolm did, at times, appreciate frankness like that. Especially when it concurred with his own conclusions. "Keep me posted. How are the military preparations going otherwise?"

The duke could see the major's shoulders lift slightly. "They have set things forward just in case there have been any leaks. It should, however, take a while for the rumor, let alone news, to percolate through to Western Australia. They're waiting on a last fuel delivery. Unfortunately, the vessel has been delayed at sea."

❊

Rested, rehydrated, even better fed than he'd been in a while, but very stiff, Jack struggled to get walking that evening. The cold, cooked big lizard tasted rather more like lizard than chicken in the afternoon. They'd wrapped it in leaves and buried it to keep the flies off, so it had added eucalyptus flavor and sand crunch. It was food, however, and they ate as they walked. Once his muscles warmed and loosened up he began to try to draw the boy out as they walked west under the stars.

"Once we get away from the soldiers where are you going to go?" Jack asked.

"Not sure. Got some cousins down Jericho way working as stockmen. That's what Pa did when me ma was alive. Maybe I'll go to look for them. I'd go to me uncle, but he got killed by some railway-man near Boulia. Railway-man was out shootin' and he saw my uncle and shot 'im. He was good bloke, my uncle. My ma's people. He took me in the bush, taught me how to be a man. I live with him for three years. Otherwise . . . I don' know. My da's woman, she don't want me back, 'cept to steal for her. And she tol' the coppers I done it and it my fault." Lampy scowled. "It wasn't. When the drink gets in him he was bad. Ain't going back there. Anyway, that's where they'd come look for me."

"Won't they look with your cousins?" asked Jack.

"Aw, they think we all look the same. And me cousins ain't going to tell them me name."

Lampy didn't look particularly like the other aboriginal prisoners to Jack, but he kept his council to himself. It worried him, though. The boy had kept him alive.

"And you, Irish?" asked Lampy.

"Call me Jack. I am going to look for my family. I suppose . . . if I fail to find them, I'll try to get back to my own country."

"You should bring 'em here. Best country in the world," said Lampy sincerely. "You get to know it, and everything a man could want is out here, my uncle say."

He meant it. Despite the fact that they were in a desert, where if you were out in the sun in January it could easily get to a hundred and twenty degrees where man could die of heat, and Lampy was a second-class citizen, or by the sounds of it, worse, in Westralia. "It's pretty warm," Jack said.

"You learn to live with it. The plants and the animals—Hush." The youngster stiffened like a bird dog catching the scent or sound of prey.

Which was appropriate, seeing as what he heard was a bird.

A very big bird, on a nest.

"We need a boobinch," said Lampy.

Jack's sense of humor was beginning to reassert itself. "Now, I knew I'd be needing one of those! What the devil's a boobinch?" he asked quietly.

"We go back to the river," was the nearest he got to an explanation.

So they went back to the dry watercourse, and Lampy scavenged among the dry wood debris, coming up with a hollow stick about fourteen inches long and about three inches in diameter. The bottom was blocked with some slightly damp clay that was the only sign that water had been there. Lampy hastily flattened off the top. "You hit like this, see." He showed Jack how to tap it. It made an odd booming sound. "Now you go there, down that little gully. You hit the boobinch till I tell you to stop."

He gave orders well, thought Jack. "What are you going to be doing?"

"Stealing eggs from the emu. You stop and I get kicked. He thinks you his missus, and he'll come look."

Jack had some idea of the size of the emu, and he knew being kicked by a six-foot-tall flightless bird was no joke. He hoped it wouldn't be disappointed to find he wasn't its missus.

But to his relief it was Lampy rather than the male emu who came along first, with four eggs—*big* eggs, dark in the moonlight. They walked on, talking about the country, about the wildlife, about the dingoes, and about what had got them into this situation.

"I suppose I made some choices. It was either me or Padraig, and I believed that the rebellion would be less hurt by me being in jail than by him," said Jack. "I hadn't really thought too much about what it would mean to me . . . or my family."

"Yeah. You can't really get what being inside means until you're there," said the boy.

※

Lampy wondered just why he'd started talking. He usually carefully avoided mentioning he could read and write. It only brought you trouble. But when Jack asked he admitted to it. "I been to school. Mission school. We lived next to the mission for a while before ma died. Them nuns!" He shook his head. "They was strict. *Were* strict. But you can't talk like they want, or people think you all up yerself."

"Heh," said Jack. "I learned to speak a broad south Irish brogue for that very reason. It was almost like having two languages. One for school, one for playing with the other boys back at my father's place."

Lampy had been slightly surprised to find out that it wasn't just him who had done this. "True, an' then you get careless an' one slips into the other, and you get into trouble. Mind you, some of it goes back around. Even them nuns called me 'Lampy' because ma did. Ain't the name I was given. She just called me that."

"Why?"

Even as he said it, Lampy wondered why he was explaining himself. Maybe because no one had ever asked before. It was private. A last thing between him and his mother. "The nuns taught us this song 'Give me oil my lamp keep me burning, burning, burning' and I come home singing it. I was just a little 'un just starting school. Ma loved it. Made me sing it all the time." He didn't say: *Even when she was dying and I was twelve years old.* "She called me her little Lampy, and pretty soon everyone did."

"It happens like that."

"I stick by it, now she's dead. It's kind of respect."

"It is," said Jack. And he seemed to understand. Or at least that's what Lampy read in it. "How old were you then?"

"'Bout twelve. Pa went off the rails, well, more than before then. Moved around, nearer to the city on the coast. Me uncle, he came an' took me away. Back to me mother's people. I stayed with him, we'd move around, work a bit, go back to the bush a bit. It was good. Did that for two, two and a half years."

"Then what happened?" asked Jack.

Lampy walked silently for a while, then said, "Then he got shot and I went back to my Da." Which was a very short version of despair, anger, and hurt. "He got him a new woman, but he was drinkin' real bad. They neither of them was glad to see a half-abo son turn up, but he give me a roof. He was all right until the booze got him. Couldn't hold a job though, and they was makin' do . . . with stealing and selling mostly. I'd learned to be good with sheep, see. So he send me out to get one when there was no food in the house, and they'd eat, sell meat, and be all right for a bit. I just decided I was going to cut out of there, go lookin' for me cousins . . . but I fetched them one last sheep. I got back with it . . . he'd been on the grog and was layin' into Carol, that tallow-haired woman of his, and she see me come in, and I sing out to him to stop it, I'd brought the mutton. And she runs to me. He comes after her with a stock whip and I tried to take it off him. Only there was an axe and he grabbed that instead. And . . . and we fought. He was bigger than me, an' we fell over."

They walked in silence for a while. Jack didn't chase it, just waited for it come out.

"He got cut, really bad. And she run and got two coppers. I should have run too . . . but I was trying to stop the blood." There had been so much blood.

"The judge said I was a black thief and had killed a white man, see. But I'm under age to hang. So they put me in jail to die."

※

Looked at one way, Jack could see that the boy was a thief and murderer. Looked at another, he was a loyal son who did what his father told him to do, who had then tried to protect his stepmother from his drunken father. The worst part, for Jack, was that Lampy saw himself as the former, at least some of the time, and hated himself for it. And now that he was getting to know the boy, he was also coming to realize that "being inside" was tough on any man, but for Lampy it had been far worse. Jack could see it by the way he touched the land and tasted the air. It must have been like caging an eagle.

"For what it's worth, I think you did what any decent man would have done in the situation."

Lampy shook his head. "I should have left there, straight off, when I see what he was doing. I knew it wasn't right."

"It's easy to be wise after the fact. There are plenty of mistakes I wish I hadn't made. I reckon you paid a high price for them already. Nothing to deserve dying on the railway, in chains."

"Never gunna let anyone chain me again."

CHAPTER 14

It was already getting hot by the time Clara finally figured out the problem . . . and that her use of the horn was at least partly to blame. The water supply to feed over the burners was low, and they had, she assumed, some kind of a pressure switch that had levers that choked the fire and stopped it melting the copper pipes.

The cooling steam fed through a big cooler, and recondensed and fed back into the system. It did have one major escape, as far as she could work out: through the steam whistle.

Now all she needed was more water, and to get the burners going again, and she would be able to move. And she did have water in a huge tank on the tender . . . it was just how to get it from one place to the next? But in finding this she also found that she'd used quite a lot of the fuel.

It took some time to work out that there was a tap, a hand pump, and an indicator just behind her seat in the cab. Obviously the second member of the crew of the scout mole was supposed to see to the water level.

Now that she had the water situation sorted—and had used rather a lot during the refilling—she merely had to get the burner going. That should have required priming and half an hour . . .

It took her a lot more than that, and a fair amount of the primer fuel—some kind of alcohol that made her feel odd, just smelling it in the fire box. She had a horrifying moment when the steam mole started to trundle . . . and she wasn't in it. She had to clamber desperately along the frame, burning her hands on the hot pipes, to swing into the cab and pull the levers back. The gauges still read no pressure at all, and really, the steam mole had been going slower than a crawling baby. She could have jumped off and walked to the ladder up to the cab. It was late afternoon before she was ready to start the steam mole moving again. Now, knowing she was lost, knowing that only chance would let her see Tim or Tim see her, she kept the steam mole rumbling along the plain, as she stared out.

Come full dark, she stopped and smothered the furnace with its damper choke. She had, in her exploring and learning how it all worked, at least learned how to do that. She would have to reprime and get it all going in the morning, but at least that too had no mysteries anymore.

She ate and drank frugally, spread the bedroll in the cab, and opened the door slightly.

Sleep was a refuge from all the uncertainty and fear.

Unfortunately, sleep was a long long way off. She really didn't know what she should do in the morning. Gnawing at her was the fact that she'd failed. She hadn't found Tim. There was a chance, maybe, but a chance that she wouldn't let herself let go of, that he'd found his way back to the power station. But by now she knew that his chances out here were very, very small. It was hard not to feel sorry for herself, and to cry, for him, for her mother, and for the father she was not sure if she could ever reach. Now that she'd seen and been in the desert, it was quite a different concept to somehow rescue her father from a prison somewhere on the other side of it, with no resources but a stolen steam mole, and that probably wouldn't get that far.

※

Tim's other discovery had been a broken egg shell that led him to climb up to a bird's nest. It was empty, dashing the hope he'd had of eggs. Then it occurred to him that an empty little egg shell could at least make a tiny bowl for the slow drips from the seep in the crack. The egg had lost its big end, and he propped it carefully, positioning it so that the drops—about one every minute, landed in it. It was better than lying on his back with his mouth open waiting, or licking it off the rock, both of which he'd tried. Gradually through the day, he got egg-full after egg-full to drink, as he sat in the shade, dozing, not daring to sleep too long.

As the heat began to burn off with the sun dropping red onto the horizon, Tim knew he had to move on. He knew he had nothing like enough water, so there was no point in staying there. Of course . . . the next place could be even worse. Temptation warred within his breast. If he stayed put overnight, he might see the fire again . . .

Or he might die of cold. If he'd had a fire or more water he might have tried. He'd tried knocking rocks together to see if he could make a spark, but had no other ideas on how one made fire.

He had an egg shell full of water, and about fifty of the little figs threaded onto a plait of grass . . . supplies!

He started walking down across the still-hot sand with occasional tufts of dead grass and one or two twisted-branched, waxy-leafed trees, so stunted they barely stood much more than shoulder height. And then he heard something. A thumping sound. A *regular* thumping sound.

The sound of pistons.

The red sunset gleamed off the curve of the roof of a scout mole a mile or so away.

With a yell of joy he started running after it.

He soon realized he wasn't gaining on the thing, and that the gathering dark was making his tired, weak half-run even more difficult.

In the brief twilight Tim staggered toward the steam mole, which trundled steadily along the plain, knowing he could never reach it, but knowing he had to try. He screamed. But he knew, even as he did it, that inside the sealed cab, with its input air running

over the coolers and the thump of the steam mole's pistons, the
driver would never hear him.

Eventually he just had to stop.

In the distance, a growing distance now, he could see the spark
of the fire box . . . and then, nothing. It must have moved into a
gully. He couldn't even hear it anymore.

He stood there, looking forlorn, hoping to see at least where it
was going, when someone spoke in the darkness next to him. It
wasn't English. And, looking hard into the darkness, he saw the
spear the black man held half-raised. He spoke again in the strange
language, repeating what he had said before.

Tim slowly raised his hands. "I'm sorry, but I don't understand.
I'm lost," he said.

"What mob you come from? What you want in our country?"
asked the stranger.

The question, and the way it was said, was . . . guarded. Not
unfriendly, just guarded.

"I don't want anything except to stay alive and get out of your
country," said Tim, not knowing what answer the man wanted and
too tired and too desperate to try anything more than the truth. "It's
not my place. I'm lost."

There was a chuckle. "Good answer, boy. How you come here?
Where you come from? Who your people?"

"I come from Under London. And I got lost from the railway." Tim
wasn't sure who his people were, besides the crew of the *Cuttlefish*.

"You a long way from the railway."

"Um. I've been walking for a few days. I'd . . . I'd like to get
back there. Or back to the south coast. Ceduna. My people are
there," said Tim.

"You Yarulandi?" asked the stranger.

"No . . . I'm Tim. Tim Barnabas." Tim stuck out his hand.
"Pleased to meet you. After walking around for days I'm just so
pleased to meet anyone."

"We know. Bin watching you from this morning." The man didn't take his hand. Then he appeared to reach a decision. "You come alonga me."

Tim did his best. But he was weak and struggled to walk at half the speed of the man with the spear. After a while the man stopped. "What's wrong, boy?"

"I'm just . . . thirsty and tired. I haven't eaten much," said Tim, feeling he was offering excuses. "Sorry. Don't mean to hold you up."

"Ah. How long since you had any tucker?" asked the man.

Tim had learned that word from Cookie. "A few days. I had some figs and a bit of a bird, but no food—real food—in a few days. I don't know how to live off the country. It's not like where I come from."

The man held out something to Tim. "Suck it. We ain't got too far to go now."

It was sweet gum and it did help, both for the thirst and for some energy. Still, Tim was very relieved by the time they saw the flicker of a small fire. Even from here Tim could smell cooking meat.

He went through the ritual that followed in a somewhat hazy state. It did involve water, which was very welcome, and having smoke fanned into his face, which made him cough. It was easier to breathe than the coal smoke in the tunnel, though. And it ended up with him getting food—cooked meat and a very odd hard bread that tasted like no bread he'd ever eaten—and the inquisition. They were very kind to him, but they were convinced that he was an Australian aboriginal, at least in part. And the sea was not something they really seemed to grasp too well. They spoke some English, to varying degrees, but their own language between themselves, most of the time.

And none of them seemed in the least surprised that someone on the railway should try to kill him. "Some of them whitefellers are mad. Kill a blackfeller just for fun."

Tim slept well for the first time since what seemed forever.

※

Lampy woke with Jack shaking his shoulder. "Bad news, son. I think I see something behind us."

It was very early morning and they'd slept on a slight rise in the ground. That was definitely a light in the distance. Lampy looked at it and shivered slightly. It wasn't, as Jack feared, pursuit so close they could see their light. But it was something that he'd last seen the last time he'd been into this country, with his uncle. "It's a min-min light," he said, hoping his voice didn't shake. "You see 'em sometimes here. My uncle, he reckoned it was bad spirits. Come on, we're awake. Let's get away from this place." Just in case Uncle Jake was right.

They walked west. Lampy had enough stories and enough horrors brought back by those lights. They stopped, ate, drank from the nearly empty bucket. It was more awkward than a Coolamon, but he'd rigged a harness for it and carried it on his back. It was coming on for the heat of the day, time to stop again, when, looking back, Lampy realized they couldn't. They'd been walking up a long, gentle slope. Knowing the way the channels ran and the nature of the country, they'd start a descent into a country of southwest-running channels beyond that. Then there was the rock country on the other side of that, then gibber plains and the tall rock Uncle Jake had taken him to. Important place that. The railroad was not more than sixty or seventy miles the other side of it, with the deep desert beyond. Only, looking back, that was dust. A little patch of it, suggesting a mob of camels or . . .

He pointed back.

Jack squinted in the brightness. "Could be trackers. I wonder just how many?

"Dunno, but even two is too many. We go on."

So they did. Down in the channels, they stumbled on a dingo kill. The dingoes . . . and the birds of prey, were not inclined to give up on the dead kangaroo easily, but a few loud noises and prods with their spears sent them clear. "If that is the chase, we'll need the meat," said Jack, severing a leg and tying it to a piece of the thin rope he'd looted from the locomotive.

"What you planning, man?" asked Lampy.

"They can outrun us. We can deal with dogs, if there aren't too many of them. We can try to deal with men if there aren't too many of them. We have no chance on both. So we need to distract the dogs, at least. And if we're wrong, we'll have some tucker."

That wasn't all they found. There was the snake, too. It was a gwarder. "Careful. They bite. It's poison," Lampy warned.

Jack seemed unworried by the snake in their path. It was too small to eat, but not too small to bite. Lampy wondered if the man just didn't know snakes. "Australian Brown Snake I think," said the Irishman, proving him wrong. "We don't have snakes in Ireland. They fascinated me as a result, I think. I used to catch them and keep them when I was a student at Cambridge. Mary did *not* approve!" He moved slowly and deliberately, breaking a long branch from the stunted mulga, and breaking twigs to make a little fork.

"What you going to do?" asked Lampy, fascinated.

"Catch it. It should fit into that egg shell."

They had one emu egg that they'd kept intact—with just a finger-wide hole in it to drain the egg out. The contents they'd eaten, but the shell Jack had in his bucket. He trapped the snake, then picked it up. Holding it just behind the head, he had the interesting task of getting it into the egg, which he plugged with some leaves.

"A few scorpions and it would be the makings of a great hand grenade," said the Irishman.

He was mad, decided Lampy.

※

Linda returned to the bungalow with Dr. Calland as the heat of the day set in. Most people would rest now, but both of them were still somewhat wound up by the events at the railroad office. They sat talking about what could possibly have happened there. The truth was, neither had any real idea.

"I'm afraid, Linda, that I am going to have to take the trip up to Dajarra," said Dr. Calland. "I'd love to take you along, but I suspect your parents wouldn't allow it."

Linda shook her head regretfully. "Not very likely, Dr. Calland. I am supposed to be back at school, and the trip will take you at least four days. My father's suddenly very keen on my education."

"He should be. You're a bright young woman," said Dr. Calland. It meant a bit more coming from her, as Linda was sure she didn't do socially polite lies very well. "I'll pursue whatever enquiries we can this afternoon and evening. I've asked Captain Malkis to book our journey on this railway, and we'll leave tomorrow. I hate wasting all this time. And thank you so much for yours."

There was a polite knock. It was Captain Malkis. "Bit of a setback, ma'am. We attempted to book two carriages on the northbound rail . . . and it appears that Discovery North Railroad has managed to take some steps to prevent it. They claim the trains are fully booked for some weeks. We could go west, via Kalgoorlie, on the line owned by Marram Rail. There's a link to Alice Springs every week from there, and then across to Sheba. The link to Dajarra is of course owned by Discovery North again. I've sent Lieutenant Ambrose around to talk to Colonel Clifford, to see if we can claim police need and requisition the carriage."

Dr. Calland got up and clenched her fists. "More time for them to cover up, more time for Clara, and possibly Tim, to get into deeper trouble. I feel every hour is precious. I was wondering . . . if it was possible for that horrible Mr. Rainor to fly someone up to this place, why we can't do the same?

"A good idea, ma'am. I'll investigate," said the captain. He turned to Linda. "I wonder, Miss, if you would know anything about it?"

"Not really. I mean, I know they fly from Boomerang Fields, and they fly patrols. They're part of the army, I think. I do know they can be hired for . . . for really important things. It costs a lot."

"There are times when money is less important than other matters," said Clara's mother, firmly. "And right now I have money. I hope it won't cost so much I don't have spare for the *Cuttlefish*, Captain, but I think this needs doing now."

He nodded. "The desert is a bit like the sea, ma'am. It'll kill you if you don't know it. If . . . if they have decided to cross over to Queensland from there, and Tim is not dead, but this is just some kind of cover-up then they're in the desert. And neither of them know it. If they're trying to cross it . . . the sooner we get there the better."

"Well, we need to hire an airship, then. Linda, where is this 'Boomerang Fields'?"

"Well, it's on the flats beyond Mandynonga. Quite a long way. And I don't think they have many airships, really. They have a few blimps, but it's where the flying wings take off from."

To the questioning look, Linda shrugged. "I don't know. They're heavier-than-air, not like airships, I think. Look, why don't you ask my father? He's involved with them . . . I know he's been off into the desert to see some experimental stuff he's not supposed to tell us about."

"And does he?" asked the captain, with a slight smile.

"Not much, no. Well. Not anything. My stepmother agonized about them blowing up and killing him. He said that was unlikely, and laughed."

"It's a good idea. Let us call Mr. Darlington."

Linda could only hear half the conversation. But the words "hornet's nest" were definitely part of it. Of course, well-bred ladies shouldn't eavesdrop, but she wished she could hear both sides. She'd put up with being less well-bred for a while.

Dr. Calland put down the telephone horn and looked at them from over her glasses, an impish smile on her face for the first time Linda could recall. "Your father thinks it would be a good idea for us to get out of town as soon as possible, before we get ourselves arrested. He will contact the Air Wing of the army and make arrangements, but he doubts if it will be possible before first thing tomorrow morning. They don't like to fly at night. Part of their cost savings has been to hire transport planes out to civilian use. He doesn't approve, but does think it very convenient for us."

"I gather Rainor is making a stink, is he?" asked the captain.

"His lawyers are. They've demanded an immediate bail hearing. So he may be a free man again by this afternoon. The hearing is scheduled for five thirty."

"If it succeeds he'll do his best to put a spoke in our wheel," said the captain.

"And if he fails, his lawyers will. Maxwell Darlington says it would be best if we simply weren't available for a few days. His friend Clifford has said there are ongoing investigations that have come out of this, but it's slow work."

※

Clara awoke, cold, from a troubled sleep, and sat looking out at the dark land and endless starscape above. Here, far from the coal smoke of Europe, and even the coal smoke of the east coast, she could see stars beyond anything she'd ever dreamed of back in Ireland. Yes, they'd seen stars at night on *Cuttlefish* quite as clearly as this, but there had always been a wary eye on the horizon in case of an enemy ship's lights.

Here there was nothing.

Except . . . that wasn't true. That red spark on the dark of the landscape, below the stars, against the dark that must be a hill . . . that red spark must be a fire.

A fire out here—where she'd seen no sign of life for days. Hope rose like a tide in her. She put it down as hard as she could. It could be someone searching for her. It could be the aboriginals that were supposed to live out here, somehow.

In the cold of the predawn darkness Clara set about priming the steam mole's furnace. It was more difficult when she couldn't see what she was doing. It was only when she'd finally got it lit that she remembered the little carbide lamp hanging on a hook near the roof. By then it was grey, rather than black out, and she had no more need of it. Now she just had to get sufficient pressure of steam to head for a fire she could no longer see.

She had a good bearing on it, though, lining up her seat and the back corner porthole. She could vaguely make out landmarks by now. She got out of the cab again and drew a long straight line on the sandy soil with the shovel. There were dry tussocks of grass out here, but they were quite scattered and not enough to stop her from making a fifty-yard-long line. Now all she'd have to do was turn the steam mole and drive down the line, then pick markers—just as they'd learned on the *Cuttlefish*—and line them up. If she could find any markers on this landscape . . . There were places where there were rocks and other features, but there was also a lot of flat land stretching into sameness.

In a few minutes she was able to get the mole moving, turned around, and travelling down her line. Fortunately, there was a twist of darker land—could be the scrubby trees of this place—and a round, low hill in front of another range of hills that she could line up and head toward. She had no idea from how far off she could have seen that fire in the darkness. She'd decided she had to keep searching as long as she could, or until she knew Tim was dead. She just couldn't bear the thought of leaving him out there.

She trundled on toward the rounded hill. There was no sign of smoke from the fire she'd seen as the sky turned from blue-grey, to red-tinged, to blue.

CHAPTER 15

The emu eggs were more than one meal for the two of them. Lampy cooked them by burying them under the sand and making the fire on top of them, and he contrived a rough basket to carry them in, disdaining the fire bucket, still half filled with water, that Jack was lugging along. "We dig some roots here. I show you. They good for water. I'm showin' you lots, cause when we see that railway, I'm gunna leave you to get to it on your own. Not goin' near them railway-men. You maybe have ten-fifteen mile to walk."

"Anyone who tries to give you problems will have to deal with me first," said Jack. "They should be pleased enough to know about that railway and the troops on it. That's trouble, and it's coming here."

"Trouble for Westralia. What do I care?" said Lampy with a shrug. "Now this is the leaf you look for, see? We dig here. You got a digging stick?"

"Wish I'd brought a shovel," said Jack, setting to work.

"Then you got to carry it. Here you find another stick if that one go break, or if you need your hands to throw a spear, they're free to throw."

Jack's ever-fertile mind absorbed all of this, as well as the fact that this young, bitter man almost certainly knew more about survival out here than most soldiers in the King's army. They could, if they were armed and motivated, make a force to be reckoned with. If the Westralians or the Empire could be bothered, it would seem that in the aboriginals the British Empire had a willing tool, given the way Lampy felt about Westralia. Jack just hoped the Empire was too arrogant to realize it. The British Army firmly believed they were the best soldiers in the world. And maybe in European and conventional battle terms they were.

Out here, with distances and small numbers, it might be a different matter. Water and supplies would be key, but a small, mobile, locally knowledgeable guerilla force could tie up a lot of conventional soldiers. The Boers had nearly bled the British Empire white, in South Africa in the 1900s, after all.

※

The Irishman was a strange one, thought Lampy. Almost not like a whitefeller, except that he also knew nothing. Well, nothing about the land. Maybe back in his own country he could do things there. He knew a bit about snaring rabbits. Uncle had said they used to be thick, back before the sun got so hot you had to hunt at night, or dawn or dusk.

It was worrying that he was so slow. They were doing maybe thirty miles a day. Lampy knew that on his own he could do twice that. A man on a horse might do eighty. Mind you the horse would need water and feed and rest, and a man might still outrun it. A man, not a whitefeller from Ireland, not even one who was practicing with a spear and a throwing stick. It was funny, but yet . . . very pleasing to hand on the things he'd been taught.

The Irishman was a thinking man. A clever one, even if the two 'roo legs were smelly stuff, making them easier for the dogs to trail.

A little later, he realized that that, too, was part of Jack's plan. By late that afternoon, they could hear the dogs, and at one stage, caught sight of the chase. It wasn't that large a group: five dogs, three men—one an aboriginal tracker, the other two troopers—and seven horses.

"They be on us soon, man. They must have stopped in the heat," said Lampy.

"One scent dog and four chasers," said Jack. "Well, we can't outrun them, so we'll have to deal with them. We need the trail good and clear and down into that channel. Let's drag the meat. I want the scent dog chasing that."

"And us, man."

"And us, while it's with us."

They set off through the spinifex and down into the scrubby trees of the braided channel, along it, dodging between the dead-wood, and to what Jack grunted was "ideal"—an in-cut sandy bank with a steep scramble up it to a fringe of malee.

"Go along the edge. As soon as you're out of sight, hang the meat on a tree, out over the drop—my shirt on it. Jump down, cut back onto our trail, and come back here. We've got maybe five minutes."

That Jack, Lampy thought, shaking his head, but doing it. The meat, with Jack's shirt on it, he hung out on a branch over the edge of the sand wall so the dogs would have to jump to and tear at it, then fall down and scramble all the way back up again. Then he took a running jump and landed way out on the sand of the dry river bed and ran back.

Jack was busy with the rest of the tough cord he'd taken from the cabin of the locomotive. The sun was down, and the cool of dusk would bring relief soon . . . if they lived that long. Lampy could hear the dogs yammering. "I need your shirt, too," said Jack, hastily. "Here, push it up on the bucket, and we need to get up that tree."

It wasn't much of a goolibah tree, but they scrambled up it as the dogs crossed the braided sand. The dogs hit the bank and scrabbled their way up it as the riders followed. Now there was no need for tracking, the blackfeller was with the horse string at the back and the two troopers rode as if this was some kind of happy fox hunt. They hunched low over their horses' necks as they spurred their mounts at the bank.

And at the top they hit the tight-stretched cord, carefully spanned between two tall, solid old dead goolibah stumps. The cord hit the lead rider on his arms and across the neck, sending him catapulting back out of the saddle. The other, ducking just in time, caught the snapping rope across his face. The second rider almost managed to stay in the saddle, lost his stirrup, and tumbled down the bank. Their horses heaved up, their momentum unchecked, and kept going, riderless and panicked.

Lampy and Jack jumped down from their hideout as the tracker, riding the center horse in the mob of spare horses, tried to haul his steed to a halt. The remounts strung on halters on either side of his horse tried to turn away, but some left and some right, with plunging heads and threshing hooves. The tracker lost his seat but managed to roll backward out of the chaos. The man who'd been catapulted was less lucky. He was under the hooves, and Lampy saw his face sliced by one.

The other trooper, face cut to the bone and shocked, still managed to unlimber his rifle . . . and fire a shot into the shirt-wearing fire bucket swinging on a branch. He worked the bolt as Jack threw his egg. It hit the rifle as he fired, and the bullet creased across Lampy's thigh as he threw his spear. Both of them screamed.

Jack had already jumped down and wrestled with the trooper, who had a spear in his side and only had one hand on his rifle. It was a short, nasty clinch, and the trooper fell.

There was no pain yet. Just shock. Lampy dived over the edge and scrambled to grab the rifle as the tracker came running up. "You stay still. I don't want to kill you, but I will," said Lampy through gritted teeth, pointing the rifle at the tracker. The pain was starting now. Like a wave of fire running up his leg.

Jack came running. "You all right?"

"Shot me," grunted Lampy, sitting down. He held out the rifle he'd grabbed to Jack and held his leg.

Jack took the rifle and knelt down next to him. "You," he said to the tracker. "Get those horses." The beasts plunged about all over the place. "Try and run and I'll shoot you." He ripped aside Lampy's bloody trouser leg and exposed the wound.

It was bleeding, a long gash about seven inches long ran diagonally across the front of his thigh.

Jack exhaled, plainly relieved. He squeezed Lampy's shoulder. "You'll live, son. Anything else hurt?"

"Uh. My ankle doesn't feel too good," he said, pointing at the opposite foot. "I landed kind of bad when I jumped down after he shot me. Ouch!" he yelled as Jack manipulated it.

"Hard to tell, as I don't have the experience," said Jack, "but it looks like you either sprained it or broke it. You got lucky with the bullet and unlucky with the fall."

The tracker seized his chance, with Jack's attention on Lampy. One of the horses had broken its halter, and he slipped himself up onto it and kicked it into a gallop.

Jack raised the rifle, fired, and then dropped it as he ran to grab the broken halter line before the other horses followed.

The man still fled, but he wasn't on horseback anymore. The horse had been creased or wounded, or just frightened, but its rider had lost his seat.

Gritting his teeth, Lampy picked up the rifle. He'd never fired one before, but the troopers might not both be dead. He was sure the second one, the one that had shot him, moved.

Meanwhile, Jack had found a saddlebag with hobbles, tether ropes, and stakes . . . and a stock whip—and just in time, because the dogs came back.

The whip changed their minds very fast about what they wanted to do. Lampy would have shot them, but Jack and the whip were in the way. Jack could use that whip, as Lampy saw when the dazed, wounded trooper sat up. Jack tied him up like a turkey with a horse tether. It was getting dark by then, and Jack found a lamp and the trooper's bag of supplies. That had some lint, Epsom salts, iodine, and some crepe bandage.

"Right. I'll see to the soldier in a minute. I reckon that hole in your thigh is bled clean. Let's bandage it up, and I'll strap your ankle while I'm at it." Lampy's thigh had a furrow about a quarter inch deep through it. "Painful? A shock, but incredibly lucky, Lampy," said Jack. "Like your ankle, it'll heal. And like your ankle, the less it's walked on, the better. Can you ride a horse?"

What other work was open for blackfellers, except being stockmen? He'd ridden nearly as much as he'd walked, since he was little. He managed a smile. "Can a 'roo jump?"

"Good lad. We're better off now, even with you hurt. We've got four horses, some water bags, some food, two rifles, flysheet, three swags, a good amount of ammunition . . ."

"And two ruined shirts and a dented fire bucket."

"Heh," said Jack. "To be sure. But I'll get the clothes off the trooper the horses trampled. They'll be bloody, too, but a hat and a shirt are necessary out here, especially for me, with my fine pale skin and all."

Jack then did his best for the surviving trooper. Lampy's spear, with its bone point, had hit the man at an angle on the rib cage and spiked down into his abdomen. It was still lodged there.

"This is going to hurt," said Jack. "I'll do my best for you, but you'll be coming with us. If I leave you here, you'll die. And it's likely we'll need the horses and the water, and I'm in no hurry for you to tell your friends, so I'm not sending you back. By the time the dogs and tracker get back we should be a long way off. Behave yourself, and you'll get to live. Don't, and we'll shoot you. You were going to let us be ripped apart by the dogs."

"Orders to keep you alive," said the man, sullenly, looking as if he might just pass out again. "Was after the dogs to stop 'em."

"Change of orders, then?"

"Yes. Should have shot you all."

"Hold that thought while I pull the spear out of you. Or would you rather I left it in?"

"Out . . . please."

"Brace yourself."

Lampy heard him scream, and Jack staggered back with the spear. He plugged the wound, bandaged it as best he could, tied the man's hands, then took on the next unpleasant task.

"I'll cave the bank in on your companion. It's the best I can do, and it might keep him from the dingoes. I can't take time to bury him properly. What was his name?"

The other soldier seemed surprised. "Corporal John Merrick. From Tyford," said the wounded man, weakly.

Jack dragged Corporal Merrick to the edge of the bank and went up and kicked down a solid fall of earth. He tied a rough cross and planted it on the pile, took off his hat, and stood there in the lamplight.

"He'd have killed you, Jack, and they don't bury us," said Lampy, feeling puzzled by this.

"I know. But I live by my rules, not theirs. And a dead man is no danger to anyone. I wanted to know his name so his kin can know, one day at least, that he's dead. The worst thing you can do to a family is to leave them wondering."

Lampy found himself nodding in the darkness.

"Right. We'd better go."

"You better know my name, too," said the wounded man. "Private Dale McLoughlin. I'm from Portrush."

"Well, McLoughlin," said Jack, as he helped the man up. "You've a choice. You can sit on the horse, or I can tie you across it like a sack. I'm hoping you can stay on a horse. You try anything and I'll have to shoot you, and your horse will have no water, even if you do get away."

"I'll sit. Look, I've orders to bring you in alive, or at least your body. I'll take you in alive, my word on it. You can't get away. It's just desert out there. You'll end up eating sand."

"Well, on the bright side, there's a lot of it," said Jack, hefting McLoughlin up onto the horse. He then did the same for Lampy.

They rode on a little, when a whicker from the dark announced that the two other horses had found them.

Lampy was glad of a saddle to sit in. Losing blood had made him feel nauseous, and riding was no pleasure with the ache in his leg.

By the moans in the darkness, the soldier felt worse.

CHAPTER 16

Tim was shaken awake. "You come. We got to go. Railway-men coming," said the desert aboriginal.

Tim blinked and sat up. He was stiff from sleeping on the ground, but his mind was feeling sharper than it had for days. His first thought was relief. And his second was what if that Vister and his friends wanted to finish the job.

Plainly the aboriginals weren't waiting around to find out. They were running off already. Tim looked. He could see the smoke and the dark shape of the steam mole—a good two miles off. Well, it might not actually come here. He'd chased it in vain last night. And they might want to kill him . . . He got up and trotted after the aboriginals. They hadn't gone that far. About four hundred yards away was some rough country with a spur of rocks. The aboriginals hid there, watching.

"Whitefellers find our spring, we got trouble," said his guide of last night. "They take all the water, then we got to go. Good country this."

It obviously depended on your point of view, Tim thought. The scout mole puffed to a halt near the waterhole. The aboriginals muttered angrily . . . and the door clanged open and out came—

Clara!

Even at this distance Tim recognized her in her chip straw hat and blond braids. But he was too astounded to say anything. He just swallowed and rubbed his eyes, staring as hard as he could. It . . . had to be her. He knew her walk, the way she stood and looked at things with her head at an angle, even with a little parasol held against the sun. He opened his mouth to yell . . . and a hard hand clapped over it. Other hands grabbed him

"You be quiet. Railway-men trouble for blackfellers."

"That's not the railway-men. That's Clara. She's a girl. *My* girl. She's come looking for me. She won't hurt you. I promise," said Tim with all the sincerity he could muster. "She's the best girl in the entire world."

Something about the way he said it must have got through, because the hands holding him eased their grip. "The other railway-man's still inside," said the older, gruff man who had stopped him yelling.

Clara walked to the side of the scout mole, took down a bucket, and walked to the water. And there she must have seen footprints because they saw her bend down and stare.

"Look," said Tim. "She wouldn't be carrying water if there was anyone else to do it. If I stay here . . . and if she does anything wrong, you can kill me, stick a spear in me, but someone just go and ask her if she's looking for Tim Barnabas. Please. Please!"

There was a silence.

"Please!" He tried for terms he hoped they might understand. "She'll take me back to my own land, to my own people. She's not a railway-man. They don't have any women here."

"Try to take our women," said the older man. But by the discussion among them in their own tongue, Tim was sure he'd gotten through to them. The older man pushed him forward. "You walk. Ten hands," he held up five fingers, "steps. No more. Call. You run we spear you. Railway-man come we spear you."

Tim stepped out of the shelter of the rocks and began walking. Counting steps. Taking as long a step as he dared. Wondering . . . weighing the risks in his mind. If someone else got out of the cab . . . if she got back in to go. He was going to chance that terrible feeling between his shoulder blades. But should he call to her? Would they use him to lure her out so they could kill or capture her?

He was spared the decision by her looking up, looking around
. . . and seeing him. And dropping the bucket and running toward
him yelling her lungs out: "Tim, *Tim!*" Her arms outstretched,
reaching.

"Clara! Clara, stay there. There are men with spears behind me."

"I don't care! I found you, I found you! Oh, I've been so worried.
Oh, Tim. Tim!" She was plainly not going to stop. So Tim turned to
the watchers in the rocks. "Kill me first. Don't kill her. Please. She's
not going to hurt anyone."

Clara kept right on running, and Tim decided that meeting her
was worth a spear in the back. So he stepped forward into her arms
and held her, keeping his body as much of a shield as he could while
being hugged, and between pants, kissed.

"I can't tell you how worried I've been," Clara gasped.

"We're not out of trouble. They're behind me in the rocks,
Clara, with spears. And they hate the railway-men."

"So do I!"

"Yeah. They tried to kill me."

"I know, I got to Dajarra and you were missing."

"Look . . . are there any other people in the mole?"

"Just me. I stole it to look for you."

"You did *what?*"

"I stole it to look for you. The railway-men are probably ready
to murder me too now."

"Oh. Where's your mother?"

Clara was silent. Then she said, in a very small voice. "Sick. In a
coma. Maybe even dead. I came to you for help."

Tim swallowed. "Fat lot of help I've been. Look . . . I think we
better talk to the aboriginals. Face them. We can't run and . . . and
they were looking after me."

"Then I'm grateful to them. It's . . . I thought you might be
dead, Tim. I was so scared."

"It was pretty close," he said, as they turned around and walked, still holding onto each other, back to the rocks. "Lots more luck than good judgment. I was a bit confused when I came out of the termite run. Reckon it must have been the lack of oxygen down there or something. My stupid fault."

"You're not stupid. They tried to kill you," said Clara, angrily. "The station boss was pretty mad about it, but not enough to actually get anyone to *look* for you."

"McGurk? You met McGurk? He's a terror. Not like Vister or that foreman, but driving everyone to get the tunnel finished."

Men were standing up among the rocks. Black, fierce-looking. Spears ready. Not smiling. Tim knew, by now, that these were people who smiled a lot. Tim raised his hand. "There is no one else in the steam mole, and she's not from the railway. She was looking for me."

"Leave tracks right to our water. The railway-men follow."

"We'll brush them out," said Clara. "I don't want them to find us either."

"Brush them? We follow that easy," said the older man who seemed to be the spokesman for the group. His tone was decidedly scornful.

"You do," said Tim. "But I don't think the railway-men could track a two-year-old child covered in mud crossing a clean floor."

And that made several people laugh, and even cracked a slight smile from the older man. A few comments in their own language, a little more slightly derisive laughter. The spear points came down a little.

"Besides," said Tim. "I think you need us to take the machine away. They can't track, but they could see it. See it from a long way off, especially from up in the air."

"I want to say thank you," said Clara. "I owe you a debt for looking after—" she held onto his shoulder—"my Tim. You're wonderful."

The older man shook his head, but he was smiling a little. "She cause you trouble, this one," he said to Tim.

Tim laughed a little with relief. "You have no idea how much, sir. But she's there when you need her."

"I've not caused you trouble, Tim Barnabas! Huh. It's only search the whole desert for you that I've done," said Clara, with a suitable show of being indignant.

"And found me, too. Still, you drove past me last night. I ran after you."

"It's faster you need to learn to run," she said, sticking her tongue out at him. She knew she was being silly, that they were still in danger, but shock, the fear she'd been coping with, and now the relief and happiness were making her want to giggle and *be* a little crazy.

Still, her behavior was also affecting the aboriginals. Most of them were grinning openly.

"You go race she," said someone.

"Ha," said Clara. "He can't run." She hitched up her skirts. "Race you, Tim Barnabas. Last one to the water is a rotten egg."

"To that stump over there," said Tim, pointing to a dead spike of wood about fifty yards off. "And I'll give you a head start. Go."

She didn't. "I'd not be letting go of you. Last time I did that you got lost in the desert."

"We find him if he get lost," said the older man, smiling now. "You run."

She did. And Tim ran after her. He had much longer legs. She might still have won, though, if she hadn't lost her grip on her skirts and tripped over them and managed a full, if unintended, somersault. Tim skidded to a halt. "You all right?" he asked, helping her up.

"Fine," she panted. "Well, I think I skinned my knee a bit. And I tore a flounce. But it got them laughing at us."

And so it was that they walked back to the mound spring with the aboriginals around them, talking, asking questions, and behaving as if they hadn't been a hair's breadth away from being speared. They all helped refill the water tank and inspected the scout mole. The older man appeared doubtful, looking at the deep indents of the endless tracks. "How you go brush that out?"

"I thought we might tie some branches behind it," said Clara.

"I'd only have to go back to where I turned, and then on, as if I didn't come here."

"I've a better idea," said Tim. "We make a brush and tie it to the drill head. That'll wipe it out."

"I've worked out how to make it go up and down, not round and round. Besides, it would make a groove in the middle before it took out the tracks."

"Oh, it'll be like the big mole. It'll need to be fired up and got spinning. Look, there are igniter holes . . ."

"It's still not going to work."

"We could make it do an elliptic."

"It's not going to work," she said firmly. "We need some leafy bushes."

They bickered amiably and eventually settled on trying his method—which made a lot of dust and thrashed the branch to pieces, and then her method, which with a bit of weight on the branches worked quite well.

They left with waves and goodwill and even some seed-cakes and a piece of cooked meat.

※

Back on Clara's track, and well away from the spring mound, Tim sighed. "You drive really well."

"Of course I do," she said cheerfully. "I taught myself. I'll be getting Captain Malkis to let me drive the *Cuttlefish* next."

"So . . . where are we going?" asked Tim. "Because to be honest with you, I don't know where we are."

"Australia."

"You're a great help, Clara Calland," he said, laughing. "A natural navigator. Now where are we going?"

"I thought I was. I can take you back to your friends at the spring. They need a junior submariner," she said, avoiding the subject. She just wasn't quite ready to explain, to tell of the disasters and her decision just yet.

She should have known better with Tim, though. He read her better than most. And he was a lot harder than the average teacher ever had been to lead off on a tangent.

"That doesn't explain why you needed my help or what you're doing here. Not that I'm not glad to see you, because I always am. Especially when you find me in the desert."

"I saw their fire. I came up to Dajarra because . . . because you understood about my father. He's a prisoner in Queensland. The letter said he'd been sick. His handwriting was all shaky. He said he loved us and missed us. He . . . always sent me his love. Never to Mother. And now I know, well, know they pretended to be divorced for me. If he said that . . . I know he must be really, really sick, so it doesn't matter anymore. And the man in Hansmeyers Emporium said . . . said if I wanted to see him alive and staying that way I needed to cooperate, and fast. Only I couldn't. And when I went back later, and the next day, he wasn't there."

"It's a trap, Clara. They want you for a hold over your mother."

"Except Mother is in hospital. They wouldn't even let me see her. She was unconscious and they said . . . well they didn't say, but the doctor told Max Darlington that she wasn't going to recover. He said it was best if I remembered her alive," said Clara, tears coming now.

Tim held her. They steered a rather wobbly course onward. Eventually, when she'd sniffed and dried her eyes, he said, "So where are we going?"

"Queensland. To break my father out of jail."

"You're just a little bit mad, you know that?" It was said with a squeeze of the shoulder, so she couldn't really take offence.

"Someone has to do something. And it was best it was something they wouldn't expect."

"So you came to get me and stole a steam mole?"

"Um. The steam mole just happened. I don't steal. I'll give it back. I came to you . . . because you were my closest . . . person."

He was silent for a while; he just kept his hand on her shoulder as they bumped across the plain. "Well," he said eventually, "we'll need more fuel if we're to get to Queensland. Not that it's that far. The aborigines say the soldiers and prisoners are about three days' walk away, working on a railway."

"The aborigines know where the soldiers are?" asked Clara, incredulous. The country here was just so vast it seemed to her that it could hide anything.

"If it happens out here in the desert, they'll know. They were watching me. And you."

"I should have asked them. We'd better go back," she said, beginning to turn.

Tim shook his head. "No point. They won't be there, and we probably won't find them. You could see they were getting ready to leave just as soon as we were gone. And they never told us where they were going. They've had some pretty bad experiences with the railway-men. And I know first-hand they've got reason."

"The railway-men were very nice to me," said Clara, feeling guilty for no good reason. "They looked after me, hid me, and fed me on the journey up."

"It wasn't so bad until Dajarra," said Tim. "But no one even really talked to me on the clanker. It was creepy." He sighed. "I wish I could talk to the captain about what to do. I'm responsible for you."

"No you're not! *I'm* responsible for me."

"Not as far as the captain is concerned," said Tim with a grin. "You're part of his crew, sort of. And I'm a senior crew member, compared to you."

That gave her a bit of a glow. They were a sort of extended family. Like the cousins and uncles and aunts she didn't have. "I told him. At least, I sent him a letter."

"Well, that's better than nothing, anyway. Now look, your steam-biscuit supply is a bit low, but these fire boxes, they say they can burn anything. While I was lost I saw some big piles of old deadwood that must have come down here with the floods."

"Why didn't you set fire to them? I could have found you so easily then."

"I didn't have anything to start a fire with. I did think about it—when I ate that raw bird."

CHAPTER 17

The major was sweating visibly in his green and gold uniform. "Your Grace, the news from Queensland: As best they can establish, Jack Calland and three of the aboriginal prisoners and an Afghan— they were brought over as camel-drivers—are still loose. One of the recaptured men said Calland talked of going southwest. He was behind the breakout, Your Grace. They got twenty pairs of men, and aboriginal trackers and dogs, all out scouring the southwest. It's desert or semi-desert out there. The officer commanding insists that everything that can be done is being done. But if Calland is with the aboriginal escapees . . . well, that is their terrain. If anyone can find water, they will."

Duke Malcolm steepled his fingers. He sat silently while the officer sweated and waited. "Well," he said. "We will have to modify the orders. I think if Calland or the others are sighted, and there is any chance of their escape, shoot first. Only attempt to capture if the prisoners are unable to flee. Now, what news of the state of readiness of the strike force?"

"Uh. They're still waiting on more fuel. Otherwise they're ready, Your Grace."

"And news from our spies in Ceduna?"

"Well, they evaded capture, Your Grace. One of them works in a railroad office and actually observed Dr. Calland. She seems to be in a vendetta against one of the railroad companies, but . . . but if rumor is to be believed she displayed her ammonia synthesis technique to some high officials of the Westralian government."

"I see. Well, it becomes paramount to weaken them rapidly, then. Order an airship deployed from the nearest base to assist in the search for Calland. He is an intelligent man, and it's possible he has worked out just what the railway is for. Obviously, the airship is to shoot to kill. They cannot capture."

※

Linda felt rather forlorn that afternoon, when they were all making plans for the flight to the north—her father had been successful, and it appeared the cost, while exorbitant, was not ruinous. "We have the use of a flying wing called *Wedgetail* for eight hundred pounds a day, and a bond of ten thousand pounds against damages," announced Dr. Calland after the call.

Ten thousand pounds sounded ruinous to Linda. You could buy two respectable houses for that sum, but it appeared that it did not seem ruinous to Dr. Calland. Then Linda had to leave her and the captain to it, and go home

At tea, while they ate, she tried to draw her father out about just what was happening. He smiled and shook his head. "The corridors of power sound a bit more like a schoolyard at the moment. There are a few of the captains of industry who are clamoring for Rainor's release and measures to rein in the police. Others are being, well, privately well pleased. He isn't a widely liked man, and not just by his competitors. I'm not in favor of government interfering too much in business, but business needs to behave in such a way that people don't want the government to do that. There'll be all sort of legal jumping around tomorrow, and I think some dismay when they find that they can't interfere with Dr. Calland and her plans, as she'll be airborne. It'll take them a while to establish that, by which stage, with any luck, it will be too late. Now, I was going to say, I've been looking at your school reports, and I hadn't realized just how well you've been doing. But you slipped last term. I've spoken to

Leonid Borin at the university. He's got a promising young mathematician looking for some extra work, so I've signed you up for some lessons with him in the next few days. I went and had a few words with him." He looked at her with a hint of amusement. "You're too young for him, miss. He must be three years older than you."

What would her father say if he ever found out about Nicky, who was a lofty twenty-four?

"But Maxie," said her stepmother, "being thought too clever could ruin her chances. And our friends Arthur and Jane and their dear little Melanie and Walter are coming back to Ceduna. I'd hoped—"

"Ha. 'Chances,'" said her father expansively. "She'll have as many as she needs. Anyway, she's far too young to even worry about that, and any man who doesn't appreciate her mind doesn't deserve her."

"I don't think this woman scientist has been good for either of you," said her stepmother, repressively. "A girl needs to think of her future."

※

Linda was tucked up in bed, half-asleep, when someone tapped at her window. She nearly called out. Then it occurred to her it might be Clara. She wouldn't know her mother had recovered and was home. She leapt out of bed and, in her nightdress, opened the window.

Only to find it wasn't Clara, but her boyfriend.

"Nicky! You can't come here. My father . . ."

"I need to talk to you, Linda. It's urgent. Really important," he said.

"But you can't come here. I'm in my nightdress. Tomorrow. We can meet in the gardens at the Tivoli at nine."

He shook his head. "I need to talk to you *about* tomorrow. Mr. Rainor's lawyers need you to testify. That stupid magistrate threw the bail appeal out."

"What?"

"Hush. We need you to prove that statement was obtained under duress. I . . . er, told them I could arrange it, when they were asking me about the terrible incident. Mr. Cheswick was delighted. It'll mean a big promotion for me."

"What?" She couldn't believe what she was hearing.

"Yes, that should let them have countercharges pressed to get that vicious woman and those submariners arrested." He sounded very pleased about that.

"Go away. Go away, or I will call my father."

"Oh no you won't," he grabbed her arm. "You need to testify tomorrow at ten o'clock. They'll come around to subpoena you in the morning. You'll tell them they threatened to kill him if he didn't write that statement. That he tried to refuse but that captain twisted his arm and threatened to break it. And if you don't do it . . . I'll, I'll send your letters to your father."

"Let *go* of me!" she yelled.

"What's wrong, Linda?" called her stepmother, from somewhere in the house.

Nicky fled, leaving Linda to fall back into her bed as the door opened. "What's wrong, Linda?" repeated her stepmother worriedly.

Linda could still feel the imprint of his fingers in her arm. Her heart raced and her mouth was a little dry. "Just . . . just a nightmare. I . . . I was being chased."

"It's all right dear. You're perfectly safe."

"I know. It was just a bad dream."

"There, there," soothed her stepmother, comfortingly. "This is Ceduna, safe as can be. Do you need a hot drink?"

"No, thank you," said Linda, her heart still hammering. She realized she wasn't scared, just furious. Furious and . . . and used. Betrayed. And . . . just a little worried already. "I'll be fine. It was just a shock."

The door hadn't been closed for more than two minutes before

Linda was up. She didn't put a light on, but the moon was bright. She dressed, collected her supply of money from the little drawer, and left a note in its place—written by moonlight and in pencil. Hopefully it would be reassuring and not helpful.

She knew her way to the station, and if luck was with her, the trains were still running out to Mandynonga.

If being airborne would keep the lawyers away from Dr. Calland, then it would keep them away from her.

She was certain Dr. Calland would not agree to this. But she'd been to Boomerang Fields a number of times. She knew where the vast hangars were, and she knew the name of their flying wing.

What she hadn't known, an hour later, was just how far it would be to walk, in the dark, on her own, by moonlight. She'd hidden from several cyclists and three carts, ducking down and kneeling in the fields, getting mud on her dress from the drip-irrigators. Fortunately, she could hear the carts and see the bicycle lamps—and everyone had been coming toward her. Her beautiful red calf-skin mules were never going to recover from this . . . if her feet did. The gates of Boomerang Fields were welcome . . . and a problem.

The gate was, naturally, closed. It was a lovely ornate iron double gate, with stylized eagles pressed out of the metal.

For a moment she was stopped. Then she worked out that, in Westralian style, the gate was just latched, not locked, and it was not that difficult to unlatch it, push it open, and squeeze through. Unfortunately, it didn't latch from the inside—at least that she could see in the moonlight. She hurried on as it swung open, ponderous and creaking the alarm. Only no one seemed to hear it, which was just as well because she could see nowhere to hide.

Then came the next complication. She knew the name of the flying wing, but there were many hangars. She could still be busy moving from one to the next until the day started. But there was one light on. She walked quietly toward it, and sure enough, there were three engineers doing final preparation to the *Wedgetail*. The name and picture were on her engine nacelles. Two of the men were just starting to pack away tools, while the other finished off. Now it was just a case of waiting for them to go, and she let herself in through the small side door they'd left by.

Inside the huge hangar she realized her next mistake. It was dark in there, away from the moonlight. She would never have been able to see the name of any flying wing in this. It was a huge craft perched on its wheels. She'd seen a ladder in her sneak-peek at it. But had they taken it down?

It seemed to take forever, and several bumps and bruises, to find it, but she did. Climbing blindly in the dark, she felt her way around, looking for a hiding place. Eventually, she just gave up and lay down on a sheepskin for a rest . . .

※

Mary Calland had asked the captain if they could have a meeting of all the *Cuttlefish* crew who had arrived in Ceduna—a good two-thirds of them—and they gathered at the bungalow. The meeting had to be held outside, but fortunately in the predawn it was still cool.

"As you all know by now, we've identified that something is rotten at the station where Tim Barnabas was sent, a place called Dajarra in the north, some eight hundred and fifty miles from here, only accessible by two days' worth of travel. They claim Tim was killed in an accident, and we think this may in some way relate to my daughter Clara, who, it appears, set off for there. We've been informed by Discovery North that, alas, there is no space on their regular trains going north. They're being as obstructive as possible. They've flown a special manager up there, presumably to try to cover up."

She smiled at her audience. "I thought if *they* could fly someone to this Dajarra place, why couldn't we? It seems there, or Alice, or Sheba, are the places we need to check now. Not here. So, gentlemen, I've hired us a flying wing. It took some intervention from Mr. Dar-

lington to get permission to do so. They're all owned by the Westralian government and they don't want them to fall into the hands
of the British Empire. Most of them are kept for military use and for
patrols, although they do have some transport vessels, which the
state does hire out in an effort to keep their costs down. They're
faster and more maneuverable than airships and have a far longer
range. We have to, of course, take their pilots and engineers, but
there is space for some twenty men. I'll need volunteers. It may be
grim work, and it will be out in the desert. It's hot out there."

Hands shot up. "I volunteer!" was an almost universal chorus.

"Either no one wants to stay in Ceduna, or young Tim is . . . or
was more popular than I realized," Dr. Calland said.

"He's one of us. Our lucky charm, the lad is. And Clara, too. She
did her ticket. Junior submariner," said one of the younger men.

"Besides," said Lieutenant Willis with a twinkle in his eye, "I've
never been on an airship, let alone one of these posh Westralian
flying wings. I'd do it even if they weren't important to us, ma'am.
But they are."

"And I can't tell you how important that is to me. I'm going to
have to ask the captain to choose a crew. I would take everybody, but
we need to consider skills and total weight."

"I'm going on a diet," said Big Eddie, one of the divers, and possibly the biggest man on the *Cuttlefish*—submarine jobs favored
small, compact, tough men. "And you never know when you're
going to need a diver in the desert."

Three-quarters of an hour later the chosen ones were out at
Boomerang Fields, ferried there in a hired motor-truck. The flying
wing Mary Calland had arranged was already being winched out of
its camouflage shed and over to the takeoff ramp. "Gentlemen," said
the flier, dressed in pale blue padded knickerbockers, a high throated
leather vest, and woolen boots—an odd ensemble for the heat of
Ceduna, although it was still quite cool. "We need you ranked in
order of size for the weighing. There are boots and over trousers on

the racks to your left, and hooded flying jackets to the right, and
scarves and gloves and earmuffs on the shelf over there. We'll need
you to be weighed with your kit. Dr. Calland, we have some ladies'
outfits through that door over there."

"We're still waiting for the two gentlemen from the Westralian
Mounted Police that Colonel Clifford said he'd send with us. They're
supposed to meet us here."

The flier looked at the new slouch hats and uniform coats of the
deputized men—somewhat more than half of the group.

"They're . . . um . . . temporary deputies," explained Mary,
"drafted in for the job." She didn't explain that after their arrest of one
of the captains of Westralian industry, the colonel had decided some
senior-ranking minders would be in order. "I think we can make it
stick, Captain Malkis," the colonel had said. "Your . . . unconventional
methods did succeed in collecting quite a lot of evidence. And since
the arrest, completely unrelated complaints and charges to that have
been laid by people who were plainly afraid to act against Rainor
before. Enough to keep him facing charges, even if his lawyers are
falling over themselves to get him out. But it would be easier if you
had a couple of men to walk you through due process next time."

"Easier for whom?" asked Captain Malkis with a smile.

"Me!" said the colonel. "I'll either get promoted or fired for this.
But news from my men on the streets is that it's done them no end
of good with the ordinary people. The men I'm sending, Inspector
Johns and Sergeant Morgan, are known for getting things done. Top
officers both, and you'll find them understanding . . . but able to do
it by the rules."

The flier looked at the submariners. "Ah. Darlington did say it
would involve the wimps. I thought you lot looked a bit on the
small side for them. They like big fellers. And they're usually late."

"Wimps?" said Lieutenant Ambrose. "Aha. WMP. I never
thought of that. No wonder they're big and struggle to get recruits.
I should have worked that out before I agreed to this."

The flier laughed. "You might as well kit up and be weighed in the meanwhile. Now, the one thing I have to emphasize: A wing is *not* an airship. We use hydrogen bags in the wing. You are inside the wing. So there is *no* smoking—no ignition of any kind. From the stability point of view the captain would prefer you not to move from your pads. Are any of you claustrophobic?"

That brought a laugh from the *Cuttlefish* crew. "We're submariners," One of them piped in.

"I suppose that saves me giving a second lecture about smoking," said the flier. "Ah. A motoring-car. That may be our policemen."

It was. The two policemen joined them, shook hands, were kitted up, and they filed into the flying wing.

※

Linda was awakened by the metallic shriek of the hangar doors opening. Blinking in the dim light, she hastily looked around. She'd slept on a pad in the pilot's nacelle, a few yards from the wheels and controls. This would surely be where they came first. There was a small hatch behind her—only about a foot high. Opening it, she crawled through into sheltering darkness again. The crawlway opened up into a long, low-ceilinged chamber—as best she could work out by feeling around in the dark—as the sounds of voices and noise of machinery began outside. She fell over something soft . . . more sheepskins and some blankets, by the feel of it. The only other thing in there was a piece of machinery she could only guess at. So she found the blankets and hid herself behind them as the flying wing started to move.

Were they about to fly?

※

Mary was in the privileged position of being in the central nacelle, with the pilot and the copilot/navigator. The rest of the crew found themselves crawling along the inside of the wing to their flight couches—sheepskin covered pads, each near a small, downward-looking porthole.

The navigator showed Mary to her seat. "It doesn't matter quite as much if you move around, ma'am. This area and the cargo hold are fairly stable. The old *Wedgetail* is a bit more finicky than the new planes, but they're only hiring out the old unarmed transporters. 'Cost recovery,' they call it. I call it too mean to spend on anything but . . . er . . . new offices for the bludgers. Anyway, the pilot doesn't appreciate weight shifts by passengers otherwise, but you can get up and move. Sit back, they're just doing a final trim on the engines. The engineers will be in their pods and we can winch away in a minute or two."

Outside the window, the double pusher-puller propellers were flung into motion, and the engines roared to life. The copilot signaled to the winch crews as the pilot checked the various brass and aluminum wheels and levers.

The winch hauled the wing faster and faster and then they left the earth below and began slowly rising toward the sun, the reds and browns of the interior ahead.

※

Linda heard familiar voices and the sway of the huge craft as they were positioned at the end of the runway. And then finally, the rush as the wing became airborne.

Well. They could try and subpoena her now. And if that treacherous, horrible Nicholas—how she hated him! It made her temples throb just thinking of him, now. How *could* he!—went through with his threat . . . well, she wasn't going to be there to explain. And she was so glad of those blankets. No one had told her it would be so cold up here! Or how noisy it was. She covered her head in a sheepskin and endured.

And then added another blanket.

※

And then, for the next eight hours, they flew.

It was quite cold this high up. It also gave Mary some idea of the sheer vastness of the country as they flew across vast, dazzling, shimmering dry salt lakes, endless lines of dunes, miles and miles of braided-dry waterways, more salt-rimmed dead lakes, wind-flayed low hills . . . and then more of the same. Wild camels fled in dust-trail mobs from the shadow of the wing or the unfamiliar throb of her engines.

"Should be at Dajarra in about twenty minutes," wrote the navigator on his pad. They'd begun to lose altitude, and from above she could see the termite run of the Westralian railroad system, a red ridge across the bleak landscape, disappearing occasionally, re-appearing on the same straight lines later. She could see the power stations too, two of them from here, sharp and narrow, dribbling smoke and steam into the blue. Beyond them the mound of the termite run speared into the rough country beyond. They flew over that, and then to where the mound coming from the north came out of Dajarra station. Low now, Mary could see the tall roof, with its complicated system of vents, and the high chimney.

The pilot pulled the power cables and the engines were silenced as the wing slowed, gliding down to the long landing strip. There were some men working on a corrugated iron structure on the edge of the power station roof.

Mary could see the faces staring up . . .

And then, with a bump, they were rolling and bouncing and jerking about as the anchors dragged and caught, and the wing came to a final halt.

Then it was a case of dropping the ladder and off-loading the passengers. The men who had been working on the corrugated iron shed had come running while the passengers were still stretching

out their limbs after the long flight. Mary was glad to shed her flying
gear at her seat, as the heat, even this late in the day, was oppressive.

The men from the power station approached them with broad
smiles and waves.

"They seem pleased to see us, anyway."

"My word. They're pleased to see coppers," said Sergeant
Morgan. "That means either they're hiding something and faking it,
or they're in deep trouble and expect us to get them out of it."

It seemed it was the latter.

"Bleeding 'eck! Are we glad to see you blokes after all," said the
leader of the workmen. "That joker Rainor sent here with his half-
dozen goons don't know what the law means and don't care. He's as
thick as thieves with that bastard Vister and his mates, threatenin'
us with blue murder and all sorts of trouble if it leaks. Well, I'm
ready to spill the whole pot of beans so long as you put the bastards
in stir."

"Too right," nodded a gangly workman in a singlet and a holey
pair of khaki shorts. "Count me in. This Ness bloke c'n tell me I
won't work again, and that the boss has the whole industry so sewn
up we'll be blacklisted and that he's got so much clout that no
charge will ever stick. But I had enough."

"Robert Rainor is in Ceduna central right now. He's been
refused bail. The magistrate was unimpressed by his lawyer, or his
threats. Said he'd have let him out if he hadn't got those. And we'd
like to make sure the charges do stick. Now, we're here investigating
the reported death of one Timothy Barnabas."

"They could have found the kid. I reckon that was a mistake
McGurk made, putting it off with the sandstorm, but by the time
we went out looking the tracks were gone. We couldn't even find the
scout mole the girl took."

Mary Calland seized on that. "The *girl*?"

The fellow in the khaki shorts blinked, taking in the presence of
a woman among the police slouch hats, and hastily doffing his own.

"Yeah, too right, ma'am. Little slip of thing came up here beggin' us to go look for the kid. And then when we go below, she takes off with the scout mole into the desert."

"I think we've finally found where Clara has got to," said Captain Malkis.

"Clara. Yeah, they said that was her name. Gutsy little thing. Rainor tried to stop us looking for her, too, but that was too much. The fellers said they'd be shot and be damned first, and he let us do a search for the mole. Trouble is, she'd gone too far for us to see her. Someone caught sight of smoke to the west, though. It could be the mole, could be blackfellers. Ness promised he'd get some blackfeller trackers onto it. Said she was an orphan, and though he wanted her found, well, she had no kin and that was why she'd come up here and got involved with some boong. Kind of shocked all of us that. Said she had a history of trouble."

"She's my daughter," grated Mary. "And trouble is nothing to what's coming Mr. Ness's way. We're here to look for her, and for young Tim Barnabas. Can you tell us where to start?"

The railway-man shrugged. "Nowhere close ma'am. It's . . . its pretty tough out there. If she stayed with the mole she's got water and some shade. She's got a chance. But the boy's a boong. They can survive out there."

"Tim, despite appearances, is not one of the aboriginals, or even of aboriginal descent." Mary Calland was getting to the point where she found this aspect of Westralia intolerable. It was like the British attitude to the Irish.

"Oh, you mean he's like one of them Iteys or something? Not an aboriginal? I guess no one knew, him being dark-skinned and all. Well, ma'am, no use pulling punches. He's dead, I'm afraid. A day out there without water will do that, two and there is next to no chance, and he's been gone more than three."

Mary bit her lip and shook her head. "He's a clever lad, but, well, I feel really sorry for whoever was responsible if he's not found alive. We can just hope Clara found him! We will have to mount a proper search. Fortunately, we have the flying wing here."

"Can't do much until morning," said the pilot. "Landing isn't safe at night and I can't keep her flying until daylight."

"Well," said Captain Malkis, "it does sound as if we have a mess to clear up here before we move on."

"Indeed!" said Lieutenant Willis. "Let's get down there."

"Hold your horses, Lieutenant," said the WMP inspector. "Let's try to do this more or less by the book."

Captain Malkis nodded. "Let's first find out what information we can and then do this quietly and so we get the most out of it." He turned to the railway-men. "Do you gentlemen mind telling us exactly what you know, and then we can try and plan this?"

So they heard about Tim being put off the steam mole and how Clara had taken the scout mole after pleading with them to go and look for Tim. They heard about how the shift captain had taken control of the winder room and negotiated an end to the situation, which had left him free and working. "This Ness feller. He just don't care whether it is right or wrong, as long as the drilling goes fast. He wants the first clankers of ore going south in less than month, no matter what."

"He was mad about the scout mole, but when McGurk wanted wimps . . . er the coppers called, he wasn't having any. Said it would hold things up and they needed men of Vister's experience and skill. Said he'd get trackers. Well, they're not here yet. I reckon no black-feller is going to come near this place."

CHAPTER 18

In the hold, Linda blessed the absence of noise and the fact that it was warmer. She was stiff, sore, and desperately in need of a drink and a bathroom, and not in that order. And she'd had a lot of noisy hours to think about her actions and the consequences of them. The level of trouble was going to be large, just like her need to get out of that flying wing. She found her way to the hatch she'd come in through and started fiddling with it . . . only to have it suddenly open. The man staring at her looked nearly as surprised to see her as she was to see him. She said, feeling it a tad inadequate, "Er. Good afternoon."

"Crikey! What are you doing in there?" demanded the airman.

"Er. Hiding."

He shook his head at her, giving her a hand to get out. "You're lucky you didn't freeze to death." He looked at her askance, his lips twitching. "Don't tell me you're the girl that Dr. Calland is looking for."

"No. She's going to be pretty mad at me, I think," admitted Linda. "But I did it for the best . . . please, I desperately need the bathroom."

He looked both uncomfortable and understanding. "Here. We don't usually use it when the plane is not in flight, but I think the ground will survive."

Linda came out to find the news of her presence had preceded her.

"Your parents will be worried stiff about you, and you could have died of the cold in there!" said Dr. Calland.

"I know. But it seemed like the only thing to do at the time. You see they were going to subpoena me to testify that you had forced that horrible man to sign that confession. If I wasn't there, they couldn't do it. And I honestly couldn't think of anywhere else to hide, or to go to."

"But, my dear girl, you simply had to tell them the truth. The captain did trick him into it, but he didn't force him."

"Nicky said he'd . . . he'd give my father my letters if I didn't say he was forced." Linda bit her lip. "My father can . . . can get very angry."

"I see," said Dr. Calland. "This is your young man? The one who told you not to tell your father about Clara?"

"He's not my young man anymore." Linda found some relief in saying that. "He's a toad. He was . . . he was the other clerk at the Discovery North Railroad office."

"The callow young one with the attempt at a moustache?" asked the captain.

Linda nodded miserably.

"I don't think you need to trouble yourself any further about him or his threats," said the captain calmly. "I've met your father, and it's not you he's going to be angry with. Well, not you so very much. The first thing we need to do is to contact Max Darlington and reassure him that you're safe. The flying wing has a Marconi-transmitter. We can at least send a shortwave message."

※

Linda really did not enjoy writing down the message for the flying wing copilot to code and send to her parents. Because of the noise, they used Morse code for messages, not voice. Dr. Calland and Captain Malkis composed it, and they didn't pull their punches. The message started by telling them she was safe and had been a stow-away on the flying wing. The rest . . . She had to tell them Nicky's full name, and what he'd wanted her to say, and what he'd threatened her with.

The copilot looked at her. "The radio op said I should hold. He was contacting your parents."

"Excuse me, Miss," said one of the two proper policemen. "Do you mind giving us a statement about all this? It could be very useful, and er, when you've done that, the lieutenant here has been hatching a plan I don't know if I should know anything about. You're . . . more or less the same age as Miss Clara Calland, and the new man who was sent up here won't know what she looks like. Lieutenant Ambrose wants to know if you'll help to give him enough rope to hang himself. He assures me you'll be quite safe."

"Why shouldn't you know?" asked Linda, wary.

"It's entrapment. We're not supposed to do it."

The lieutenant smiled. "I thought it was only entrapment if they were forced to say it."

"It's something of a grey area," said the policeman, "and they have clever lawyers. We like to do things by the book with them, to avoid a lot of hard work for nothing. I should caution him first."

"You, of course, would caution him if you knew he had actually done anything, but we don't as yet have conclusive evidence," said Lieutenant Ambrose, smoothly enough to be a lawyer himself. "All she will say is that she doesn't want to talk to him. She wants to talk to the Westralian Mounted Police. Just what a good citizen would do."

"Not in these bleeding parts, unless they were in deep trouble," said the railway-man who had been working on the shed. "Me and Tony and three of these submarine coppers will be with you, Miss. He's likely to go bark-o."

"And there will be several men just outside the door," said Lieutenant Ambrose. "The rest of the men will be taking up positions in case of any trouble. But I gather Vister and his crew are out in their mole, and they would have most to lose. They get in in two hours' time, so we want to move as soon as you have that statement, Inspector."

A little later, Linda found herself being escorted by grinning, burly men to the office of the power-station manager. There was a large, jowly, unshaven man with narrow eyes propping up the passage wall outside it. "Where do you think you're going?" he growled, fondling the rifle he held.

"Got a girl to see the manager," said the railway-man, stepping between the rifle and her.

Sergeant Morgan and Inspector Johns, who had approached, walking quietly, from the opposite direction to the group with Linda, were almost on top of him before he realized they were there. He must have heard them at the last minute and turned. Seeing two large men in the uniforms of the Westralian Mounted Police didn't seem to be quite what he was expecting. He dropped the rifle. "Ah. It's Porky Balmin," said Sergeant Morgan. "I've been looking for you, Porky. There'd better not be any live rounds in that rifle, or you'll be in stir for even longer."

The unshaven man gaped at them, then tried to turn to run, only to find himself brought up short by a hand on his collar. "You go ahead," said the inspector to the rest of them. "You're just seeing the manager, I'm arresting a known felon," he said, face absolutely prim.

They knocked and went in.

"Who said you could come in?" asked the sandy-haired man with very pale amber eyes. Linda thought his eyes looked rather like those of the Weimaraner dog down the road, but without any sign of the dog's pleasant nature.

"We're the scout mole crew. We was working topside. We brought this girl to see you, Mr. Ness." Ned pushed Linda forward a little.

Ness smiled. It was not a kind smile. "Ah. I see why Balmin let you in. Well, you can get out. I'll deal with this. You've got some questions to answer, girly."

"I'm not saying anything to you. I want to talk to the Westralian Mounted Police," said Linda, eyes downcast.

"You're in such trouble, you don't want to talk to them," said Ness. "I'll make you a deal, little girl. You tell me what I need to know, you shut your face for life, and I'll see you get a ride to Kalgoorlie. There's some places there that'll take young girls. Your mother is dead, and you've got no one. Forget you ever came here, forget your boong boyfriend, and we won't prosecute you for theft."

He looked at the men still standing there. "I thought I told you to get out."

"Can't just leave her," said Tony. "Give her a break, Mr. Ness."

"Break! She's lucky I don't tell Balmin and the boys to take her out into the desert and leave her there. And if you're not out of my office in thirty seconds I'll see you get something broken. What's your name?"

"Tony Porter. Look, yer can't do this. Yer boss won't let yer. You got no authority to do this, and me and the boys ain't leaving until yer prove yer have. Yer covering up murder, and now you want to send this poor lass to Kalgoorlie. That's a bad town, that."

"Porter," said Ness icily. "You're fired, and docked your outstanding pay. Any of you even speak of murder or about this girl, I'll get to hear about it and you'll never work again. There's no time to waste on some aboriginal kid being got rid of, and girls like this are not going to stop us. Rainor said it was to be all hushed up, and that's the way it'll be. We've got a blacklist for workers who cause trouble, we circulate it, and all the major employers work together on this. I've warned you . . ."

"Show me yer authority. Yer talking through your hat. Mr. Rainor never said you could do this. Them's crimes. We're going to tell the wimps," said the big Tony Porter, putting a hand on Linda's shoulder.

"We *own* the police, you fool. You're going to end up breaking rocks for your trouble. I've orders directly from Mr. Rainor, in person. Balmin!"

"He's been detained," said Inspector Johns, leaning around the open door. "Can I help you? Seeing as you 'own' me."

The sight of the slouch hat and uniform made quite an impression on Ness. "I . . . I was just speaking rhetorically," he said. "I meant no harm, really. Of course I was going to call the police. It's just been really important to Westralia to keep the tunneling going."

"Tell it to the judge," said Inspector Johns.

"Oh, by the way," said Clara's mother, putting her hand on Linda's other shoulder. "Miss Darlington is not my daughter. And I am not dead. Now, would you like to explain where you thought you were going to send my daughter?"

"Not unless he wants me to march his teeth out of what he sits on," growled Gordon, the submariner who'd been playing a plain-clothes witness. "Better stay in jail, because we won't need a list to remember you."

"I want a lawyer," said Ness, looking like a cornered rat.

"Mr. Cheswick?" asked Lieutenant Ambrose.

"Yes!" said Ness.

"I believe he's going to be one cell over from your dear boss for his role in attempting to subvert a witness. We'll get him to talk to you once the clanker takes you down to Ceduna. Now, we need a secure place to lock these two up, and we need to round up the rest of those who might try to stop a police investigation. I think this place could be the scene of at least one crime."

※

Linda had no part in the arrest of the shift-captain or the foreman. She was up at the wing, writing a reply to her father's message. He wanted to know if she had suffered from frostbite and if her lungs were all right . . . and nothing about Nicky. She didn't know whether to be relieved or worried that it was not being mentioned.

The WMP, however, were making sure that her ex-boyfriend's boss was not going to be happy. Linda was pretty certain it was deliberate, she just wasn't quite sure why. They declared the tunnel a crime scene and off-limits until further investigation. They declared the newly returned steam mole a crime scene. They found McGurk, who had been relegated to a back office and was steaming about that . . . and charged him, too. When the clanker came in the morning, the prisoners would all be on their way to Sheba in irons. The WMP were playing very hard, it seemed.

Linda knew, from having been on the breakfast table fringes of politics, that they didn't usually treat Westralian businesses that harshly. She had to wonder just what her father and some of his friends, like Colonel Clifford, were up to. It was more than just a murder investigation or cover-up.

CHAPTER 19

"So, what do we do when we get to Queensland?" asked Tim.

Tired, dusty, but with the tender filling up with a stock of short sections of hardwood that were, hopefully, going to work on the conveyor. Otherwise they'd have to hand feed the furnace, which would be hot and difficult. Using the axes and bow-saw had been hard work already, but it might save them later. Wood was scarce out on the plains, but quite available in the gullies. They'd stopped near a huge tangle of flood-washed, bone-dry wood in a braided river bed. They'd spent most of the daylight hours cutting wood, except during the middle of the day, when they lay in the shade, drank water, and talked. And talked. It seemed like years they had to catch up on, not weeks.

"I guess the first question is how do we even know when we're *in* Queensland?" said Clara, wishing of all things that she could have a bath. "I know there are tropical forests on the coast, but his letter said it was very hot and humid at first, but the country outside the prison was baked brown. He said he'd landed at Rockhampton and been transported as far inland as the railway would go. It was called Winton Prison, so I suppose it must be somewhere near Winton. Looking at the map it appeared to be about two hundred and fifty miles east-southeast of Dajarra."

"Well, I suppose tomorrow, really early, we better start heading east-southeast, then. And burrow if we see problems and sneak in at night. I'd start tonight, but I am so tired I'd fall asleep. I'm sorry, Clara."

"And why should you be?" she said, reaching out and giving his arm a squeeze. "It's barely a ton of wood we've shifted, to say nothing of a few little adventures with wild savages." He was like that, always thinking he should do more.

"They weren't exactly savage," he said, slightly defensively.

"It's what they'd have been called back in Fermoy," said Clara. She hadn't meant it nastily or anything. They just didn't wear a lot of clothes and used spears. Obviously Tim was bothered by it.

He yawned, then said, "The world's a bigger place, and not quite everything in Fermoy was perfect. Like that school you talked about . . ."

"Fair enough, Tim Barnabas." She yawned, too. "We're not in Fermoy. And we're not on the *Cuttlefish*, either. I'll fall asleep on my feet any moment now. Which means you get to kiss me good night."

He grinned. "It's not all bad here."

They awoke long before dawn. Clara had slept well for the first time in what felt like forever, feeling the warm comfort of Tim lying against her back. It was most improper, she knew. But then, having finally found Tim, there was no way she was sleeping anywhere but right next to him. And there were dingoes and wild aboriginals out here. She wasn't sure how dangerous either were, but there was no sense in taking any chances. She knew that the snakes, scorpions, and spiders were deadly enough.

They ate. The steam mole was provisioned for two men for a couple of weeks, but much of what there was was in the form of flour and other dry goods. Despite working in the galley for Cookie on the *Cuttlefish*, neither of them were too confident about cooking. The condensed milk and biscuits they knew what do with, however. And tea. Clara had always wondered just why her mother made such a fuss about tea . . . until she hadn't had it for a day or two. In the dawn they got the steam mole primed and going and set out. It was just so much easier with two people.

※

Jack and Lampy and the soldier, McLoughlin, had ridden for another two hours before stopping. Lampy noticed the horses were pulling south and guessed what it meant. "They smelling water, Jack. Give 'em their heads."

The horses took them to water, which was amazing in itself, nearly as amazing as water existing out here. Jack had a feeling that the billabong—which was what Lampy called the long, limpid pool that remained on this bit of otherwise dried-up river—wouldn't look so good in the daylight, but right now it saved them water, and there was a little feed there for the horses to supplement the rations they carried. It was hard to add looking after the horses into the list of things that had to be done, but Lampy just couldn't. His ankle was swelled up like a balloon. Jack had him lying on his back with it up, kindling the fire, while he unsaddled and hobbled the horses. The saddlebag had revealed, among other things, a small bottle of rum, and Jack gave the soldier some. He wasn't sure, medically, if it was a good idea, but the man was in pain. He offered some to Lampy, too, for the same reason. The young half-aboriginal lad—Jack had found out that his father had been a "whitefeller"—shook his head violently. "I don't drink that stuff, man. I seen what it does. My pa wasn't a bad feller when he wasn't drinking."

"Some people can't tolerate it. My friend Padraig was a doctor, and he reckoned the tendency ran in families."

"I'll have his," said the soldier, his voice weak and tremulous, betraying his bravado. "I feel a little rough, and it might smooth the ground."

"I'll save it," said Jack.

He let them sleep a while, and sat there looking at the stars reflected in the narrow band of water tucked between the trees. Their chances had improved vastly with the horses, water, and rifles, but from what McLoughlin had let slip there were other hunters out there, other groups searching the desert, mostly to the south of them. They couldn't be that far away. He regretted that he hadn't shot to kill the tracker. But Jack came from a background that held life as precious and not to be taken lightly, or if there was choice. But by now, the tracker could have found another party. And then the chase would be on again. The question in Jack's mind was just how far it was to the underground railway of the Westralians? Would he find it? Or would he simply ride over it? And what did he do with the boy? Lampy was so set against the Westralians, with good reason, but with that foot he was in no state to cope with the desert.

Jack dosed a bit. Some rest he had to have, but years of practice had made him quite good at not sleeping too deeply. Mary slept like the dead when she slept, and if his little Clara had called out, it had been Jack who had got up to tend to her. Thinking about his wife and daughter and being free to maybe see them again one day made that light sleep more refreshing. He woke, somewhat later, when the soldier groaned in his sleep.

Long before sun-up they rode somewhat north of due west. "Might be chased by the other soldiers," Jack explained. "If the tracker finds them and tells them. Where do you think's best, lad?"

They were on a slight rise, and in the clear sunrise they could see right across miles of flatland into the rougher country beyond. It all looked so endless, and so empty.

※

Lampy's foot and ankle felt better when he woke, but it didn't last with riding. The throbbing wasn't helping him think. But the Irishman was right, it wouldn't take the tracker all that long to find the other soldiers. They'd probably get some other men, too, now that he and Jack had guns.

Jack called him "lad." Asked for his advice. He was a different whitefeller to the ones Lampy had met around his father. Different to the prisoners and the guards, too. "Look, we stick to the side of the channel. That big plain . . . it would be faster to cross, but we'd be visible for miles.

"We go a little north. And then you can see that darker line. That's a channel. Got some scrub trees. They won't see us so easy, we won't raise so much dust. We go 'long that. In them hills over that side, we can rest out the hot time of day. If they come for us . . . we'll see them, too. We can run then."

So they turned north and then along the edge of a braided dry creek set about with scattered, scrubby bushes rather than trees, moving across the plain just a few feet lower than the skyline. It was pretty flat, this country. They crossed the broad central braid of the dry river and then went north until they found another dry course going west. It was a good part to get across before the midday heat, and it was already warm.

Lampy ached. Both he and the soldier had chewed quids of Pituri leaves he'd spotted on a nearly dead plant, which had helped a bit. But he was still sore. The sun was starting to get toward where they'd have to find some shade—maybe something in the rocks in the rough country. And then Lampy spotted the smoke trail a little to the south out on the plain. He pointed it out to Jack, who rode south a little away from the slight valley.

Jack called back, "I've never seen anything like it, but it's not chasing us."

Lampy and the soldier rode over to him, and there, out on the plain, maybe two or more miles off, in the shivering heat, was a machine, smoke coming out of its low stack. At this distance, Lampy couldn't see a lot more.

"Looks like a steam car of some kind. The question is, whose is it?" asked Jack.

The soldier was slumped on the horse, staying on more by habit than any reflection of his condition. He was as white as a ghost. "Ain't ours," he muttered. "Mus' be them Westralian bastards."

"Well, we'd better see if we can signal to them or catch them," said Jack.

Lampy held up his hand. "Jack . . . you hear something?"

He definitely could, and it was nothing he'd ever heard in the desert before. Then he worked out what he was hearing. Up in the sky was one of those flying balloons. He'd heard of them. Never seen one. It was long and white, and even from here he could see the Union Jack painted on the tail. The noise came from its motors.

"Back to the dry bed," said Jack urgently. "It's got to be hunting us."

※

Tim and Clara had made slow going across the rougher country. There were rocks and gullies and steep spots they just had to avoid. Tim saw what he'd believed was a power station in the distance two days before. In the early morning's clear dry air it was obviously just a tall, monolithic rock. They moved past it and out onto a vast, flat plain, not a tree to be seen, just a distant, heat-quivering horizon.

"Well, at least we'll be able to move a bit faster," said Tim. "No gullies to fall into, anyway. But I hope we have enough fuel. There's nothing out there, is there?"

"It's almost like the sea," said Clara. "I was thinking, the only way we're ever going to find my dad without getting caught is to get ourselves what all those old books call 'a trusty native guide.'"

"So long as you don't have any ideas that I am one. I've had being taken for the locals, just because of the way I look to the back teeth. I'm thinking of getting 'my dad came from Jamaica' tattooed on my forehead," said Tim, as they trundled out onto the plain, crunching over scattered tufts of dry grass, heading toward the distant horizon.

"Maybe you could get them to talk to us, though."

"I wouldn't know where to—What's that?"

They stared at a white object, high above them and coming closer.

"It's an airship!" said Clara. They'd both seen airships before. It was just so unexpected out here that it had taken a little time to work it out. It was also bearing straight down on them, rather than giving them the normal profile view.

Tim grabbed the igniter. "Going to start the drill. Pull the steam divert." He pointed to a red lever, grateful that it was the same on the scout mole as on the big, rail-mounted mole. He swung himself out of the cabin, along the rails past the pistons, and onto the drill gantry as sudden spurts of dust leapt in a line across the desert and something screamed off the roof of the mole. "They're shooting at us!" he yelled. She couldn't hear him, of course.

He watched for the rotation gap, trying not to think of the bullets, and pushed the igniter in. The drill head motor fired, and the drill began spinning faster and faster, showering everything with dust and flying grit. Tim felt rather than saw his way along, climbing back.

"I can't see a thing," yelled Clara as he slammed the door. "And they're shooting."

"Push the dig levers down!" Tim yelled back. A bullet hit the mole somewhere behind them with a loud *spang!*

"At least they can't see us! Are we digging?"

"I think so. Slow forward, I reckon. Listen. You can hear the drill cutting."

Tim knew that rock-drilling was quite slow, but some of the plains were clay-pan, and apparently the drill could cut those fast. He hoped this was one of those, and they were, at least, definitely going down. The scout moles could do sample drills and even dig themselves shelters, he'd heard the others say. But the scout mole wasn't like a big steam mole, it couldn't be trailing an air hose . . . or could it? He found a big spool marked "snorkel" and lifted the ratchet. It clickety-clacked out. Maybe that fed the furnace . . . maybe it was air for them. It was very dark in there. Tim felt about and found the Davy lamp and lit it, blessing the careful and systematic organization in the scout mole. If they went on digging . . .

Even that thought was put aside as the ground suddenly shuddered. They could feel rather than hear the explosion.

"They're bombing us," said Clara fearfully. "It's like being drop mined. We're going to be buried alive."

Tim took her hand. "Well, they can't sink us. And I don't think we're that deep."

"What do we do?" she asked, giving his hand a squeeze and turning back to her dials. She'd learned to make some sense out of them. Tim didn't yet know quite what they meant.

"Not sure. Do you think we can play dead? Pull the damper levers nearly down and wait a bit. That probably collapsed our tunnel. It's not reinforced or propped."

She nodded, pulled levers, adjusted a wheel, and shifted the power levers into neutral. It got quieter, and the vibrations basically ceased. "The drill is turning at dead slow . . . I hope we can go again, or we're buried down here. And I have no idea how deep that is."

She got up, took down a small axe from the rack, and gave Tim her more usual smile. "But the first one to come digging his way into our lair is going to regret it."

Tim couldn't help smiling back. "I think I love you because you're crazy."

"It's a fine one you are to talk, Tim Barnabas. Climbing out there to start the drill while they're shooting at us."

"Someone had to."

❋

"Someone had to."

That was Tim, thought Clara, looking at him in the dim lamplight. He'd never think that that someone didn't have to be him, and he'd do it, not because he wasn't scared, but because "someone had to," and he was there. There were worse people to buried alive with, but not likely many better. "How long do you think we need to wait?"

"Dunno. I don't think they'll stick around too long. They'll either come and have a look or go on. I wish we had an earth periscope!"

It was scary, simply lying doggo, waiting. They'd done it on the submarine of course, but the captain had had the decision to make about when they moved, not them. Then something more alarming happened. The low grumble of the turning drill head stuttered . . . and stopped.

"What's happening?" Clara asked.

"I dunno. It sounded a bit like the drill stopping when the steam moles go back to the power station. They do it gradually to stop it flying apart when it's pulled out of the drill face."

"So why did it do it?"

Tim shrugged. "Could be it was just turning too slow. Could be lack of oxygen for the furnace. I think . . . I think I had better try and see if it'll start again."

"But you'd have to dig there."

"No, we're dug into a bit of a tunnel, even if that bomb has shaken everything loose and down on us. Open the dampers some, give her some fuel, and see if we can move backward at all, and then I'll try. Looking at the 'snorkel,' it looks like we get some of the air and the rest goes to the furnace."

"The air will be unbreathable out there."

"I can hold my breath for that long. If the way to the drill head isn't blocked."

"I'll do it," said Clara. " I can hold my breath for longer."

"Yeah, but I know what I have to do, and it's a bit hard to explain."

Clara watched the pressure dial, then pulled the control levers back. The mole quivered, moved back eight inches or so, and stopped moving. "We're stuck."

"Tunnel caved in, I suppose. And the mole's not designed to dig backward," said Tim. "We may be able to dig out, if we can get the drill going, or if the mole's stuck, we can try to dig ourselves out."

And then, thought Clara, they'd be in the middle of the desert with nothing. But she didn't say that. She just opened the drill head throttle slightly as Tim stood, taking deep breaths. Then, taking the lantern, he opened the door and squeezed himself out. Clara was left alone in the dark. Only it wasn't quite dark . . . a little light came back from the lantern. She counted resolutely to herself, "One-and-two-and . . ." She'd give him ninety seconds, then she was going after him.

They were long seconds. The door opened again after about thirty of them had passed. Tim slipped in, closed it, and panted.

"What's up out there?"

"I had to clear a bit of fallen stuff. Got to the drill head, but I have to wait for the rotation gap to stick the igniter in, and I thought I might run out of breath. I also thought wrapping something around my head might be a good idea, because the noise will be pretty bad."

"So will the flying bits of stone and dirt. There are earmuffs and goggles back there in the drawer."

Tim put them on and went out again. This time they were rewarded by a stutter and then the drill head starting its previous rumbling roar. Tim came back, grinning and bleeding from a cut above the eye.

"Good thing I had those goggles! There was stuff flying every-where," he said, pushing them up on his forehead.

"I'm tilting the head up and pushing forward," said Clara, easing the levers and increasing the drill speed, and then pushing the forward levers slowly . . . and slowly they began to dig.

"Hope we don't choke on our diggings . . . there's no place for the tailings all to go to. We used to take loads out with the big moles, the stuff that wasn't used for the wall stanchions," said Tim.

Clara said nothing. She watched her pressure gauges, and they weren't doing well. She guessed the furnace was being starved for air. But the mole lurched forward, and the roar of the drill head changed pitch.

"I'd say we're breaking out!" yelled Tim.

"That has to be outside light, even if it is red," Clara shouted.

"Dust!" yelled Tim.

She pulled back the throttle on the drill head They kept trundling forward. The dust was yellow-red now, and she cut the throttle right back. Dust swirled like their own personal sandstorm out there, but at least they weren't stuck underground anymore.

"Where are you going?" she asked, seeing Tim grab the brass door handle and pull the goggles on.

"To see if I can see the airship," Tim explained. "We use a lot more fuel drilling."

"Stay in! They'll shoot at you."

He shook his head. "We need to know."

He came back moments later, letting in a cloud of dust. "Can't see much more than from in here. I think we can cut off the feed to the drill head. If they were close I'd see them, and if they're far they'll see our dust."

Clara cut the drill, and it rumbled to a stop. The mole trundled on.

"I guess that's it over there, going south," said Tim, pointing into the distance as the dust settled. "Look, I think we need to cross this plain tonight and brush out our tracks. If we trundle back, slowly, not raising dust, then if it doesn't turn around, we can make a dash for it. It must be a border patrol or something."

"Then we're closer than we thought."

"I dunno. They say it's cooled down a bit here in the middle of Australia, but it was just so hot no one even tried to cross it since. I'd heard the flying wings do patrols. I'd forgotten about that. I suppose it's logical the British do the same. But no one wants to fight a war out here," said Tim, keeping a weather eye on the distant airship. It continued flying south.

"If this is cooler, I don't want to be here when it turns hotter," said Clara.

"We've still got a couple of months before the real hot. Then they get the wet, too, sometimes." He peered at the airship. "I wonder why they're flying south?"

"Because it's too far to walk?" said Clara, cheerfully. "I wonder if we can find some shade."

"Not much, unless we go right into the hills. And even there . . . the mole is too big to tuck under an overhang.

"We could dig our own. That would hide us."

"I guess we could make a little cave . . ."

CHAPTER 20

Lampy watched helplessly as the airship shot at the Westralian machine . . . and the sudden willy-willy of dust the machine kicked up.

"That has to make shooting tricky," he said.

"Yes," replied Jack. "But I don't think it can save them. I think shooting back with tracer bullets might. I wish we could help, but our rifles are next to useless. Ordinary bullets just go straight through the envelope. At least it's doing something good. While they're looking at that mole, they're not looking for us. Let us go over there, where there's a bit of a sand wall cut by the flood. They would have to get right above us to shoot at us, or even see us, from that height."

Lampy nodded. "Or come from the north or west. We could dig a hole, I suppose."

They retreated and tethered the horses, looking for a few washed-out rocks to hide under, both for shade and for shelter from the airship's bullets.

Then the air shook with an explosion, followed by a plume of smoke.

"They've bombed them!" said Jack, hobbling off to look. The riding was telling on him. "Well, that's the end of them." He watched for a while longer. "The dust has settled. I can't even see anything left. Must have copped a direct hit." He sucked his teeth and shook his head. "I suppose it was quick. Ah. The airship is moving. The luck of the Irish is still with us, it is going south. We'll give it a few minutes and see if we can get among those hills before we take a break."

So they did. Lampy gave some more Pituri to the soldier, who was flushed and glassy-eyed. He really didn't seem too aware of his captors at all, but rather somewhere in the whitefeller's dreaming. He muttered to himself. But he still managed to stay on a horse.

It was maybe a mile farther on when Lampy, as he did by habit, looked back to check for dust . . . and saw lots of it. "Look, Jack!" he screamed, trying to keep the panic out of his voice. From the bomb crater a willy-willy rose, and in the middle of it . . . something. Something dark with bright flashes.

"Holy . . . I don't believe it!" said Jack. "It's coming out of the ground!"

So it was. Lampy began wondering about those rainbow serpent stories uncle told. But it was that machine, a trickle of smoke oozing from it, and it was turning, heading for the hills. Just like they were. Or was it hunting them?

"Airship is heading back this way," said Jack. "A bit west though."

✳

No one woke Duke Malcolm Woldemar Adolf Windsor-Schaumburg-Lippe, Duke of Leinster, Margrave of Waldeck, Earl of Northhamton, and baron of a dozen lesser estates, English, German, Canadian, African, and Australian. He did have a telephone instrument, right there in his bedroom, but it had been some years since it had rung during the night. Its insistent jangling woke him from a deep sleep. He turned on his bedside lamp and found the telephone. He heard the operator say "You're through" . . . and someone said, "Your Grace, Major Simmer speaking. I'm sorry to wake you, but there are developments in Australia that I think are urgent."

"What is it, Simmer?" asked Duke Malcolm, reaching for his cigarette case.

"Your Grace, my night crew alerted me that we'd had messages from Australia they deemed important. I think likewise, Your Grace. The airship you ordered into the search made contact with one of the search parties. They signaled to it, and a message was passed from them. The escaped prisoner, Calland . . . one of the search parties found their trail and caught up with them."

"Did you wake me up to tell me this Calland has been captured?" Duke Malcolm said testily, lighting a match.

"No, Your Grace. It's a lot more serious. There were two prisoners, and they managed to outwit the soldiers and kill them. Only the tracker got away on foot. He ran until he found another party. They're collecting another search party, but Calland and the other prisoner are armed and have horses and water now. And, Your Grace, they were heading due west rather than southwest—straight toward the Westralian tunnels."

The duke hastily shook the match out before it burned his fingers. He worked out the implications for himself. "Well done for alerting me, Simmer. Consider yourself promoted. I'll be at the office in twenty minutes. We need to get the strike force in action now."

"There is more, Your Grace. The airship had seen a Westralian steam vehicle in roughly the same area the escapees were heading into. It did destroy the vehicle, but is now returning to check for survivors."

"I'll be there in twenty minutes. In the meanwhile, tell the Marconi operators I want a voice line to General Von Stross in Queensland."

Duke Malcolm knew that immediate action was all that could save years of work from being wasted, worst of all work on a project that Ernest had bragged to the privy council about being nearly in the bag. No matter how unready they were, those trucks at the railhead, under the camouflage netting . . . well, they must head out, right now. An elite force of three thousand men would have to spear their way through any resistance, preferably before the Westralians could be warned, and certainly before they could reinforce their holdings.

※

Getting the flying wing airborne again here, in the middle of the desert, and not on the airstrip and ramp at Boomerang Fields, was a lot more complicated. The steam moles transported the extra material from the tunnel to the power stations, and they did have ramps and landing strips—the flying wings needed fairly short strips, fortunately—but the wing had to be moved to the ramp and then positioned and chocked so it didn't start moving too soon.

A sand anchor had to be planted and the catapult on the wing cranked up. The engines weren't quite powerful enough to get the wing flying. Once it was moving fast enough, the air provided lift. A good steady breeze helped, and fortunately there was one.

The props were swung, and once they were moving at full blurring, throbbing revolutions, someone yelled, "Chocks away!"

The flying wing began to accelerate, and then, as Linda peered through the navigation window, it lifted slowly from the ground. The pilot was a tense mass of concentration until they were several hundred feet into the air. No one would have dreamed of disturbing him, least of all Linda. She was still in trouble for spoiling his balance yesterday. He'd had a worrying flight, correcting a tiny bit . . . he was that in tune with his aircraft. He'd assumed they'd got the weights wrong when distributing men out into the wing.

Linda's flying gear was somewhat less rudimentary than the blankets she'd rolled herself in yesterday, but not much. Spare earmuffs and scarves were something the flying wing carried, but not woolly boots or padded trousers and hooded sheepskin jackets. So they'd had to do their best to cut out and sew an outfit out of blankets and make a sort of foot sleeping bag from sheepskin. At least, today, there were no plans to go very high, so the temperature wouldn't be an issue. She could see out of the aircraft, the earmuffs reduced the noise a great deal, and right now, she was unpleasantly warm. Soon Dajarra station was a tiny smoke spot on the desert below.

The searchers flew a grid pattern, which involved some precise navigation, as they had few landmarks to work off. Following the compass or tracking the termite runs were all the pilot really had. And they had lots of eyes staring down, looking for any sign. They got nothing to the west or the south. They spotted a family group of aboriginals to the north and nothing to the east. So they began a wider circuit.

And then again. Fortunately, the flying wing was very fuel efficient, or so the pilot said, and could refuel at Sheba before the flight back.

It was nearly ten thirty in the morning, just when habit said to Linda that one should have tea and start looking forward to a little sleep in the heat after lunch, except it wasn't very hot, when the slow process of searching suddenly became a lot more lively. A note was passed along from the wingtip. It read: "Tracks spotted off to the west-southwest."

The *Cuttlefish*'s topmast men had eyes like hawks.

The *Wedgetail* began a slow circuit, getting lower, and there, sure enough, was a line of double caterpillar tracks, heading due west. How someone had spotted them from that height was almost unbelievable to Linda. But from three hundred feet up, they were quite easy to follow . . . until they got onto the gibber plain, where the stony country made it difficult. They were doing their second pass, and one of the crew was pointing down, when Linda looked up at the horizon and grabbed the pilot's shoulder. One didn't do that, by his look of extreme annoyance. But she pointed at her reason . . . and he began to climb as fast as possible from the few hundred feet above the desert floor.

What Linda had seen was an airship. It wasn't that far off, either. They'd all been focusing their attention on the ground while it sneaked up on them.

The copilot took one look, whipped his gloves off, and worked the Marconi-transmitter while the pilot steered them upward in a slow spiral, working his controls with a deft and delicate touch.

※

"The airship," said Tim. "I think it's heading back."

Clara turned her head to look, and as she did a distant flash in the sky caught her eye. "There's another—low and bit north of us!"

Tim peered, too. "I think . . . that's not an airship. It's one of those flying wings. The Westralian's have them."

"Maybe they can keep each other busy."

"I'd guess that's what they're planning to do. The airship looks like it's heading for them, not us. It must be able to see our smoke, but I guess the other aircraft is more important.

"Let's get to those hills, and we can get ready to dig in and try to hide our tracks while they do that. You watch them, we seem to be having a temperature problem. The pressure is dropping."

"It's probably one of those bits of wood jammed. I'll go out and have a look. I'll be able to see better from there, anyway," said Tim, going to the door and out, leaving Clara driving. He came back a minute or two later. "Need the pry bar. It's good and jammed up, up there. I'll manually feed some wood first. The airship is definitely heading for the flying wing."

Up on the top of the tender, Tim hauled wood and dropped it into the feed for the furnace. He then lifted the cover and set about trying to break apart the pieces of limb that had crunched themselves into a tangle and somehow got a branch into the roller-wheels. It looked like the flying wing and the airship were going to battle it out.

※

The airship closed in on them, and also rose as fast as it could. Linda could see sudden puffs of smoke from the gondola. The flying wing banked sharply, then the pilot jinked the other way. The flying wing shuddered as if something had slapped it, but continued to climb. So did the airship. The flying wing had the edge in maneuverability and speed, but at climbing, well, the airship was doing better. And it was doing better at shooting at them. The flying wing slewed viciously again, then began to dive. The wing certainly could move a lot faster than the airship. It would easily outrun it, Linda thought.

Only it couldn't outrun bullets. The starboard engine suddenly blossomed flames and smoke as the pilot fought for control.

※

Jack, the soldier, and Lampy kept heading for the rough country. "Whatever that Westralian machine is, it's tough. Survived that bomb. I would have thought it would blow it to smithereens," said Jack. "It should keep them off us, though. Keep the airship busy."

"I think that airship got its own problems," said Lampy, pointing. "That's one of them Westralian fliers. I saw them patrolling when I was here with my uncle."

"Well, maybe we should make contact with the Westralian machine. If they can survive that bomb they must be quite something. Could give us shelter. I reckon they'll be quite glad to hear about the lot we escaped from," Jack said, glancing at their prisoner. But McLoughlin was beyond noticing. He was white-faced and clinging to the horse's mane.

"He's going to fall off just now, I reckon," said Lampy. He'd never thought he'd feel sorry for a soldier, but he did. One had to admire the way he stayed on a horse, if nothing else.

"Better reason to get him to that machine," said Jack.

"I ain't having nothing to do with them Westralians, Jack.

They'll shoot any blackfeller they see. Prob'ly shoot you, too, with that hat. Hello. Look. One of them has climbed on top of the thing."

And then Lampy swallowed hard. The man—and he wasn't particularly large—wore railway-man clothing.

Only . . . he was black. Well, as black as Lampy anyway.

And then, suddenly, even from here they could hear the gunfire.

It was coming from the airship. Lampy could see the little puffs of smoke from the cabin-thing that hung underneath it. The flying wing was behaving like a bat trying to get away from an owl.

✳

The engineer climbed out of his nacelle and down the struts to the wing itself, clinging desperately, but at least away from the flames. With one set of engines out, the *Wedgetail* turned back toward the airship. And then Linda realized it was more than the engine sending them back. The pilot steered them in a sharp arc.

The captain of the airship must have realized what a burning engine would do to his great bag of hydrogen, and tried to turn away, venting hydrogen and dropping as they hurtled toward him. That might have been a mistake, as the flying wing now had more height and more maneuverability than his craft . . . and looking out of the window, Linda saw that the engineer clinging to the strut in the hundred-mile-an-hour wind had been joined by another—the copilot. And they were working on something, hauling at levers, despite being about a thousand feet up and out on the wing. The pilot flicked his eyes at them, and then, out on the wing, as they were racing ever closer to the airship, the copilot managed to wave. The pilot signaled to them to hold on.

The pilot dropped the wingtip and side-slipped. Linda hung on for dear life as the flying wing flipped over. They all fell about, except the pilot. He clung like a monkey to his levers as the flying wing shuddered, as if she'd been slapped, and began to dive and turn hard again. And as she fell toward her seat, Linda saw the still-burning engine fly on without them, like a burning cannonball, straight for the airship.

She watched, time seeming to drag out, as the burning engine plunged toward the airship. The captain of the airship must have dumped all his ballast at once, and the airship rose.

It was going to miss—

And it did.

It missed the gas bag.

It hit the engine and steering vane instead, sending a tearing shower of debris and flame arcing downward. The airship went on rising, as the pilot of the flying wing tried to stabilize his craft. He beckoned Linda close and yelled in her ear, "Get ten men onto the starboard wing. Right!"

※

As they watched the aerial battle unfold from where they were hidden in the little fold in the landscape, Lampy glanced across the open flats to see that the Westralian machine had stopped. And a second person had joined the first on the roof of the tender. Even from here Lampy could see that this person had yellow hair . . . and wore a dress. He had barely time to take this in when the last act in the aerial battle took place.

"Mary McCree!" said Jack, shaking his head. "Did you see the poor fellow on the wing fall! That was some skill! But I think they've paid a dear price for it. They're losing height."

The flying wing, which had changed from a bat fluttering away from an owl to a swallow fluttering away from a hawk, was indeed coming down. The airship wasn't. It continued to rise, but seemed to be drifting rather than flying. It certainly wasn't coming back this way.

At that point, McLoughlin did fall off his horse.

"I think," said Lampy, as Jack got down to him, "we need to go to that steam engine. I go fetch 'em."

"I'd better go," said Jack, laying the groaning, semiconscious man flat. McLoughlin clung to Jack's hand.

"I'll be right for it," said Lampy, hoping he was right about what he'd seen. At the same time he laid the rifle on its sling off his shoulder and forward onto his saddle bow. He rode closer. He sang out from a good three hundred yards off from the steam machine. Them dopey Westralians hadn't actually even seen him, they were too busy watching the flying wing coming down and the airship drifting off. But that was definitely a blackfeller . . . in the clothes of a railway-man. Sooty and dusty clothes, but railway-man clothes, and the girl was wearing a little straw hat, and yes, pleated skirts. They didn't look as if they were even his age, either of them. Mind you, there were plenty of men working at his age.

※

Linda scrambled into the crawl way to the wing. She got to the first submariner, pulled his earmuff aside, and yelled in his ear. Then she moved on to the next until she had ten moving over. Then she went back to the pilot's nacelle. The copilot was back, looking grim. He wrote: "Have to crash-land. Pass it on." Then he wrote it again and gave her the two notes, pointing at the wing crawlways. He went back to the pipes he was working on, under the floor panel he had open.

Linda went to deliver the messages, then got herself back to her seat—to be handed a piece of rope.

"Tie yourself to the seat," Clara's mother yelled in her ear.

Linda did her best with the rope. They were much lower . . . and moving far slower now. The ground was still going past rather fast. Linda looked out the forward window and braced herself. In the distance, she could still see the airship. They were barely fifty feet above the gibber plain now, with the pilot fiercely intent, huddled over his controls, fighting for every last bit of air to slow them down and to put the flying wing down safely. They cut the surviving engine . . . and the next instant they were bouncing, and slewed wildly across the ground. Linda was wacked back into her seat and then slammed forward with her face onto her knees as the aircraft came to a stop.

※

The black-skinned railway-man and the woman were surely very surprised to see Lampy. Neither reached for guns. They waved instead. A little warily, it seemed to Lampy.

"Day-ee. We got a hurt man back there. You want to bring this machine closer. I don't think he can ride no more."

"How far?" said the blackfeller, nodding.

"Maybe six hundred yards. Maybe a little more. He's hurt bad. You follow me, an' I show you."

"I suppose we'd have to help, then. I was thinking we should go to that flying wing. It must have landed hard," said the girl.

"These people are nearer," said the blackfeller on the cab of the machine. "Who are you?"

"My mother was Tialatchari. Who your people?"

The bloke looked at the girl and laughed. "*Cuttlefish*, I guess. We'll follow you, we just need to get the steam up."

"There anymore o' you?" asked Lampy, staring at the windows of the machine.

"No, it's just us," said the girl. They climbed down the iron and brass ladder and into the cab, and a few moments later the big machine gave a belch of smoke and began to move.

Lampy trotted the horse back toward Jack and McLoughlin. Puffing and clattering, the steam machine followed.

※

"Well, that was clever of you," said Clara. "Looks like you found us a trusty native guide after all."

"More like he found us. He had a rifle, don't know if you noticed. This could be trouble, Clara."

"When is there ever anything else?" she said wryly. "It's more empty than I thought it would be, this desert in the middle of Australia."

"When you're walking around lost in it, it's pretty empty," said Tim with feeling. "Ah. There's someone else there, waving. Didn't even realize this fold of land was here. It's much less visible than where we were out on the plain."

Clara slowed the steam mole. "We'll not quite stop until we can see them, and all around them."

But that wasn't hard, once they got closer. If there was an ambush it would have to be a very clever one. There were a bunch of tired horses, and a man knelt next to another fellow lying on the ground with a bloody bandage and a pallid, almost yellow face. The man seeing to him had a ragged beard and a gaunt face, with very blue eyes. He raised a hand to them. There was something oddly familiar about his face.

"Looks harmless. Like the real thing. Better let me go first," said Tim.

"Don't be silly," said Clara. "I'm coming, too." She pulled the dampers down, stood up, and they climbed out of the cab together. Tim did manage to be first out. Just. She'd have to train him better.

The man who'd been seeing to the injured fellow stood up and dusted off his hands. "I wasn't expecting a young lady out here. I'm glad to see you. My name is Jack. Jack Calland. And this lad's Lampy Green. We've got a wounded soldier here."

Clara felt the ground go wobbly under her feet, and it was only Tim's arms catching her that stopped her falling over.

"What's wrong?" asked her father, stepping forward.

It was him. He was older, exhausted, gaunt, bearded . . . but the eyes. She would always recognize those eyes. She couldn't say any-thing, the lump in her throat was too big. But she could smile and reach for him.

He blinked. "Er . . ." His face was a study in confusion.

"She's come a long way to find you, sir," said Tim. "This is your daughter, Clara."

"Clara?" he said as she took his half-outstretched hands.

She nodded. "It's me, Daddy," she managed to croak around the lump in her throat.

He folded her in his arms then, saying her name over and over. Then he held her away from him, looking at her, his eyes wide, as if he wanted to see as much of her as possible. "It's big you've grown, girl," he said thickly. "I didn't even recognize you at first. Is . . . is your mother here, too?"

There was such hope in his voice that Clara couldn't speak again, Just shake her head. It was left to Tim to say, "I'm afraid Dr. Calland is sick. Um. She may be dead, sir. That's why Clara came on her own."

"Mary? What's wrong?" His voice was desperate, shaken to the core.

"We don't know," said Clara quietly, misery rising into her hap-piness and flooding it. "She . . . was in a coma. They . . . they think it's some tropical disease. She was in quarantine and . . . and they said she was never going to get better. And they said you were dying, too. Your letter . . . I thought you were."

She closed her eyes. "Mother's dead, Daddy. I know it, I just didn't want to admit to it to myself. She loved you so much." Which was enough to start both of them crying again, holding onto each other.

There were still tears streaming down Jack's face, and Clara's, when he pushed her away a little. He squeezed her shoulder. "I've lost the love of my life," he said quietly. "I hoped . . . prayed that I'd see Mary again before I died. But at least I've found my girl. And that was more than I ever really thought to do. But for now . . . we have an injured man here, and we'd better go and see if anyone sur-vived that crash. And you'd better introduce me to this gentleman."

Clara nodded and looked at him again, the new image putting itself firmly over the cloudy one of long, long ago. "Daddy . . . Oh. I never thought I'd be saying that again. Daddy, this is Tim. Tim Barnabas. He's my . . . friend. My *boy*friend." She saw the look on his face and added, "And Mother *approved* of Tim! Just so you know."

Tim awkwardly extended his hand. "How do you do, sir? I was one of the crew of the submarine that brought your wife and daughter to Westralia."

"He saved my life. A couple of times!" said Clara.

Her father took his hand. "Then I am in your debt, but I think she's rather young for a boyfriend."

And Tim, the traitor, nodded. "Yes, sir."

"I am not!"

Her father shook himself like a dog coming out of the water. "I suppose it has been some years since I went to jail, and you are older now, little one. Now, Lampy injured his foot, so do you think you can give me a hand getting McLoughlin into the cab, Mr. Barnabas? Is there space for him to lie down? What is this thing, anyway?"

"It's a steam mole, sir, a scout mole, to be exact. And yes, there is some space. There are some swags we can put him on. I've got some laudanum in the cab, too. What's wrong with him? His hands seem to be tied. Is he . . . confused?" asked Tim, joining hands with Clara's father to carry the semiconscious man.

"He's delirious. He's tied up because he was one of the soldiers chasing us. We couldn't just leave him, so we brought him along."

With difficulty they got him up into the cab of the scout mole and laid him down on the swags.

"Right. I wonder, what we should do with the horses?" said her father. "It's a very smart machine this. How did you come by it?"

"I stole it," Clara said.

"Ah," said her father. "I did wonder how you and Tim came to be wandering around the desert alone."

"I stole it because they wouldn't go to look for Tim, and then when I eventually found him, we went to go and get you from Queensland."

Her father blinked and shook his head. "You're so like your mother."

"That's what she said to me, but about you, every time I did something outrageous," said Clara.

"Yes, but every time Mary did it to me, I just didn't expect it. She didn't look like she would. She looked so . . . well, angelic," said her father. "We have a lot of catching up to do."

"Well, sir," said Tim. "I've never been on a horse in my life, but how about if Lampy and I ride and you talk to Clara? She's a really good driver."

Her father looked tempted. "No. I'd like to, but if you've never ridden, it would not end well. I'm sore enough, and I used to ride almost every day, once."

"I'll ride," said Clara. "Tim can drive. It's been a few years since those riding lessons, Daddy, but at least I have ridden a horse before!"

"Skirts," said Tim. "Dunno if you can ride in those."

"Pooh. They're broad enough to spill over."

"There are some spare breeches back in the locker there. You could put those on," said Tim.

"I'll do that. I hope they're not too big."

"Keep your skirts on, too."

"You want to boil me?"

Her father nodded. "Boiled will be better than chafed. We could try it for a little anyway. Lampy could come and put his foot up. He's sore, poor lad. Now, you said you had some laudanum drops. We could try some on McLoughlin here. Can't make him worse, surely."

CHAPTER 21

Tim set the steam mole in motion. He was not as familiar with it as Clara was, but he liked machinery, and he noticed things. Clara and her father had already mounted fresh horses and were ahead and to the right. Tim didn't have a lot of concentration to spare for her, but it looked as though she was a lot less comfortable on a horse than in the steam mole. He said so to his new companion, who chuckled. Lampy had a warm laugh that reminded Tim of the aboriginals who had rescued him after he'd failed to catch the mole.

"I reckon she needs to ask for her money back from that riding school," said Tim with a grin.

"Too right," said Lampy, putting his foot up against a strut on the wall. "Didn't know there was any blackfellers working on the railway."

"They tried to kill me for it," said Tim.

"That sounds like them bastards to me. Shot me uncle," said Lampy.

It was hard to know what to say to that.

Eventually, Tim said, "I hope they caught whoever did it."

"They don't care. We blackfellers are like 'roos to them."

"That's not right. Mind you, that Vister seemed to think he could kill me. It's different where I come from. Tough in the tunnels, and I had some fights because of it. But not just . . . killing."

"Yeah? So where you come from, man?"

He and Lampy fell into easy talk, both finding the other's world so different from their own, and oddly fascinating. And Tim did a little fishing about Clara's father.

"Jack's a bonza bloke. Madder than . . . I dunno, the maddest thing you ever met. But he's decent, see. Buried the bloke what got killed, did his best for McLoughlin. Wouldn't let the others kill that Quint." Lampy looked askance at Tim. "Wouldn't want to get on the wrong side of him with his daughter, though."

"She's fairly crazy, too. I mean, she came up here to cross the desert to get her old man out of stir. And she'd have probably done it, too. She doesn't know what 'give up' means. She'd be loyal to her last breath. Best girl in the world," said Tim fervently. "I hope her father doesn't mind me . . . Well, I don't know what I'd do."

Lampy grinned at him. "Sounds like you're in deep."

Tim didn't pretend not to understand. "Yep. Mind you, we've had some good fights. She won't admit she can't do anything. She usually can, too."

"Looks like some smoke over there," said Lampy, pointing. "Maybe that's where the flying thing came down."

They headed toward it.

※

Duke Malcolm listened, stony faced, to the transmission from Australia. Then he turned to the head of the Australia section, who, like himself, showed signs of having hastily donned his uniform. The duke had had a sleepy valet to help him, but Major Simmer, by the looks of him, had done it himself. "So. The vehicles have already left Camp Baltimore?"

"So the general said," replied the major. "They should be ready to leave the railhead by four o' clock this afternoon, their time, Your Grace."

"It's not certain that the flying wing was able to communicate, or would grasp the significance of one airship. But they're bound to send more up to search for the crash. And it is possible that they will have put these 'power stations' and Sheba onto an alert footing." He picked up the microphone. "General Von Stross, this is Duke Malcolm Windsor-Schaumburg-Lippe. You are hereby instructed to have your troops use the tunnel option. I hope your sappers are up to it."

The general reassured him.

Duke Malcolm was too wise to military doublespeak to believe him entirely.

He wondered just how much the crew of the airship actually knew. They'd lost their motors and part of the gondola and were now drifting west. Into the desert and into Westralian territory. Territory the Westralians relied on the desert to hold.

※

For a few moments after the wing had come down, Linda just sat there, holding onto her knees. Then she sat up.

The copilot, bloody-faced, said, "Right. Better get everybody out, in case of fire." He looked rather as if someone should get him out.

Linda could see the rocky ground through a hole in the fuselage. She already had the rope knot loose, and dashed into the crawlway to one wing. "All *out!*" she bawled at the top of her voice. And then she did the same on the other side, before coming back to the navigation nacelle. Dr. Calland lay very still in her seat, with a little blood on her forehead. Horrified, Linda knelt next to her, wishing she knew more about medicine. She felt for a pulse and was rewarded by feeling one. Then a submariner shooed her out and carried Dr. Calland out. The hatch was jammed onto the ground, but someone had broken open part of the wing, and they took her out of that.

Linda saw the advantage, very quickly, in the fact that almost all the men were submariners and used to working to orders and keeping calm. Lieutenant Ambrose and the captain directed the evacuation of the people from the wing, Lieutenant Willis had already set up a first aid station, and he was doing his best to deal with injuries.

Linda went over there to help. There didn't seem much wrong with her, besides some bruises.

"Nearly made it down," said the copilot. "We'd have done it in one piece if the undercarriage had come down. But those first shots must have hit that. Still. What a piece of flying! I hope Dan is all right."

"I can't believe what you did on that engine," said Linda.

He sighed and shook his head sadly. "Mickey, the starboard engineer, didn't have time for a safety line when they hit the engine and he had to get out. I couldn't have detached the engine without him. He was pretty badly burned, and he came off with the engine. A good man gone."

"So brave!"

"I was scared out of my wits," he said. "Yes, Lieutenant?" Lieutenant Ambrose had come up to them.

"Captain wants to know what the risk of fire is, and whether we can try to get supplies out of the plane, and if there's a system for signaling distress."

"I got a Marconi message out. Said we were under attack. There'll be fighter wings coming, I would guess. Poor old *Wedgie* was just a transporter due for retirement. I can't believe what Danny managed to do with her."

"You fliers did magnificently. But the captain needs to know how safe it is. And whether we can make a fire for signaling."

"If she hasn't caught fire yet, she probably won't," said the copilot, getting to his feet and staggering a little. "I cut off the fuel to the port engines. There's a fair amount of fuel there if we need to make signal fires. But I'd like to get to the Marconi set . . ."

"Sit down, man," said the lieutenant, sitting him down firmly, "and stay there. I know a Marconi set when I see it. I'll bring it out if it is intact. Not going to generate sparks in there. And we'll keep the number of men going in to a minimum. The captain's got most of the men backed off to a hundred yards now. There's no one still on board."

"I could use a fire, Amby," said Lieutenant Willis, binding a nasty gash, "and some boiled water and sterile dressings. And a couple of men as runners."

"I'll get some men onto it, Bob," promised Lieutenant Ambrose, leaving at a run.

"Can I help?" asked Linda. "I don't know anything about band-aging, but I could do the smaller cuts and things. I could try, anyway."

"If blood doesn't worry you, I'd like another set of hands," said the lieutenant. "I like to at least see the patients, Miss. I've got them ranked in priority here."

"Is Dr. Calland going to be . . . ? I mean, is she . . . ?"

"Hard to tell. She's concussed, at least."

The Marconi set was in fragments. The fire that Lieutenant Willis wanted for sterile dressings was kindled and tended with amazing speed as they worked their way down the line of patients.

"Except for the pilot's nacelle, the landing did us less damage than you'd think. The pilot stalled the wing almost perfectly at the last moment. Most of our injuries come from that loop-the-loop. I know why he did it, and I know it took great skill . . . but I wish we'd all been strapped down. I got out unhurt by being squashed between Gordon, here, and Tamworth, and they ended up with Big Eddie on top of them. I prefer softer cushions," said the lieutenant, feeling Gordon's nose. "Yes, it's broken. There is a lady present. You don't have to use words like that. You'll live."

So far, with the exception of the poor engineer, and possibly the unconscious pilot and Dr. Calland, it looked as if most of them would live.

Linda knew just how lucky they'd been. Or rather, how good their pilot had been, and how brave the copilot and the unfortunate engineer had been.

It made her little troubles back in Ceduna seem so small.

Her relief at seeing Dr. Calland trying to sit up and being made to lie down again, as some of the crew constructed a sun shelter over the patients, was enormous. So was her relief when one of the look-outs called, "Looks like the Westralians are onto it all quicker than we thought. Steam car coming."

The steam car—Linda recognized it for what it was, a scout mole in the colors of the Discovery North Railroad—slowed as it came closer. There were some horsemen with it, too, riding just out of the dust.

Only one of them wasn't a horse*man*.

She had blond plaits under a straw hat, and one of her plaits had come undone.

"Clara!" called Linda, as the door to the mole opened and a young man bounced out "Ahoy, *Cuttlefish!*" he bellowed.

"I see we found Tim Barnabas, or he found us," said the lieu-tenant with a smile, as several of the crew carried him on their shoul-ders up to the captain.

"Over here," yelled Linda, waving as someone helped Clara down from her horse. She looked like she needed help. And by the looks of the way she walked, holding on to the bearded man with her, she might need Lieutenant Willis's medical skills, too.

❋

Clara was surprised, but not amazed to see *Cuttlefish* crewmen around the wreck of the flying wing. Captain Malkis had obviously done his magic with her letter. She *was* amazed to see Linda. Was Mr. Dar-lington also here? Or her stepmother? Or had they . . . the thought was put aside. Linda looked far too happy. She bounded toward them like one of those kangaroos. "What's wrong, Clara?"

"Horse riding," grimaced Clara. "It's for nothing I'll tell you, Linda, a riding school hack in a paddock in Ireland two years ago is no training for Australia. I didn't realize it until we slowed down. I don't think I'll be able to stand tomorrow, let alone walk."

"Oh. I thought, well, I thought it might be something serious. Look, come quickly. Your mother is here."

"What? Where?" Clara wasn't too sore to try running, and neither was her father. He virtually carried both of them along.

The two of them dropped to their knees next to Mary.

"What's wrong? Is this the coma she was in?" demanded her father. "Dear God, Mary." He touched her face as you might the most fragile piece of porcelain in the world.

"No," said Lieutenant Willis, who had come up, too. "Concussion, I hope. She was awake a little earlier. A bit confused. She's not to move."

As if ordered, Mary Calland opened her eyes and blinked. "My glasses."

"There love. You don't need them right now. Lie still. We're here. You'll be fine."

Clara's mother tried really hard to sit up and was held firmly down.

"You're not to move, Mother," said Clara.

"Being dead really is a better place," said her mother dreamily. "Or am I just dying? I'm still sore, so I'm just dying. I thought I heard my Jack, and my baby."

"If you're going to call me a baby, I'll go and get lost again," said Clara fiercely, holding her hand. "You're not dying. You can't die. I've brought Daddy back to you."

"Just what hurts?" asked her father, calm and caring.

"My head. And my hand. Is . . . is that really you Jack-love?"

"It is indeed. Our girl found me and brought me to you."

"Clara. Little Tim. I'm so sorry . . ."

"Tim's fine, Mother. Actually, I think he found Daddy."

"T'was a group effort, I think," said her father. "Now lie still. Everything is fine."

※

Tim saluted Captain Malkis. "I can't tell you how glad I am to see you, sir, no matter what kind of trouble I'm in."

"I can't tell you how glad we are to see you, too, Barnabas. I'd half convinced myself they'd killed you. I gather your death was a bit exaggerated."

"Only just, sir. It was touch and go that my own stupidity killed me. But we have found him, sir."

The captain tugged his beard in the way Tim knew meant he was laughing. "And who have you found for us, Tim?"

"Clara's father, sir. We found him, a prisoner, and Lampy . . . uh, an aboriginal boy, sir. He'd be great on the crew. Um, the prisoner is quite injured, sir. He's lying in the steam mole. Maybe Lieutenant Willis could have a look at him?"

The captain nodded. "Of course. Is it possible to move him or should he see him there?"

"Well, moving him hurt him, and I think we'll just have to keep him there, sir, if we're going to take him anywhere. He can't ride. Mind you, I don't know what we'll do with transporting all these people. You don't have water, do you?"

The captain turned to one of the other submariners. "Nichol, will you ask the lieutenant to come to the steam mole, please?" He put a hand on Tim's shoulder and began walking them back to the steam mole. "I am a little sore from our crash. Now, tell me all of it, Barnabas, because I am the captain, and if there is any reason you might be in trouble, I need to get you out of it. When did Miss Calland find you?"

"Yesterday morning, sir. I was found by some aboriginals, and they were found by Clara. She saw their fire."

They'd arrived at the steam mole, where Lampy sat on the step, looking wary. "Ah," said Captain Malkis. "This must be one of the gentlemen who rescued you." He reached up, offering his hand. "Thank you for looking after him. Tim is a valuable member of my crew, and I'm very grateful."

Lampy looked confused, but he took the extended hand and shook it. "Not me, Mister. I didn't have nothing to do with it."

"That wasn't Lampy. He's the one who escaped with Mr. Calland."

"Oh. Well, I am still pleased to meet you. I see you're injured, too. Lieutenant Willis is our medical officer from the boat. He's not a doctor, but he has some experience."

"He's good at it," said Tim. "Let him have a look, Lampy. He's coming to see McLoughlin."

Lampy jerked a thumb back into the cab. "He's out of it. Doesn't know where he is, Tim-o."

"Cookie calls me that," said Tim, grinning. "Is he here, sir? I've missed his food."

Lieutenant Willis arrived as the captain shook his head. "We couldn't bring everyone, Barnabas. For which I am grateful. You bring up a good point about water for thirty-four people."

"I think you need to go and talk to Jack Calland, Captain," said the lieutenant. "He was telling the copilot about the troop build-up the British Imperial forces have in the desert. Calland is of the opinion they're getting ready for something soon."

"Yeah," said Lampy laconically. "Those jokers are up to something."

"That's what the aboriginals who found me said, too," said Tim. "They said there was a big army camp and a railway about three days walk away. Mind you, that's their walk, not mine, but it's quite close, really. And the Westralians back at the power station didn't know anything about them. Someone said there weren't even any people closer than this side of the dividing range, you know where the rivers either flow back to the east coast or into the desert. Well, Clara's letter, the one she got from her father, was from near Winton. Which is this side, a long way, from what Lampy says, and the railway the prisoners were working on . . . that's still further west."

Captain Malkis turned to Lampy. "How good are you at judging distance, young man?"

"Reckon I know 'bout how long it takes to walk a mile," said Lampy with a sketch of a grin. "We be maybe a hundred mile at most from the railway. An' that maybe . . . three hundred mile from the dividing range. That's where you find a few whitefellers again."

The captain looked thoughtful. "Surely the Westralian authorities know all about this. I mean, if the aboriginals do . . . surely they'll tell them?"

"The people won't go tell 'em," said Lampy, scornfully. "That's these Westralian blokes' problem. Make no difference to us, see."

The captain nodded slowly. "I had gathered there was something of an issue," he said. "I think we need to go and talk to the copilot, and Mr. Calland. No wonder they had airships out searching the desert. They really don't want this news getting back to Westralia."

"Shows how stupid the Westralians have been," said Tim.

"That, too. But we all do that. Some of us learn from it. Mr. Lampy, would you come with us to explain? By the looks of it Lieutenant Willis will be busy for a while." The captain mopped his brow. "Phew, it is hot. I thought we might use the flying wing for shade, but that's probably fairly risky if there are going to be other airships."

"It's Mr. Green, Captain. And he's got an injured foot," said Tim.

"My ma called me Lampy. Everyone does."

Lieutenant Willis raised his head from cutting aside the dressing. "I'll need hot water. What happened to this man?"

"Lampy speared him," said Tim, unthinking. It was only when he'd said it, and saw Lampy's face, that he wished he'd kept his mouth shut.

There was a moment's silence. "He tried to kill me. I stuck him with my spear," said Lampy, his knuckles tightening on the rifle he held.

Lieutenant Willis didn't notice that. He just went on cutting carefully. "That explains it."

"Um . . . I could use the mole to dig a shelter in that hillside, sir," said Tim. "Make shade, and be safer from bombs. The airship bombed us, but we were underground and that seemed to protect us."

"That would be a good idea. And if you drive it past the lieutenant's makeshift hospital, we can speak to the rest and maybe move those who can't walk. Can you operate the machine safely enough to stop there?" asked the captain.

"Oh, yes, sir. But Clara is a much better driver, sir."

"You would say so, Barnabas. If you can let us up, Mr. Green, and the lieutenant can let us have the time it takes? How long will it take, Barnabas?"

"She's still warm, sir. Let me just see the pressure. Ah. Two or three minutes, sir."

※

Lampy had expected trouble, real trouble, when they saw he was still holding the rifle. But they didn't even seem to notice. It was, he supposed, because they were Tim's people. He hadn't really quite understood all of what Tim had told him, but their accent was different from Australian whitefellers. So was Jack's to theirs. It was good that Jack had his family. Odd that Lampy felt a little left out about it.

Then he'd gone and told them he'd speared the soldier. He'd expected . . . he didn't even know why he'd admitted it, except that Tim had already told them. And they had acted like he'd said he had tea that morning.

Tim was busy getting the steam mole going, and the lieutenant was carefully cleaning and prodding the groaning soldier. And the captain said, "So, tell me about these soldiers. Can you describe their headgear?"

He didn't seem to care that a blackfeller had stuck a whitefeller with a spear. "Shakos. And black little hats with a pom-pom and little tassels, and checked ribbon, and big floppy green berets."

"Hussars, Lowland Dragoons, and Inniskillen Fusiliers," said the captain. "Some of the British Empire's finest troops."

"He said he was a sapper," said Lampy. The words came out in a rush. "I'm sorry I speared him. But he was shooting. He would have killed Jack or me, otherwise."

The captain patted his shoulder. "There are times when we have to do these things, boy. I can see it upsets you, but it wasn't as if you set out to murder someone. You did what had to be done. We'll look after him as best as possible."

The man didn't understand at all. And yet . . . the way he didn't understand was important. Lampy began to see why Tim was so lit up when he talked about the '*Cuttlefish* crew,' they were pretty good.

The mole trundled over to the lieutenant's makeshift hospital, Tim driving carefully. Lampy could see that he really wanted to show this captain how good he was. They pulled up, and the captain said, "After you, Mr. Green. You have a sore foot."

So they got down from the mole, Tim last, as he was shutting things down. There was Jack sitting with a woman who was as blond as his daughter, lying with her head on his knee. All three of them looked as if they'd still be smiling next week.

"Lampy!" said Jack. "Come here, will you? Mary is not to get up, and I'm doing pillow duty."

So Lampy did, feeling very awkward.

"Mary. This is the lad I was telling you about. Without him I would never have got here. Never crossed the desert, never managed to break out in the first place. I must tell you about what he did on that train!"

She beckoned to him. "They won't let me get up."

He squatted down next to them. And she sat up and put her arms around him. "You're supposed to lie down," said Jack, as Lampy tried to stay upright, too. "Here, Mary, lie down for heaven's sake."

"I owe you more gratitude than I can ever repay," said Jack's missus. She had one of those posh voices, like the nun who had taught him back at the mission school, and that made Lampy feel a little odder than being hugged and thanked did, and that was strange enough.

"'S nothing, ma'am. But you lie down see."

She did, but held onto his hand. "Jack tells me you're an orphan, and very worried about Westralia. Well, you brought my family to me. We're your family now. And if anyone, just anyone, dares to raise a finger to you, they'll have us to deal with."

Lampy swallowed, shook his head, not quite knowing how to deal with this. "I'll be right, see. I got some cousins down near Jericho. I reckon Jack can spare me some horses now. They ain't going to catch me."

"Your ankle is hurt, and you need to sit down and have it seen to," said Jack. "Make him sit, Clara."

Lampy wasn't used to being pushed around by girls, but from what Tim said, he'd better get used to it from this one. She started to get up, so Lampy sat down. It was much easier on the ankle. "He learns quicker than Tim," said Clara, grinning. "Don't even try and argue until you're able to run. Ask Tim."

"Too true," said Tim, who had been standing behind them.

"Tim Barnabas!" exclaimed Jack's missus, trying to sit up again.

"Stay down, Mary."

Tim squatted down next to her. "Hello, Dr. Calland."

She reached up for him and he leaned forward and gave her an awkward kiss on the cheek.

"I was so afraid for you, Tim."

"I was so upset about you, ma'am. Now, if you'll excuse me, I have to go and dig a shelter with the mole."

"I'll come with you," said Clara. "Hello, Captain Malkis!"

"You've led us a merry chase, cadet," the captain said. "I gather you're the expert driver. We'll need shelter, and then I suspect we'll need to send the worst of the injured back to the power station." He squatted down and held out a hand to Jack. "Captain Joaquim

Malkis. You're the luckiest man alive, Calland," said the captain. "I can see your daughter in you."

"And from what I can gather from my daughter, you're best the captain of the greatest crew that ever lived."

"That's about right," said Clara. "Except when he's wrong, of course."

"I shall ignore that, cadet, until I can assign you to slops duty," said Captain Malkis. "Now Mr. Calland, I believe you saw these troops?"

"Yes. They're readying for action, and we saw motor-trucks coming in on the railway."

Lampy kept quiet, thinking about it all. Thinking and wondering, as Jack gave the details to the captain. He was a noticing feller was Jack. Counted things . . . Lampy noticed something himself. The mole hadn't moved.

Then the lieutenant got down, in a hurry. Came up to the captain. "Sir. Pardon me for interrupting, sir, but the patient in there is delirious. Insisting he has to be back before the eighteenth . . . *for the attack*." The lieutenant paused. "That's tomorrow, sir. I don't think we can dig holes and wait it out. If it goes ahead, if they succeed, sir, we'll be trapped out here, even if the Imperial forces don't find us. And the summer is still coming. We'll need to get back."

"Moving thirty-seven people. Some of them injured," the captain pointed to Lampy. "But not until you've seen to that foot, lieutenant. I'll get Ambrose and start to get things in train."

"Give him the instruction, sir, and you're to rest. MO's orders," said Lieutenant Willis.

"And the MO trumps the skipper," said the captain. "Very well, Willis. My back hurts a bit, I'll admit."

The lieutenant was deft and quick . . . and it hurt like billy-o when he moved Lampy's foot. "I'd guess you have a broken fibula, the smaller of the two bones in your leg. Breaks of the tibia or fibula when jumping or landing awkwardly is one of the more common fractures, and I'm fairly certain that's what you've done. We need to splint and immobilize that. You're not moving it for the next three or four weeks, son." He turned to the girl who hovered next to him. "We need two of those splints. I'm going to put one either side. He really needs plaster-of-Paris, but strapping in is the best I can do." He turned back to Lampy. "You need to keep the foot up as much as possible. That'll bring the swelling down."

"Will . . . will I be able to walk again?" Lampy was ashamed that he let his fear show.

"Oh, yes. I should think in six weeks you'll be right as rain. If you don't keep it still, preferably in plaster-of-Paris, it won't heal and you won't ever get mobility back again, though."

Lampy kept his foot dead still through the strapping process. He needed that foot, to hunt and to live as a man should live.

CHAPTER 22

"It's going to look a sight, sir, but I think we can do it," said Lieutenant Ambrose to the captain. "We can get most of the seriously injured inside the vehicle. It'll be crowded, but possible. There are handrails and running boards on the outside of the mole. We've collected some rope from the launch gear, and we're trying to unbolt the landing gear, and we'll make a sort of trailer. Then we'll put the horses on a long string behind that, just in case. We're not going to move fast, just steadily westward. As the crow flies, or rather, the *Wedgetail* would have flown, we can't be more than thirty to forty miles out. Of course, we have to collect more fuel, and it isn't going to be a straight route back. But five or six hours should do it."

Tim had a feeling the lieutenant was thinking of travel by sea or by air. But he wasn't going to comment. It didn't matter that much, did it? He and Clara were back together with the *Cuttlefish* crew, and that was the important thing. Clara seemed to quite like making decisions. Tim made them if he had to. He was happy to have people he trusted making them for him, after the last while. But of course the captain noticed and asked his opinion.

"Uh. Probably longer, sir," Tim answered. "The up and down and going round seems to take more time. And the steam mole can probably push through anything, but it's not worth it. If we get stuck we have a huge problem, so we need to take care."

"I told you he was officer material, sir," said Lieutenant Ambrose.

"I'm not so sure I want to be!" said Tim, truthfully. "It's . . . it's a lot of responsibility."

That made the captain smile and the lieutenant laugh. "I think if we could get rid of candidate officers who didn't realize that, we'd start with half as many and be twice as well off," said the captain. "Most of them only learn that later. When will we be ready to start loading?"

"Two hours, sir. The question I have is what happens to the flying wing?"

"Ask the copilot. They may hope to recover it, or destroy it to stop it falling into enemy hands."

So Tim was sent to do so, while the lieutenants and the captain organized rosters of who would be where and do what.

The copilot was with the surviving engineer, helping to unbolt the two wheels from the flying wing, with half a dozen of the submariners helping. He was glad enough to step aside and speak to Tim.

"So you're the lad who wasn't dead," he said cheerfully. "The wrath of heaven was nice compared to that skipper of yours talking to the mob at Dajarra about what they'd done to you."

"Uh. His crew is pretty important to him."

"I got that!" said the copilot. "Now, what do you want, youngster?"

"The captain wants to know what needs to be done about the flying wing when we leave here. Do we set fire to her or something?"

"Standing orders are to destroy it, if possible, only if we fall behind enemy lines. And this is still part of Westralia. They might send a lifter-airship and haul her out. She's not that badly damaged, poor old bird. We'll take what we need and leave the rest."

"Has she got anything we can use as fuel?"

The copilot laughed. "I'll ask the engineer what he thinks of the possibility of running your machine on aero-fuel. We can get the two final reserve tanks out, easy enough. They're only twenty gallons each. I reckon flying wings from down south will be over here and searching by midmorning tomorrow. Might be useful for signal fires if the steam contraption doesn't make it."

Tim found himself feeling defensive about the "steam contraption," but left it at that and went back to the captain to report. And an hour and forty-eight minutes later the steam mole and its contrived trailer were ready to go. Tim found it quite funny that he and Clara were the only two with any experience driving the steam mole, and so would take turns in doing so.

"Besides, you're fairly small, and the cab is quite crowded," said Lieutenant Ambrose cheerfully. "You get to hang on the outside first, though. Clara's driving."

"It's rough country here, and she's better than I am," said Tim. "She's had more practice."

"So she told us when someone suggested the engineer from the flying wing might drive," said Lieutenant Ambrose.

Tim was assigned to the makeshift trailer, which had been bolted together and then roped onto the back. All it had to save the passengers from bouncing as high as the moon was the fact that the mole flattened the bumps with its endless treads. The bars had been padded with some of the sheepskins from the flying wing, and Tim was grateful for them. He'd have been more grateful for some springs on the wheels. He said so to the copilot.

"It's worse when you're landing. One rock and she wants to dig her wing tip in."

"I hadn't thought of that," admitted Tim.

"The new wings have this arrangement of a magnet in a tube, but I'd have to get the engineer to explain it to you. Flying and navigation is my thing!"

He was only a few years older than Tim, and they fell into conversation about navigation first and then the rest of the world. He was intensely curious about that. Tim found him easy to talk to, not like most of the Westralians who had avoided talking to him. He said so.

"Ah. Depends on who you get in with and where they come from. I grew up on a farm in South Australia, and I only had black kids to play with, and my da made a point of getting on with the local tribe.

But some farmers didn't, and also the railway . . . well a lot of the workers are scared blacks will take their jobs. Bit stupid when there are three jobs for every willing man, but the bosses encourage it. 'Give trouble and we'll get the blacks in.' Leads to nasty situations. But I never really heard of it going to murder before."

"It happens more than you know, then. Lampy's uncle was shot for fun down at someplace called Boiler or something." It had been niggling at Tim like a toothache since they got to *Cuttlefish*'s crew and he'd been told by several of his friends what a good time they'd had in Westralia. If it didn't affect you, you didn't know about it.

"Boulia! There was a big fuss about the railway-men shooting some old abo down there. But it all turned into a tall story. There was one witness who swore black-and-blue he'd seen it, and laid charges. You should talk to Sergeant Morgan about it. He was the investigating officer, and nearly got himself tossed out of the force because he insisted it did happen. But they never found a body, and the bloke who was accused denied it, and so did his mates. Morgan searched the area himself. I mean there have been a few incidents, but it is against the law."

"Yeah, like what the shift-captain tried to do to me. They'd have got away with it, too, if it hadn't been for luck and Clara, and the *Cuttlefish* crew," said Tim.

The copilot absorbed this. "Well. Westralia's not perfect. The abos can't vote like they used to do in Vic and New South Wales before direct Imperial rule, but they fall under the same law as everyone else here in Westralia. Not like in Queensland, with the aboriginal statute list. That's better and worse. But the truth is, I suppose, the police and magistrates turn a blind eye to a lot of the abuse."

"The people who picked me up out of the desert didn't think much of them. Oh. We seem to be stopping."

"Looks like a good spot to collect fuel."

It was. A tangle of long-dead trees from somewhere farther north had been left here by a long-ago flood. It was hard to imagine all of this under water, but the railway had been built to withstand it.

There were lots of people, but still only one bow saw, an axe, and a hatchet. The lieutenants were organizing so that they all got maximum use, but it was still going to be slow going. Tim looked at it and had a bright idea. "Sir, we could start the drill head and chop it up a bit," he suggested to Lieutenant Willis.

"And give me a whole lot more patients, probably," said the lieutenant. "Hoy, Amby, what do you think of this idea from young Barnabas?" He explained it.

"Ask Thorne. We haven't got anyone higher up from engineering here," said Ambrose. "Might work. Might turn it all to sawdust."

Thorne suggested they try it on one of the edges, so they did.

The results were . . . interesting. The wood, old and dry, got flung, rather than cut. Quite a lot of it did get broken. Some landed on the mole, and the dust made it difficult to see. "Not exactly brilliant," said Lieutenant Ambrose, "but worth trying on the main lot."

"If everyone stands clear," said Lieutenant Willis. "*A long way* clear."

So they did that, and then it was more a case of hauling the smaller, broken pieces of wood back to the tender and even onto the little trailer. It took a lot more wood than coal to run the mole. In the gathering dusk Tim walked off to go and collect some more pieces, when a voice called him from a few rocks on the side of the dry watercourse. Tim went over to see who wanted what, not thinking twice about it.

It was only when he saw the spear and the black face of its wielder grinning at him that he realized it hadn't been one of the crew, but the man who had taken him to the camp on the first night. "These your people, Tim Barnabas?"

Tim nodded. "Yes, they came looking for me on the flying wing. I'm trying to get them back home."

"We see them fall out of the sky. You tellem go quick-quick, 'cause lots of soldiers in trucks comin'. Maybe seventy trucks. We goin' north. Thems comin' down your tail, maybe a day's walk back now. They're coming faster than we walk." At this he turned and slipped away.

Tim turned and ran himself. This news needed to get straight to the Old Man. And Clara, because she was driving, and was good at backing him up when he needed it. "Captain Malkis, sir. I just had one of the aboriginals, the ones that saved me out there, come up and tell me that the convoy of soldiers is coming. I don't know how well they counted them, sir, but he says seventy trucks are a day's walk away from us."

Tim had been afraid that the captain might not believe him, but the captain showed no such doubts. "Tell the lieutenants to get a move on, Barnabas. How well does this thing do at night for lights, Miss Calland?"

Tim heard Clara say "pretty good," as he ran to find the lieutenants. Any thought of stopping or slowing for the night was not happening.

Soon they were bouncing on their way again.

※

Clara focused on driving. The steam mole's steady thumping helped to drown some of the more distressing groans when she hit a bad bump—things she'd barely noticed on her search for Tim. Well, they might have been in a flatter piece of the desert. She'd realized by now that it wasn't all the same. Lieutenant Willis, poor man, was trying to pad and strap and protect people as they trundled along. He'd used most of the precious supply of laudanum, and still McLoughlin and the two men with compound fractures were in considerable pain. McLoughlin was delirious and babbling—alternating between blowing up things and talking to his mother.

The moon helped, but it still took a great deal of concentration to pick the best and smoothest path possible. The one headlight stabbed ahead in the darkness, and they tried to keep a compass bearing. And then news came from those perched on top of the tender.

There was a ribbon of lights far off in the desert.

"Will they see our light?" asked Clara warily.

"It's not that likely, Miss. We're looking back at them, and our light shines forward."

"Where are they?"

"They're behind us, somewhere out on the plains a little to the southwest of us. They must have scouted a route."

"We've been going uphill slowly but steadily," said Clara. "Tim said the termite run went along the higher ground to avoid flooding."

"Well," said Nichol, who had climbed down to report this, "we're guessing they're still about as far off as we can see. They disappear every now and again."

"I just don't think we can go any faster," said Clara.

"The mole is built more for endurance than speed," said the captain. "We need to get news to the power stations and Sheba as soon as possible. I'm just not sure why the vehicles would be south of us. Sheba is to the north."

"Rougher country for driving up that way, maybe," suggested the flying wing's engineer. "Maybe they want to take over the clankers and arrive by surprise."

"Maybe their trucks can run on rails," said her father. "It wouldn't be that hard to engineer for. I assume there are rails in the tunnels?"

"Monorail overhead, two below," said Clara.

"Well, they can move really fast if they can run on rails . . . until they meet an oncoming train. That could be ugly."

"Not if they cut the cable," said Clara. "Then the Westralian trains won't go anywhere. They're hauled by cable, not locomotives."

"Well . . ." said her father. "How's the foot, Lampy? We can ride a lot faster than this and give them warning."

"Someone else can, sir," said Lieutenant Willis. "Not you. You're staying with your wife. Both of you under my eye. I've been told you fell over during that wood parade."

"Lack of food and a lot of exercise," said her father. "And not having ridden for some years, I admit. I'm pretty stiff. But I could still do it."

"That may be, but we have thirty-seven people, and twenty-six have no injuries at all," said Captain Malkis.

"But how many of them can ride well?"

"Ah. Most of my men are from Under-London."

"I can ride," said Linda. "I used to ride every day until we moved into Ceduna. I still ride two afternoons a week. I was hoping to take you, Clara."

"We can't send you, Linda," said the captain, putting Clara in mind of his reaction to her volunteering to do the diving on the submarine. "Ask around. Get young Barnabas onto it, and no, I won't believe he can ride. Besides, I think he needs to take over from the driver a little. I need real riders, not heroes."

But the answer that Tim brought back was not what Captain Malkis wanted to hear. The only person who had ridden at all was the copilot, and that not for a good five years.

※

Lampy heard this with mixed feelings. He had no love for Westralia, but he knew what the army would do to Jack, Jack's family, and the rest of them if they caught up with them, let alone to him. The rest of these people . . . it was odd, but maybe because they were used to Tim, they treated him, if anything, with respect. And if the soldiers captured Sheba, and the *Cuttlefish* people were still free . . . well, there was no way they could survive living out here in the desert. Not with summer coming.

It seemed Tim understood, too. "Sir," he said to the captain. "If you're going to ask this of Lampy . . . he needs some protection.

They shot his uncle for no reason. Sir, I see some of the men are wearing police uniforms. Could he at least have that to wear? They won't shoot at the uniform, and he could go with the copilot."

"I'll do that, and better," said Lieutenant Ambrose, clinging just outside the door. "You remember, sir, I still have some temporary commissions. And as the ranking representative of the Westralian Mounted Police I am authorized to use them. I can make you into a policeman, Lampy. Anyone shoots you, besides the fact they will have to answer to us, they're shooting a policeman. You are entitled to shoot back, and I gather the Westralians will hang anyone who shoots a policeman, no matter what the reason."

"Me? A policeman?" Lampy could scarcely believe his ears.

"Too right," said the copilot. "And you could even make them investigate your uncle's murder."

"I'm a blackfeller. I can't be a policeman." Still. It was an odd thought. Something to show that old nun back at the mission school who had said he was born to be hanged.

"You could," said Jack. "It'd be a good thing, I think. It will change the way people see you."

"You'd be with me," said the copilot. "I just am not sure about finding my way on my own."

"And me," said Linda, firmly. "They won't touch you while you're with us. And yes, I am going, sir."

"If they ride north they'll be farther off from the invaders, and moving faster than us," said Clara. "When we hit the termite run we'll go south unless we can see the power station. If they go north Linda will be farther away and safer, and we won't have all our eggs in one basket."

"Two horses apiece, nearly full moon, three of them. I think they'd be reasonably safe," said Mary. "Yes, Captain. I worry, too. But Clara is right. Linda might just be safer without us."

"Provided you can find her some trousers that fit better than those ones I had," said Clara. "I'm rubbed raw in a few places, and that was only for an hour or two."

The girl was bigger than Jack's kid. A swap for the railwayman's trousers and with one of the smaller submariners and she'd be right. Lampy was just surprised that she was willing to do it. She was Westralian, not one of these *Cuttlefish* people. Jack's 'change the way people see you' was still running around his head.

"I'll do it," he said slowly. "If you make me a policeman for that. Are you sure I can ride with this thing on my foot, Mr. Lieutenant?"

The lieutenant nodded. "Your foot will swell and be sore, but it's not going to be a disaster. Just don't fall off."

"It ain't something a bloke plans on," said Lampy, grinning. "I'll do me best to land on me head if I take a purler then."

They laughed. But they laughed with him. And a lot of them said things like, "Good for you, Lampy."

A bloke could get to like this mob. Even a bloke in a new policeman's slouch hat and jacket, with a letter in the top pocket, saying he was now a special constable and a member of the Westralian Mounted Police.

⁂

Linda wondered just how clever her bravado had been. She wasn't really like Clara, much as she'd like to be. Clara, she was sure, would have jumped to be able to ride off into the dark in borrowed trousers. Right now Linda would have rather jumped back onto the crowded steam mole. But instead the three of them rode off in the moonlight, with no real way of knowing how far they had to go.

She also wondered just what her father would have said. He was the one who encouraged her to ride. Little had he ever guessed what she'd do with it, she thought. Lampy had got the measure of them very quickly, she realized. He might just be an aborigine, but he rode as if he was a part of that horse, and it was he who set the pace, and he decided when they stuck to a fast walk and where it was safe to go a little faster. It was obvious the copilot Ned could ride, but he seemed happy to take orders. Linda might have felt a bit different about it otherwise, but soon realized he was dead right, and Lampy was no fool.

When they slowed to a walk, Ned said, "You know, Lampy, Tim was talking to me about what happened to your uncle. I want to introduce you to Sergeant Morgan. He tried to find your uncle's body. He couldn't get any trackers to help him, and the man that shot him said it never happened."

"It did, Mister. I was there," said Lampy grimly.

"I believe you. That's why Morgan needs you. He only had one witness come forward, and the others all denied it had happened. And they never found the body."

"Uncle's still there. I went back. He was like my father to me, that man. I wanted to bury him proper. Couldn't bring myself to do it. I was just a kid."

He isn't that old now, thought Linda, absorbing this.

"Well, I think it would be time to do it. And to bring the person who did it to justice."

Lampy was silent a while. Then he said, "I reckon."

"I'll back you up," said Ned.

"Um. Me too," said Linda.

Lampy flashed them a grin in the moonlight. Touched his hat. "I'm a copper now. I'll do it meself."

There was another pause. "Thank yous, both," he said awkwardly.

※

After the riders left, Tim had taken a spell of driving. Then, when he'd felt his concentration was not at its best anymore, Clara had taken over. The convoy out in the dark was closer now. The topmast men reckoned they were about five or six miles back now, but still southwest a little.

And then when Tim was just coming in to do a second spell, to their relief, the headlight showed the mound of the termite run.

"Which way do we turn?" he asked.

"I thought we said south unless we can see a power station," said Clara, peering at it.

"It's a gamble, really," said Tim. "We have no way of knowing where we are on the line. We could be, say, nineteen miles from one side and one from the other. Or worse, if we're on the last section, the termite run hits some deep ground for a few miles, no mound on the surface, and then comes to the surface and ends. We could get there after the invasion, if they're going straight to the power station."

"Nonetheless we will bear south," said the captain. "We can see the convoy lights. We can turn and flee. They have bigger fish than us to fry, I suspect."

"Ah. I think I see an answer," said Tim. "That's an emergency exit hatch, sir. If we stop for a minute I can go down and see if there's a cable running there. If there isn't, we're on the section they're drilling and need to go north."

They stopped, and Tim took the Davy lamp, and along with Submariner Gordon, climbed down. It made Tim feel uneasy and claustrophobic, going back down into that tunnel. "We'd better hold our breath," he said, before opening the inner door.

They both took several deep breaths and went in.

To Tim's delight the cables were there, and running. That meant he'd held his breath for nothing, but that wasn't so much to ask.

The steam mole turned south. Now they ran without their lights, because they would be visible.

They could see the dark bulk of the power station chimneys before they got to the next emergency hatch.

But they could also see the lights of the convoy turning north. Were they heading straight for the power station, too?

CHAPTER 23

Linda had been so glad to spot the ridge of the termite mound and head north after about an hour's ride. They'd occasionally caught sight of the single light of the steam mole at first, and since then, nothing but darkness and the moonlit desert. She'd begun to wonder if somehow they'd missed it, or had much farther to go than she'd imagined.

"All right! We change horses," said Lampy, plainly also relieved.

"How are you doing?" asked the copilot

"Foot's gettin' a bit sore," admitted Lampy. "But I c'n ride. That soldier, he stayed in the saddle even when he was passing out. I c'n do better. Can't have far now."

"What do we do with the horses we've ridden?" asked Linda.

"Hook the reins up an' leave 'em," said Lampy, already gingerly lifting his sore foot over. "They follow us or they don't. We need to make a little speed see. Those blokes are goin' straight to where they goin'. We done one side of a triangle."

"Oh," said Linda, absorbing this. "So they have less distance to do. I hadn't thought of that."

"Yeah, them nuns taught me a few things," said Lampy, managing a smile by the flash of white teeth in the dark. You could hear he was sore, just in the way he spoke. "Think we can manage a trot."

They did several sessions when the moon showed flat ground and no obstacles, making more speed. Eventually Lampy said, obviously through gritted teeth, "I think I keep to a canter or a walk now."

"Is it bad?" asked Linda.

"Nothin' I can't manage," he said tersely. "If I have to stop, yous go on without me. Can't be far now. I reckon we done maybe eight-ten mile."

"It's twenty miles between power stations," said the copilot.

"I'll try to stay in the saddle, eh?" said Lampy.

But he wasn't the one to fall off.

It was the copilot. Something must have made that tired horse stumble just as Linda smelled something utterly delightful: coal smoke.

They pulled their horses up as the copilot sat on the ground, using words he would be embarrassed for his mother to hear. His horse had trotted off into the dark a bit and stopped, standing and looking at them.

"You right?" Lampy was already starting to dismount.

"Don't get down," said the copilot. "Just keep going. My legs . . . they've had it. I can't stand up, and I've done my wrist. But I'm all right. You keep going. That's an order. They can fetch me." Linda got down. "Mount up, Miss," said the copilot. "Lampy can't go on alone. And there are a lot of people relying on us."

"But . . . but we can't just leave you."

"Go and get help! Ride, the two of you."

"We be back," said Lampy. "Bin able to smell the place for a while now. Reckon it's not more than a mile."

They cantered now, and, sure enough, there was the dark bulk of the power station ahead. They rode straight to the upper doors, and Lampy didn't even get out of the saddle. He just leaned down and opened them, and they rode into the corridor that led down into the power station on horseback, both of them yelling their lungs out. They got quite far in before doors started opening. Obviously at this time of morning most of the power station staff was fast asleep.

A bleary-eyed man in a singlet stepped into the passage and looked at them. "Bloody hell! It's a drunken boong! I'll beat the . . ."

Linda prodded her horse forward. "You idiot!" she screamed at him.

He rubbed his eyes as Linda jumped down in front of him. "Uh. Miss . . . ? Who are you?"

She was shaking with rage and reaction, and slapped him. "Half the British Army is behind us. And we've got an injured man out there. Get everyone!" She jibbed her horse. "Quickly!"

"Better do it, man," said Lampy. Linda saw he was swaying in the saddle.

"Help me get him down!" she said to the man she'd just slapped, as another fellow in his nightclothes appeared.

"What's going on? What's the boong doing in a wimp's clothes?"

Linda and the first man helped Lampy down. She felt like a volcano of rage was bubbling in her. "He *is* a policeman. And he's a hero who has ridden halfway across the country with a broken leg to save us. You *will* treat him with respect!"

"Uh . . . what?" said the man, plainly nonplussed.

"Can either of you ride?" she demanded.

"Yeah," said the first man. "Sorry Miss. I . . . wasn't really expecting this."

That, thought Linda, was one of the silliest things ever said. "Get up on Lampy's horse," she ordered. "The copilot of the flying wing is out there, about half a mile away. I'll go with you. You!" She pointed at the other man. "You need to get everyone up and see to Lampy. He'll tell you everything, but you need to see Sheba is warned. There's a convoy of trucks full of British soldiers coming!"

"Bloody hell!" said the third man on the scene. "We heard about the wing being down last night, Miss! A clanker come through with the search party. Here, Fred, get moving. We need the Puffing Billy fired up. Johnny, go with her, jump to it."

And things began to happen.

On the ride back to find the copilot with the man she'd slapped, Linda started shaking. "I . . . I'm sorry I hit you," she said.

"No worries, Missy," he said, laughing. "I been slapped before, but not with as good a reason. How far are we going?"

"I hope we can find him. It's just over the ridge."

They got up there, and her fellow rider gave a mighty, "*Coooeee!*" yell into the darkness.

They got a call back. The copilot came toward them with three horses accompanying him. He clung to the saddle with one hand. "I was coming. My thighs have gone into spasms."

The railway-man jumped down and stopped him tumbling out of the saddle. "Here, mate. You're nearly there."

"I reckon I must be," said the copilot. "Have you blokes got warning off to Sheba yet?"

"Puffing Billy will be ready by the time we get back I'd guess," said the railway-man. "Now, I'm going to get up with you mate. You hold onto me."

It didn't seem so far now.

※

Lampy felt very exposed, on his own in the railway place. But the third bloke on the scene in the power station said, "Here, take my arm, sir. Let's get you somewhere to sit down. I'm Sidney Harris, the manager of this station. Um. Could you tell me what's going on?" They stepped into the first room and Lampy lowered himself into the chair. "Are you all right, sir? Can I get you anything?" the station manager asked.

"I just got a broken leg," said Lampy, lifting it onto the desk, not caring that it was some whitefeller's desk all full of papers and his foot wasn't clean. It was swollen and sore, and it throbbed. "You got to tell 'em in Sheba, they got a few thousand British Hussars, Dragoons, and Fusiliers on their way. They're maybe seven-eight mile from the railway."

"We'll send you with the service locomotive, sir. My men will do their best to defend this place, but we have only ten rifles in the store. Um, what was it that the young lady said about the flying wing? Are there any other survivors?"

"Yeah. They're with the steam mole. Most of 'em alive, except one bloke. Some injured quite bad. They're making for the line. We come on ahead to give warning. They'll go south. What is there south o' this?"

"Dajarra, sir. There are quite a lot of men there, they came through last night for the search."

There was a clatter of hooves. "Ah! They're back, I hope," said Lampy. "I told Jack I'd look after that girl."

The station manager smiled despite everything. "After what I saw out there, I don't think she needs help."

"Too right," said Lampy, thinking about it too. "Go see, man."

It was them.

And five minutes later Lampy had his first Westralian train trip, as Linda did her best to strap up the copilot's wrist. As the engineer and his fireman pushed the little loco as fast as they could, Lampy had time, finally, to think about being called "sir." They'd left his rifle with the station. The station manager looked at it a little oddly. "Took it off a British soldier," said Lampy.

"I didn't even know the wi—Westralian Police were out there."

He might have wondered why they all laughed at him. But he had a station to defend.

※

Men with lights came running out of the station when Clara had the bright idea of sounding the steam whistle, as the steam mole trundled closer.

There were a lot of them, and some on horseback. "Hello!" called the first one to reach them. "What have we got here?"

He appeared, in the moonlight, to be a mounted policeman.

"People from the flying wing!" yelled Lieutenant Ambrose.

"Hooray! We were coming to look for you! It's the blokes from the flying wing!"

Cheers spread.

"We've got half the British Army on our tail!" yelled the lieutenant to the Westralian policeman riding next to them.

By the time they got to the station, that, too, had spread. They were greeted at the entrance by a Westralian policeman in uniform with pips on his shoulders.

"Evening, Inspector Johns," called the lieutenant.

"Lieutenant Ambrose! I'm glad to see you. I see you found the missing steam mole." The inspector took a deep breath. "But for heaven's sake tell me Max Darlington's daughter is all right, too."

"She was last we saw her. She went ahead with the horses, going northwest a couple of hours back. They might be at the next station along by now. She's got two good men with her, an aboriginal and the copilot."

"Right. Well at least she wasn't killed in the crash," said the inspector, looking as if that was a huge weight off his shoulders. The rest was something he could deal with. "Now, what was this about the British Army?"

"We've got a convoy of a few thousand Hussars, Lowland Dragoons, and Inniskillen Fusiliers in trucks a few miles to the east," said the lieutenant.

"Should be able to see them from the top of the cooling roof," volunteered Tim.

"Good lad," said Captain Malkis. "Take one of the topmast men up there. We need to know where they are. As you can see, Johns, we've found our prodigals! But we have some injured men . . ."

"There are two doctors here, down from Sheba," said the inspector. "Sergeant, get the doctors up here on the double!"

Tim had Gordon with him. The submariner had one of the best records for sighting ships at sea. The two of them raced up the steel ladders into the high roof, leaving the organization to happen below. They were able to climb out onto a platform put there to service the high cooling vents, and to look across the dark desert.

They could see the lights of the convoy. Only they weren't quite where Tim had been expecting. They were heading north. The two of them watched the convoy in silence. "If they keep going that direction," said Gordon, "they're going to hit the tunnel somewhere between this station and the next. We'll be cut off."

"Might just be avoiding some of that rough country," said Tim, thoughtfully. "We just drove more or less straight, but the mole will go over things a truck won't."

"Could be. You shimmy down and tell the skipper. He better organize a watch up here."

So Tim went.

Down below things were in a ferment. Some of it involved shouting. Captain Malkis, however, seemed to have assumed overall command just by being himself. Tim ran up, saluted, and reported what they'd seen to him. The captain gave orders and soon Gordon had a second watchman and a set of men to relay messages. Tim found himself coopted for another job. "The steam mole is being refueled with coal. Unfortunately, Mr. Barnabas," said Inspector Johns, "we didn't anticipate having it back or needing it. And we deputized the normal driver and his fireman to assist Sergeant Morgan in taking the prisoners back to the lock-up in Sheba. They didn't come back, as the clanker was used to transport the men and the horses for tomorrow's search. We've got two aboriginal trackers, and the idea is to use the mole to transport the injured away from here, as it will possibly be attacked. We need you to drive the steam mole."

"Clara could do it." Tim thought he was being quite clever. It would get her away.

"Er. Legally that might be a bit tricky. You're still an employee of the railroad. She isn't."

Tim looked at the man. This didn't seem like the time to argue about petty legal points. "I guess you'll have to forget the law and choose the better driver . . . sir."

"I could send both of you," said the inspector with just a trace of irritation. "Look, if we manage to brush through all of this—and the flying wings will be here by midmorning—I want that young girl in the minimum of possible trouble."

"That's it! Excuse me, sir. I need to go and speak to the captain."

Tim ran and found the captain sitting down. "My back is a bit sore, and I made the mistake of telling someone who asked," he explained without being asked. "At the moment I am giving orders and arbitrating. The police, miners, railway-men, and *Cuttlefish* crew don't take orders from each other very well. The police should be in charge, but it turns out the militia have the final authority in war, and the railroad employees are automatically militia members. And the miners don't like the police anyway. So here we are, facing danger, and they're bickering instead of organizing their defense. They come to me, and I tell them to listen to Inspector Johns, who is doing a good job. About all that has happened that is effective is the Puffing Billy has been sent to carry warning."

Tim didn't want to tell the captain he had been resisting authority, too. "Sir, I think I've worked out what they're doing, and why."

"Ah. Tell me."

"Well, sir, you remember Clara's father said they might want to get inside the tunnels and use them to move? And McLoughlin is a sapper. They plan to blow their way straight into the tunnel. It won't take much in a lot of places. It only runs half below the surface. The tunnel is a sun shield."

"Yes, they could do that, but they could access them from the power stations," said the captain, thoughtfully.

"Then they'd waste time, sir. And daylight is not that far off. A flying wing that was armed could shoot their convoy to shreds. The copilot was talking to me about their fighters, with Gatling guns. The British airships use machine guns and bombs, the Westralians use

Gatling guns and rockets. Once the convoy is inside the tunnel . . . they're safe and invisible. That's what they plan. And everyone will be defending outside . . . and they'll come up inside and underneath."

The captain got up. "Lieutenants," he bellowed.

Then he turned to Tim. "We can't fight them above ground. We've got twenty-one rifles and fourteen Westralian police with revolvers. But in the tunnels . . . we can. We have a steam mole. And we have experience."

"The Westralian policeman wanted me to take the mole with the injured away into the desert, sir."

"Well you can't," said Captain Malkis, firmly. "That idea worked best for defense of the indefensible. There is no point in moving people. The British are not coming here. I need it. And you, and probably Miss Calland, and some horses. And someone who knows the lay of the land along the tunnel. We need a deep section. Get me Johns as well. We need to stop his crews from attempting to block the northbound tunnels. We'll be going that way."

CHAPTER 24

Duke Malcolm was in his headquarters listening to the report from General Von Stross. The truck convoy carried a Marconi transmitter and their progress was being relayed. So far the information obtained about the flattest route had largely been accurate. The scouting work, with aboriginal trackers, had been good, it seemed. The strike force would be safely under cover before dawn. Even if, somehow, the Westralians had word of the impending attack . . .

The duke heard someone shout, "Atten . . . *shun!*" He turned to find his staff coming to attention and clicking their heels and saluting. He rose and bowed respectfully.

Even he had to do that when the King just . . . dropped in, with Albert in tow.

"I asked Field Marshal Viscount Von Belstad to tell me what was happening with this gold mine, Malcolm. He said the whole thing was underway already. You promised to tell me."

"I had to set it forward in the early hours of this morning, Your Majesty," said Duke Malcolm. "And how is your new boat?"

"Now, Malcolm, don't distract me," said the King. "I've ordered one of those new hydroplanes. What's that fellow interrupting us for?" he said, pointing an irritable finger at the speaker on the Marconi transmitter.

"It's the radio report from Australia. From the strike force I have aimed at Sheba," explained the duke. Ernest was capable of ordering the machine's summary removal to the Tower of London.

"Ah. Well, how is it going?"

As if he were deaf, thought Malcolm. "Well, Your Majesty, I believe the sappers have just blown a way down into the tunnel and the engineers are busy making it drivable. The vehicles are all fitted with double-ridged tires and will be able to use the rails as a roadway. They should be able to cover the fifty miles to be inside Sheba an hour after dawn."

"But it's nearly four in the afternoon. Jolly slow effort, Malcolm. My new boat would do that in forty minutes."

"It's five in the morning there, Your Majesty. Now about this hydroplane of yours . . ."

Duke Malcolm led the King away from the radio room to a drawing room, where the King could tell him all about it.

※

The telephone line to Sheba had been busy with official calls for the last ten minutes or so. Alice and Port Wyndham had been alerted, as had the military command of Westralia. They were a long way from their help, Linda knew. Still, the armed flying wings had been scrambled. Some were possibly flying already. Two armed wings and three search craft had apparently left at about two that morning anyway, after the incident they weren't sending unarmed flying wings here again. Now, at last, the operator put her through.

"Hello. Mrs. Leonie Darlington speaking, who is calling?" came the voice from three-quarters of a continent away.

"It's me. Linda."

"*Linda!*" the shriek came down the telephone line. "Darling, are you all right? Max! Max! It's Linda!"

"I'm fine. Safe in Sheba." Linda was rather surprised at just how happy her stepmother sounded.

Then her father's voice came on the telephone. She wasn't used to it cracking like that.

"No, I'm not hurt at all. Father, teaching me to ride was the best thing you ever did for me."

"Make that the best thing he ever did for Westralia," said the copilot.

✳

The sky to the east was beginning to pale. Tim and Clara would have known that if they'd been above ground. Instead they were digging. Well, the little steam mole was digging. The rock was rather hard for it, and Tim just hoped they had enough time.

He'd heard the explosions a little earlier, as the Imperial troops blew their way into the tunnels about four miles south. He wondered if they could hear them digging in here, or if they would work out what it meant.

"The drill sound has changed. I think we must be through into the tunnel," said Clara. And sure enough the little mole lurched abruptly forward and nosedived into the tunnel, her endless tracks spinning.

✳

For a horrible moment Clara thought they were stuck. She put the tracks in neutral, then twitched and wriggled each one. They didn't have time for this . . . but it had to be done. She cut power to the drill head, and the steam mole gained traction and pushed into the tunnel.

She heard Tim sigh with relief. They bumped down the tracks into the darkness . . . only that was definitely lights in the distance, coming toward them.

"Nearly there," said Tim. "Yep. There it is."

Clara pulled the little scout mole to a halt. The tunnel was dead straight and those were oncoming trucks . . . at speed. Would the mole have time?

Thorne, the artificer from the *Cuttlefish*, was already screwing the sealer into the steam whistle pressure valve. Other men shoveled extra coal into the boiler.

The lights were coming closer. Something tinged and ricocheted off the ceiling. And then there was a flare of light farther down the tunnel. It was only aero-fuel burning, but Clara just hoped it would hold them. They ran back to the emergency exit and left the dark of the tunnel, climbing up into the grey, cold desert predawn.

Behind them, down in the tunnel, coal fed at its fastest along the conveyor into the furnace of the little steam mole. It sat jammed across the deepest section of tunnel, where the drillers had cut through rock to keep the grade nice and gradual. Steam pressure built in the mole's boiler. It would have nowhere else left to go very soon.

As for Clara, Tim, and the rest, they did have somewhere to go, and very soon, too. The horses were waiting.

They were three hundred yards off when the horses took fright. The ground shook, dust rose, and a dull boom echoed. Clara clung to her saddle. So did Tim, but he, crazy boy, was laughing. "You never told me this 'riding' was such fun."

That, Clara was sure, was not what the men underground were having. The Imperial soldiers had cut the cable. They thought they couldn't meet an oncoming train . . .

They hadn't thought of one from behind. The tunneling steam mole had been put on the turntable and was coming from Dajarra, steaming toward them, drill head turning, smoke belching, using up the oxygen in the tunnel.

Captain Malkis had been sure the sappers with the Imperial forces would stop it with explosives before it crushed them and their vehicles. It wasn't fast, just heavy and solid. And the second steam mole was ready and waiting if they broke through that one.

Clara was glad she wasn't facing the mole coming puffing down the tunnel. They probably would stop it. But that would leave them trapped in a deep section of the termite run. There were escape hatches . . . two of them, which the policemen, miners, and railway-men with the twenty or so rifles they had, and Molotov cocktails, could seal quite effectively. They planned to let them surrender . . . and come out one-by-one.

That was the idea, anyway. The only way the few armed Westralians could handle the numbers of Imperial soldiers was to let them out in a trickle. The captain had contingency plans in case it all went wrong. He said battle plans almost always did.

Clara and Tim had no part in this, however. They were with the desert group, just out from Dajarra, watching for signals.

"You have more desert experience than the rest of them," said Captain Malkis firmly when she'd tried to protest. "Leadership goes where it is needed most, not where it wants to, Cadet."

It was a kind of compliment, really. From him, it was enough to make her glow with pleasure and not even try to argue.

※

Duke Malcolm drank his second glass, and Ernest and Albert were onto their second bottle, and quite merry, with the duke quietly glancing at the clock, when Major Simmer burst in. "Your Grace . . . sorry to interrupt, Your Majesty . . . Uh, Your Majesty, I need to speak to His Grace on a matter of utmost urgency."

"So. An accounting of Sheba? Those uppity Westralians asking for terms?" said King Ernest, who could absorb alcohol like a sponge. Prince Albert beamed vacantly. He could not, and seldom drank at all.

"Er . . ." The officer stuck his finger in his collar. "I need to consult with the duke, Your Majesty . . . on, uh, another matter."

"Spit it out, man," said Ernest.

"The strike force. They're in trouble, Your Majesty. Some of them managed to break out of the tunnel, and the flying wings are hunting them. That's all we know, Your Majesty. Transmission ended abruptly."

※

He would never have thought it possible, but Lampy had fallen asleep in the cab of the Puffing Billy. They'd given him some of that laudanum stuff. He didn't like it. It had grog in it. They'd also made him a space to lie down with his foot up. He'd contributed a bit to the stories being told to the driver and engineer, telling about the work on the prisoner railway and people dying there, telling about escape and crossing the desert with Jack. Leaving out his spearing the soldier . . . and then the dark, the voices, the clickety clack of the rails . . . he'd fallen asleep. He'd only awakened, feeling muzzy and a little confused, when they came into Sheba. The way the driver was blowing that whistle would have awakened the dead.

It seemed to wake enough people in the station. "Call out the militia!" shouted the driver who had a voice to carry for miles. "The British are coming!"

And things got a lot noisier from there. A little later Lampy noticed a Westralian cop, a sergeant, pushing through the crowd, a big feller with ginger hair. Lampy was worried by what was going to happen now, what the bloke would do about a blackfeller in his mob's uniform. But there wasn't exactly anywhere to run, even if he could have run. And he reckoned these two, the girl and the copilot, weren't going to stand back and let the bloke get too rough.

What he wasn't expecting was to be saluted. He fished the papers out of his pocket and held them out to the bloke. "They made me a special constable," he said warily.

"Good-o," said this sergeant, smiling broadly. "You're supposed to salute me back, Special Constable."

Lampy did, hastily, nearly dropping the papers, standing awkwardly on his bad foot and hurting it, wincing a little.

The sergeant noticed. Lampy soon realized there was pretty little he didn't notice. "I think we'd better get you to the hospital."

Linda must have overheard that. "Yes! He's got a broken leg. He shouldn't be standing on it," she said. "Oh, hello Sergeant Morgan. This is Lampy. He saved Clara's father and led us to the station to bring warning."

The sergeant beamed. "Your parents are going be very, very relieved, Miss. But he's Special Constable Lampy to you. I'm going to see him to the hospital. There's a ward for the Westralian Police."

Lampy looked at the scene, at the people. "I wouldn't say no to a bit of tucker, Sergeant. But I don't need no hospital. Just gimme a horse and a rifle, because there are a lot of them bastards coming."

Lampy didn't realize that his voice had carried above the hubbub.

There was an odd silence. Then someone said, "Blooming 'eck. That's a tough copper."

The Sergeant grinned. "You'll get them, Special Constable. But I still want two strong fellows to help Special Constable Lampy to the hospital to see the doctor first."

Lampy got six, and there must have been thirty volunteers.

He got a plaster cast, food, and had to wait. About three hours later, or so it seemed, the sergeant came in person to take him to the barracks to collect a rifle and a horse. The underground town at Sheba was big enough to ride them around in.

"The flying wings are on their way. And a clanker of more Westralian Mounted Police from Alice," the sergeant reported.

He looked at Lampy. "You did the WMP proud down there. And I've been talking to the copilot of the flying wing. You and I need to have a talk when this is over. You're an answer to my prayers, I reckon."

Lampy had been on patrol, put in charge of ten whitefeller militiamen as the dawn had come up, and he'd seen the first flying wings arrive.

He hadn't really found out what happened until they were relieved by regular soldiers. He'd been glad to go to that hospital then and rest with his foot up and with nurses fussing about him, just like he wasn't a blackfeller.

Sergeant Morgan had come to see him that afternoon, after he'd had a good sleep. The pain was just a dull ache, and he was getting pretty tired of being in the hospital already. They'd treated him well, it was just . . . lying there.

He saluted the sergeant first, this time. The sergeant saluted him back. "The doctor said there is no reason to keep you here, and seeing as the people at Dajarra did such a good job stopping the invasion before it got here, all we have is patrols, and I'm off duty. I thought I'd take you down to the WMP mess and we could have our tea and a natter."

Lampy was grateful to get out of there. Hospitals smelled. "So they stopped 'em did they? Good mob, them submarine blokes. That Tim said he'd speak to the captain for me if I wanted a place with 'em," he said as they walked. The sergeant had brought him a pair of crutches to use, and it wasn't that easy or fast. Still, they said he'd need another plaster-of-Paris cast in two days, once the swelling went down, and he was not to put this one on the ground.

"As it happens, that's what I wanted to talk to you about, Special Constable. Ned—Edward Pascoe—the copilot, came and had a long talk with me. He was recommending that you should be asked to make that uniform permanent. To join the force properly. It's something I agree with him about."

"Me? They just gimme this to stop anyone shootin' at me," said Lampy.

"That's the other thing I needed to talk to you about: righting old wrongs. He told me about that, too."

They walked down the ramp to a doorway with the WMP dingo badge on it and went inside. It looked like a good tack-room . . . with tables and a bar. The sergeant helped him into a seat and got him another to put his foot on. "Can I shout you a beer?" said the sergeant.

"Don't drink. Don't do grog at all, mister. Sorry."

The Sergeant smiled broadly. "I'm going to pull out all the stops to get you into the force, Special Constable Green. I'm sorry I called you Lampy earlier. I didn't realize it was your first name."

"Everyone calls me that."

"No. When you're in uniform, your friends call you that. Everyone else calls you 'sir,' or by your rank and surname. It's respect. We need it. And so do you. Although, after talking to Miss Darlington and Ned, I think I'd be proud if you ask me to call you Lampy one day. But I'd like to make you Constable Green first. We, the Westralian Mounted Police, need you, firstly because of what you've showed you can do, and secondly because you're aboriginal."

"On'y half. Ma was from the Tialatchari people. But I'm a black-feller, yeah." It was odd having this held up as a reason to join the police. The entire thing was crazy. They probably wanted him as a tracker, if anything. He wouldn't mind that so much, but . . .

"We need you because . . . hell," said Sergeant Morgan. "Let me explain. I got called on to investigate the case in which some railway-men, drunk and 'hunting,' were reported to have shot an aboriginal man, near Boulia."

"Me uncle."

"I couldn't find the body. I couldn't get a single aboriginal tracker to help me. I couldn't even get anyone to talk to me. The witness who reported it said there had been a boy with the man. I couldn't find out from any of the aboriginals in the area who was missing, who this boy might be. I wanted to see justice done. I wanted to help. They wouldn't even talk to me. With the end result that the murderer got off, and the man who'd stuck his neck out to report it got hounded out of Ceduna and treated as a liar. They won't talk to me, but they would have talked to you."

"I was that kid, Sergeant. You know that from the copilot, eh? My people just thought they was protecting me. The police don' help us and we don' trust them."

"Which is why we need you. I've been talking to my boss, Colonel Clifford, in Ceduna already. He's agreed to let you work with Inspector Johns and me, if you'll take it on. And our first task is reopening that case at Boulia. Your uncle."

Lampy was silent, transported back to that place, to his anger and his fear. He only came back when someone put a plate of good-smelling mutton in front of him. He sighed. "I will show you where to find my uncle's body, but I can't be no policeman, Sergeant Morgan. I'm . . . I'm a thief. And a murderer. That's why I was in jail in Queensland. And I speared a man. A soldier."

"It seems you know what right and wrong is, son. Where did all of this happen? In Queensland?"

"Yeah. Well, the soldier was when we was running away."

"That's a different country, Special Constable. And you're entitled to use force to defend yourself and your country from invaders. But tell me about it."

So, while the food grew cold, Lampy explained how when he came back from the desert his father had sunk deeper into the grog, and in with this new woman. How he was sent out to bring home a sheep every few weeks. They'd eat, and the rest would go for alcohol.

"Which is why you don't drink," said the sergeant.

"Yeah. Me dad wasn't a bad bloke until he'd been drinking. I don't want to be like that. When he had the booze in him he . . . he used to be real wild. I come back one night with the mutton . . . and he was beating up that woman of his. She got away and was screaming for help, and she run to me. Me dad . . . I tried to stop him. He tried to hit me with the axe from the woodpile, and . . . we was wrestling for it and we fell over. Cut him here. On the neck." Lampy shuddered. "He bled a lot, and some coppers come in with his missus. They heard her screaming as she run off. And then his missus said I done it. And I did do it."

The sergeant looked at him and nodded slowly. Lampy felt dreadful, but the effects of that old nun back at the mission school were still with him. "So it ain't borders that matter, see. I know what I done. And I know I killed him."

"Let's get you some hot food. That's gone cold. And some tea," said the sergeant. "Let me tell you this. I was pretty sure we needed you in the force before. Now I am absolutely certain we do. Firstly, I doubt if any jury in Westralia would convict you, and certainly I wouldn't, and secondly, well, you will blame yourself, no matter what we say. Putting you in jail didn't fix any of it. You already know the difference between right and wrong. But as a serving policeman you can square that against your conscience. Because you already have saved more and better lives than you blame yourself for. And there is lot more of that work to do."

Lampy sat there as new food was brought. Not talking, just thinking, eating, and drinking tea.

At the end of the cup he said, "Reckon you could call me Lampy."

"I think you can call me Tom, then, Lampy," said the sergeant, holding out his hand. "The pay is terrible, but the food's not bad. And your uniforms are free."

"It's good tucker. I'll talk to Jack about it," said Lampy, feeling strangely light and at ease, but not quite ready to jump, as he shook the big hand. What was it his uncle had said? Yeah: "When the water looks nice, it's got crocodiles."

That hadn't stopped either of them from swimming.

CHAPTER 25

Linda had been a little nervous and surprised by her stepmother's reaction to that relatively short phone call. She'd been hugely grateful to the copilot for organizing things in the underground mining town. She might have known how a respectable young lady behaved in Ceduna, but she was a lot less knowledgeable about how one coped with Sheba. Where one ate, slept, and how one got home. Fortunately, Ned had taken this into his hands, starting by speaking to her father. He'd arranged for her to spend the morning recovering at the home of the mayor's wife, one of the few women in Sheba, at least of the kind her stepmother would approve of, and to fly back to Ceduna with an empty troop carrier going back for more men. He'd said he'd see her at the riding school . . . sometime.

"I've rather let riding slip, since growing up on the farm," he'd said cheerfully. "So what days do you go, Miss Darlington?"

She'd still been wary about the response she was actually going to get at home. What she hadn't expected was for her stepmother to run onto the airstrip, beating her father there, and hug her so hard and then simply refuse to let go of her.

Her father had to content himself with patting her on the back when he arrived.

"I didn't think you'd miss me quite that much, Stepmama."

"I don't think she slept after we heard the wing had been attacked," said her father. "Now, dears, we've got to get back. The jarvey is waiting."

They began to walk, her stepmother still holding onto her. Some inner demon prompted Linda to say, "But I thought it would be better for you without me around. You'd have Father to yourself." It was said lightheartedly, but she'd always felt it.

Her stepmother stopped dead, jarvey waiting or no. "Linda . . . I thought you knew. I married your father *because* he had a daughter. I can't have children of my own, dearest. You were the nearest I was ever going to get."

"Your stepmother was one of the most courted women in Ceduna," said her father. "She could have had any one of half a dozen suitors. But she proposed to me. It was a leap year, mind you. I thought it was because I was a handsome fellow. But she told me that you needed a mother and she needed a daughter, and she'd put up with me for that."

"Oh, Max. It wasn't quite like that!"

"Close," said her father, tugging his moustache and smiling.

Linda was silent for a while, absorbing this. Then she hugged her stepmother. "I feel I've been such a bad daughter after that. I thought . . . well, everyone says things about stepmothers. I'll try to be better. Tell me when I'm not."

"The only thing I would ask is for you to call me 'Mother' some-times. And, of course, to have grandchildren for me."

"Just not quite yet!" said her father. "And it would be nice if we knew who . . ."

Linda's stepmother put a hand protectively on her shoulders. "That's for us to know and deal with, and for you to stay out of, Max. Isn't it, Linda?"

"Er . . ." Linda really wasn't too sure how school was going to go after the stories that would get around from all of this inevitably started behind her back. "Yes. Thank you . . . Mother."

She wasn't prepared for her stepmother to burst into tears and hug her again even more fiercely. Or for her father to say, while handing over a handkerchief, "Dry your eyes, my dear. We have to get along to the court."

"Court? Am I in trouble?" asked Linda. Had the subpoena arrived?

Her father smiled broadly. "No, your st—your *mother* is. She's up for assaulting your last boyfriend in the street. The doorman declined to press charges."

※

Nothing ever ended quite tidily, or all at once, thought Clara, as she prepared the cups, saucers, small plates, and cake forks for tea in the guesthouse. The loose ends in Westralia were going to take quite some time to tie up. The Imperial soldiers who had been trapped in the tunnel were still, some of them, being hunted in the desert. Their vehicles had been destroyed, but there were a lot of men on foot out there. The aboriginal trackers were now in high regard and higher demand. The soldiers came out of the escape hatches when given the chance to surrender, but that had been a ruse. Their sappers had blown a hole and let nearly two thousand of the three thousand escape . . . only the flying wings had been overhead by that stage, and their lumbering trucks were easy targets.

Then the *Cuttlefish* crew all had to get out of Dajarra—which was now cut off with a wrecked tunnel and a desert full of desperate soldiers around it.

They'd had to stay put there for two days, on guard and wary, before a troop of Westralian soldiers arrived to relieve the place. Linda had already gone south, but was waiting at Mandynonga station to meet them . . . along with half of Ceduna, it seemed. She was very firmly between her stepmother and father, holding their hands.

"I want to introduce you to my mother," said Linda with a sparkle in her eye. "The popular jailbird."

It was odd to see how Linda had changed—and how the relationship with her stepmother had changed, too.

"Oh, you . . ." said her stepmother, blushing furiously. "The nice policeman said he only did it because he had to."

"She poked the doorman at Discovery North in the tummy with her parasol. And she chased Nicky out into the street and pulled his trousers down and spanked him with it. The parasol was exhibit A," said Linda, proudly.

"The magistrate was very understanding," said Linda's stepmother. "Linda is my daughter. I had to deal with that poisonous little toad."

"And ask her if people didn't carry her out of the courthouse on their shoulders."

"It's because I have a heroic daughter. There was a piece on the front page of the *Westralian* about her ride," said Mrs. Darlington, obviously so proud.

"That was all Ned's fault. The copilot," said Linda airily.

Clara wondered if there'd be secret letters there, too.

Her father still looked like he'd been given a piece of pretty glass that had turned into a diamond, though.

Clara had had her own share of the court system of Westralia. Discovery North Railroad, it appeared, had badly needed to finish the line. Really, really badly, and not just because it had a nasty managing director, but because it was on the verge of bankruptcy. Building the line was very expensive, and they'd done some shady things. And when the line suffered a serious hold-up, and creditors started demanding money, it had all fallen apart—and the audit had been all the Westralian police had hoped for so far. It would be a little while before powerful businesses would start riding roughshod over people. But that was too late for Clara. They'd already charged her with theft.

"We should be able to reduce the charge to unlawful use of company property," said the lawyer. "You returned it in good order to a railway employee."

"But I stole it. I had to."

He looked at her over the top of his glasses. "Never admit to committing a crime, young lady."

"I did it."

"I can't defend you if you plead guilty."

"Well then it's guilty that I am," she snapped, knowing that she was getting more Irish as she got madder.

"You'll end up with a criminal record," squawked the lawyer.

Her father patted her shoulder. "I hear they used to send you to Australia if you had one of those."

The magistrate hadn't been quite as understanding as the one Mrs. Darlington had had. Mind you, he had admitted that her actions had had extremely desirable results, and as her father said, the poor fellow would have been lynched if he'd tried to throw the book at her. But the fine for unlawful use seemed a fair enough thing. After all, she had done it. And they didn't put her in jail.

There was a knock at the door. It was Tim, looking polished and nervous. He was scared of her father.

Ha. He didn't know he had to be scared of both of her parents. Clara had cheerfully eavesdropped on their plans for Tim. It was all right. She'd see he did precisely what he wanted to do, not what they planned. They were talking of education, not submarines. And the future was still a far-off place. She had ideas of her own that they weren't going to like either.

She ran to meet him, to kiss him on the doorstep, before Daddy and Mother came. It had been days since she last saw him. They only had an hour before the ceremony. And then he would be away a week with the *Cuttlefish* before they all went to Port Lincoln for Lieutenant Ambrose's wedding to his Sally, with just about every crewman from the *Cuttlefish* in attendance.

Sometimes it took having thought that someone must be dead to make you realize what they were worth, she thought, hugging him again.

※

Tim found his second bite at Westralia quite different from the first. People knew who he was now. The newspapers had had a full day of it. The Westralians might welcome a submarine, however, the people who saved Sheba, they were heroes. And yes, there were still the ones who turned away and ignored him. But there were the ones who now went out of their way to make him feel welcome, too. And he realized that just as he was changing the way he saw them, and their country, he was doing the same to them.

Westralia was Clara's home now . . . not *Cuttlefish*. Tim had had a sudden realization that being a part of something never went away, it just sort of moved around you. And the crew, too, changed. Lieutenant Ambrose was even talking about staying here now. He'd been offered the captaincy of a Westralian submarine. That would be . . . different.

On the other hand, it might also be good, too.

One could change the way one felt about things, even Westralia and the desert. Lampy had asked him and Jack and Clara and her mother to come out when he'd laid his uncle to rest. And Tim had realized, as he'd stood there on that red sand and was welcomed to the place, formally, that he'd put a piece of himself into Westralia, too. It would always be a part of him, and he of it.

※

In the late afternoon, the Westralian southern cross flag fluttered above the parade ground of the Westralian Mounted Police. There were, Lampy realized, a lot of people watching. He'd never had boots that had been worth polishing before. This pair he had polished until they were nearly like mirrors, even though he was only wearing one. He still had a cast on the other leg. Every brass button, too, had been polished to perfection. He could have shaved with the ironed creases on those breeches. He buffed the dingo badge on the slouch hat a last time. Sergeant Tom Morgan came along and boosted him up onto the saddle, and Constable Lampy Green rode into the parade ground with the rest of the troop. Sixteen WMP men had been in Sheba when the British raid happened, or had taken part in the Dajarra battle, and were all due to receive their honors for it. The Westralian Mounted Police had come out of that engagement proud, and very much more respected than when it went in.

Without moving his head, Lampy let his eyes take in the crowd. There was young Tim . . . with the girl. Eh. The boy must be a year younger than he was. There was Jack and his missus, Jack smiling and waving. Lampy nearly forgot himself and waved back. Linda and her parents . . . and Ned Pascoe standing next to them. There were *Cuttlefish* crewmen. Couple of blokes from that power station they'd ridden to. That manager bloke, Sid, had come all the way down for this. It was good to have them there.

But it was the rest of the crowd that Lampy realized was really important. About half of the people were blackfellers. They'd come to see this ceremony. This honor.

"And for exceptional courage and in recognition of the honor he brought to the Westralian Mounted Police, Constable Green . . ."

They said big things that washed over him like the sea. Lampy Green knew he wasn't standing there just for Lampy Green, though.

He'd been talked into this by Sergeant Morgan and Jack. And finding Uncle Jake's body, with a bullet lodged in his spine, a bullet which could be matched to a gun.

Jack was right. He needed to do this. And he could and would. It was a heavy load, but he didn't carry it alone, or just for himself.

APPENDICES

GLOSSARY OF TERMS

Billabong—usually a cut-off oxbow lake. A body of water that remains after the river has dried up.

Boobinch—an emu caller, made from a hollow piece of wood.

Boong—an insulting term for a native Australian, which was in use in earlier years.

Coolamon—a shallow, curved-sided container, usually longer than wide, for gathering food.

Dingo—Australian wild dogs.

Flying wing—in the sense used in *Steam Mole*, a tail-less, fixed-wing aircraft, deriving some lift from the wing shape and some from lighter-than-air gasbags in the wing.

Goolibah—(AKA coolabah, coolibah) *Eucaluptus coolabah*, a eucalyptus tree.

Perente—(AKA perentie) *Varanus giganteus*, a large monitor lizard or goanna, a favorite food for desert aboriginal peoples.

Magnetic termites—a kind of termite whose mounds always align north-south

Min-min lights—mysterious lights, possibly an optical illusion, or *fata morgana*, seen particularly in the Australian Channel Country.

Mound springs—tumulus mounds formed where water from the Australian great artesian basin comes to the surface.

Paperbark—trees or shrubs of the genus *Melaleuca*, with a bark that is like many sheets of paper. Has antifungal and antibacterial properties.

Pituri—a substance made from the dry leaves of plants of the genus *Duboisia*, used in traditional aboriginal medicine as an analgesic.

Termite way/run—a covered railway tunnel in which the clankers (cable-trains) are hauled, keeping them cool

Tucker—food. Bush tucker is food from the wild and can include insect grubs, fruit, and seeds. It takes knowledge and skill to live off it.

Scout steam mole—A smaller drilling machine intended for surface travel, with endless tracks, rather like a tank or bulldozer.

Sheba—A very wealthy mine, producing lead, copper, sliver, and zinc. In our world, Mount Isa.

Steam mole—A tunnel-drilling machine intended to build termite runs.

WMP—Westralian Mounted Police

Westralia—A rebel republic set up in the western two-thirds of Australia when the British Empire retreated to the eastern seaboard. Encompassing the our-world states of Western Australia, Northern Territory, the western half of Queensland, and South Australia as far as the Spencer Gulf. Parts of Victoria and New South Wales on the west are disputed lands.

ON THE WAY THE *STEAM MOLE* WORKS, AND WHY

I've always preferred science fiction that could possibly work. The science of the *Cuttlefish* and *Steam Mole* universe is supposed to be just that—science that took a different turn.

You may have noticed that temperatures are always given "in the shade." In a hotter world, shade is going to be even more important. The mineral wealth of central Australia is not going to be possible to get to without that shade. It's not a new problem, and the opal mining settlement of Coober Pedy shows a solution. The people live underground. In *Steam Mole*'s Australia there are whole cities underground and the methods of using architecture to cool them is well advanced. It's something we don't really do in our world, which could save a lot of energy.

Termites—also called white ants—help to provide the Westralians with a way to overcome the heat. Termites are very temperature sensitive and cannot really cope with more than minimal exposure to sunlight. Yet the desert and semidesert have huge colonies of them. In particular, the magnetic termites (*amitermes*) build high north-south mounds going down into deep "basements" with a complicated arrangement of vents and tunnels to allow the mound to stay both cooler by day and warmer by night than the desert. Termites also build "termite runs"—little mud-roofed passages up trees and across places where the sun would kill them. The rail system for the mines in the hot heart of Australia is based on this. The steam moles cut a shallow groove, with gentle gradients and few turns along the highest ground. The groove is roofed over, becoming a true tunnel in places because trains do not perform well on steep gradients.

A steam mole is a rail-mounted tunneling machine. In front there are concentric discs of spinning cutters, making a cone that cuts and pours the fine-cut material (fill) back onto conveyors. The fill goes to the carriages behind the mole, and some material is used in building the shoring that stops the shallow tunnel from collapsing. Some of it will go into a roof if the groove is very shallow.

Of course, a round drill cuts a round hole. And that means either it is a very big round hole, or you cut two of them or . . . well, you have one line and trains can't go both ways at once. Or . . . you could use the top half on a hanging rail going one way, and the bottom half on a pair of rails going the other way. This works particularly well if your carriages are not trains, but cable cars, pulled on an endless loop of steel cable. After all, when one side of the cable is pulling a carriage north, the other side of the cable loop is coming south. In a world run on coal, that is how the Westralians have got around the problem of clean air in the tunnels. A steam engine down there would soon make the air unbreathable. So they have power stations every twenty miles. Each powers a cable loop ten miles to either side of it and blows cool night air into the tunnels.

This is fine once you have made the tunnel, but the steam mole must take its power with it, and a long air hose, too. It must be as airtight as a submarine, because the new tunnel will be so full of coal smoke that the air inside would be unbreathable.

There is a smaller version of the mole, too, a scout intended to travel on endless tracks (like a tank or a bulldozer) and able to travel, without rails, over rough terrain to drill, sample, and prepare the path for the steam mole to follow.

ON ALTERNATE HISTORY

Alternate history is a form of "what if." It's not wish fulfillment or pure imagination, it's logically taking "what if" to a plausible conclusion. We really don't understand space and time very well. Perhaps there really are universes where your mother never met your father and you do not exist. And maybe that universe isn't all that different from this one. Or perhaps your not being there changes everything. Perhaps every chance or choice has its own universe. There are two ways of thinking about what happens then. If you believe individuals don't matter, then things gradually go back to being the same in both universes. If you believe individuals change things . . . well, then the farther you get from that point, the more the two universes are different.

I see it like a pebble dropped in a pond, with ripples of "what if" changes going out from the original choice or breakpoint. The more time passes, the more things are different, because we're built on the past. Some things will happen no matter what. The day will still take the same number of hours, people will still experiment with machines, and they will find the same things . . . but at different times. The *Cuttlefish* and *Steam Mole* universe diverged about fifty-five years before the stories. To see something positive in two world wars, they forced a lot of scientific and mechanical development. They also caused huge social changes, as women went to do what was considered "men's work" and did it perfectly well. It mixed people of different cultures and races, too, breaking down the walls between them. This has not happened to the same extent in the *Cuttlefish* and *Steam Mole* universe. The catastrophe of the Melt has frozen social evolution at where it was in 1935, and even then it was twenty years behind ours. Racism is alive and well. Women "know their place." This is why terms used, and attitudes reflected by, the characters in these books are not what they are now, or even acceptable in the here and now. The point is not to offend; this is not a universe that I daydream of living in. It is to take "what if" to what could possibly have happened. There are other possibilities . . . infinite ones. If you don't agree with mine, or you think it impossible . . . please write your own. I believe it helps to see where we've come from and where we still want to go.

A SHORT-SHORT HISTORY OF THE ALTERNATE TIMELINE FOR *CUTTLEFISH* AND *THE STEAM MOLE*

Most alternate-history stories revolve around a battle coming out differently or a famous general dying—about military events changing the world. However, wars are not the only things that have changed or can change our world. Scientific discovery has done so far more often than wars. One chemical discovery in the early 1900s changed our world in so many ways it's almost unrecognizable. That invention was the synthesis of ammonia.

Almost all modern industry and commerce rests on this: from computers to farming, from explosives to the paint on fishing boats. These days the Haber-Bosch process is as ordinary as a coffee pot, but when the method was developed, it involved working at pressures several orders of magnitude higher than had ever been achieved. And the leading expert of the day said it was impossible. This discovery changed wars forever, changed who controlled the world, prevented more than half the world's population from starving to death . . . No war, no general, no president ever had this big an effect on the world.

Cuttlefish's history branches off not as a result of a general changing his mind or being killed, or a battle going differently, but with a simple premarital argument in 1898. Dr. Clara Immerwahr (a brilliant chemist and a very unusual woman for her time; she was the first female doctorate from the University of Breslau) had an argument about the purpose of science with her intended, Dr. Fritz Haber (something that would happen in the marriage and result in her untimely death in our timeline). As a result, she broke off the engagement. In this alternate history, her family, one of the leading Jewish families in Breslau, felt this a disgrace and sent her off to visit relations in England. In our timeline, Clara Immerwahr married Fritz Haber, remained in Germany, and her contribution to the synthesis of ammonia is unknown, although we do know she translated her husband's papers into English.

We do know it was an unhappy marriage, as Fritz expected this brilliant woman just to stay home and be a housewife, and the two of them disagreed about science and what it should be used for. Clara believed strongly that the purpose of science was to make the world a better place, and not for war. Fritz was a German nationalist and wanted science to help Germany, the kaiser, and German military might.

In the end, during World War One, Fritz was the driving force behind German poison-gas warfare. His wife found this abhorrent, and they argued. Her death was recorded as suicide—with *his* service revolver.

It is notable that Fritz's chemistry thereafter did not show the genius displayed in the synthesis of ammonia. In the *Cuttlefish* and

Steam Mole timeline, Clara Immerwahr never returned to Germany, married happily in Cambridge, had a daughter in 1907, and took a different direction within chemistry, working on fabric dyes. Cloth dyeing, then, was an enormously important part of British industry, with huge fabric mills exporting across the world. Many dyes, like indigo, were very expensive and had to be collected from natural sources.

Fritz Haber never recovered from this blow. He began drinking too much and changed his direction from working on the synthesis of ammonia to the extraction of gold from seawater (a direction he took anyway, after the apparent suicide—well, death—of Clara). In our timeline, other continental scientists were working on ammonia, or rather nitrate synthesis, but they were somewhat behind Haber and using different, more energy-expensive methods. The Haber-Bosch process was up and running by 1911, and able to supply the German war machine with feedstock for the manufacture of nitrates. This was not true in the *Cuttlefish* and *Steam Mole* timeline. The British Empire controlled access to the main natural supply of nitrates in the world (the Chilean caliches deposits), and World War I was a very short, damp squib (as it would have been without artificial ammonia synthesis).

Despite their use of the Birkeland-Eyde process (a way of making artificial nitrates), the Central Powers, having badly hurt Russia, began to run out of munitions after four months—at which point it became a race between the Austro-Hungarian Empire, the Ottoman Empire, and the Germans to see who could reach a peace treaty first, knowing that would be to their advantage. In our timeline, World War I dragged on until 1918 with terrible loss of life and much hatred. The cost of reparations for it—a huge bill handed to the losers, especially Germany—planted the seeds for the rise of Adolf Hitler and World War II.

In *Cuttlefish*'s timeline, the Austro-Hungarian Empire won that race and suffered a minor breakup of its territory. The Turks found the cave-in fraught with uprisings and lost much of their empire to the French and English, or to the rise of independent states.

Germany . . . The British Empire was determined to see it did not threaten them again. This meant breaking it up into states again and getting rid of Kaiser Wilhelm II. The "agreement" was to say he'd had a mental breakdown, which would allow him to "retire" gracefully. However, his abdication would have made his sons rulers, and the British Empire was having no more of that. So the remaining German states were placed under the regency of Adolf Schaumburg-Lippe. This minor German prince, with his vivacious, very pro-British wife Viktoria (a granddaughter of Queen Victoria) was so adroit at reconciliation and in dealing with the German High Command that a Royalist uprising by Wilhelm II's sons was successfully put down. France, however, seized the moment to invade a small German principality. Thanks to Prince Adolf—and especially to his wife—the British Empire intervened on the side of their historic ally, Germany, in the process mending many fences. The result of this was an arranged marriage between Edward VIII of the United Kingdom (who in our timeline married Wallis Simpson in 1937 and had to abdicate to do so) and the daughter of Prince Adolf and Princess Viktoria (in our timeline their only child was stillborn), Princess Alexandria, in 1916. And thus a new Imperial line was founded, in which the German Empire and British Empire largely became one. Russia still had something of a revolution—but the Mensheviks won. France, having alienated Britain, found itself mired in colonial wars. And the world had no synthetic ammonia, and the British Empire, dominant in coal, saw to it that coal, not these newfangled oil-derived fuels, stayed dominant. The Windsor-Schaumburg-Lippe family controlled vast coalfields—and had the means to slap punitive taxes on oil and control and tax the shipping of it.

Coal ran the Empire.

But coal is a very dirty-burning fuel, and as Europe had neither World War I nor the Spanish flu, it had many people and much energy use. Emigration, particularly to Africa and Australia, went full-steam ahead. Colonialism and racism flourished. So did the massive infrastructure of a steam-driven world.

By 1935, things began to go wrong environmentally, just as the British Empire began cracking under the strain of too many people and too little food—synthetic ammonia was the basis of much of the fertilizer used in our timeline. The coal-based society was pouring out massive amounts of soot (particulate carbon), causing substantial ice melting in the Arctic, particularly in Russia. And that led to a methane burst (where methane locked in by ice or pressure reaches a point where a lot of it is released) in the tundra. Methane is a short-lived (breaking down in the atmosphere) but very effective (around seventy-two times as effective as carbon dioxide) greenhouse gas.

This caused real environmental catastrophe: massive melting of ice, more out gassing methane, and a warmer world. Over seven years average temperatures rose seven degrees. It proved a disaster for Earth, but the saving of the British Empire.

Governments failed to cope as heat waves ruined agriculture and their coastal cities and plains were flooded. World weather conditions became erratic, causing the collapse of already-overstretched agriculture, widespread starvation, wars, and mass migrations. Elected governments in many countries failed. Government was suspended and martial law imposed in the British Empire, with authority returning to the royal family. Military intervention was largely brutal and self-serving—except that the British Empire, with more military might and infrastructure than any rival, did a generally better job of restoring order and seeing that people at least got some help. More if you were white and British, of course. In India the suffering was terrible. But Commonwealth countries who tried to go it alone—Australia, Canada, South Africa—rapidly became chaotic, soon begging the Crown to intervene and restore direct rule. Which it did, managing to stabilize things over the next few years (as the weather was resettling, though at hotter levels). The

Empire had its finest hour—along with some colossal failures—but these were less than the disaster's impact elsewhere.

Slowly (by about 1942) things began to return to a new form of normal: a normal where London is largely flooded, but not abandoned. Like Venice, her streets have become canals. The British Imperial House was not ready to hand back the power it had been given or taken. The Canadian Dominions, with vast new arable lands and new settlements in Newfoundland and Greenland, was a major engine for the British Empire. The restive factories of India provided goods. In Australia, the western settlements had suffered withering drought and had been abandoned, with forced resettlement to the east coast and Tasmania.

At home, Ireland seethed. And coal, the driver of the Empire, began becoming more difficult to source and more expensive. In the tunnels and tubes under the drowned city, anti-imperialist republicans and Irish rebels, part of the Liberty—the people who would see a return to older values and free elections—eke out a strange existence.

They are served by a fleet of Stirling-engined submarines. After the 1914–1915 War, submarines were outlawed by the Treaty of Lausanne, as the Kaiserliche Marine submarines had inflicted considerable damage on the Royal Navy and were thus hated. But the revolutionaries, the Underpeople, operate a small, clandestine fleet, smuggling illegal goods like chocolate, teak, and quinine.

The year is 1953.

This is when *Cuttlefish* is set. The *Cuttlefish*—carrying Mary Calland (Clara Immerwhar's daughter) and her daughter Clara—have escaped the Mensheviks and British Imperial forces and brought the secret of ammonia synthesis to the rebel Republic of Westralia—a country built on the land abandoned by the British Empire as uninhabitable by those who refused to leave and those who flee the Empire.

Steam Mole takes place in the Southern Hemisphere during the spring of 1953.

ABOUT THE AUTHOR

Dave Freer is a former marine biologist (an ichthyologist) who now lives on an island off the coast of Australia. Besides writing books he is a diver and a rock climber and perpetually has his nose in a book when he's not doing those three things. With his wife, Barbara, two dogs, three cats, three chickens, and other transient rescued wildlife, they live a sort of "chaotic self-sufficiency and adventures" life, sort of down the lines of the Swiss Family Robinson, only with many more disasters. He also has two sons and two daughter-in-laws who will all tell you he hasn't grown up very much.

A lot of Dave's time has been spent (and still is) in small boats, or in water that no one in their right mind would get into, full of everything (sometimes entirely too close) from hippopotami (in Africa) to sharks (he was the chief scientist working on the commercial shark fishery in the Western Cape, once upon a time) and lots of interesting creatures like the blue-ringed octopus and a poison-spined gurnard perch.

He's written a slew of fantasy and science fiction novels, some with Eric Flint; being a scientist, he likes the strange creatures and machines he comes up with to work.

You can find out quite a lot more at http://davefreer.com/